Green

Also by Norma Rosen
JOY TO LEVINE!

Green

❖

A Novella and Eight Stories

❖

Norma Rosen

 Harcourt, Brace & World, Inc., New York

To Robert

"Green . . . Unripe, immature. . . . Not fully developed. . . .

C. F. HALE *Life with Esquimaux* . . . Being a stranger in the place and a green hand, I found it very difficult to get a berth. . . .

DICKENS *Mart. Chuz.* . . . I've been and got married. That's rather green, you'll say. . . .

Lett. fr. Madras . . . Ladies who are very blue are apt to be rather green. . . .

HUGHES *Tom Brown at Oxf.* . . . Most readers . . . will think our hero very green for being puzzled at so simple a matter. . . ."

—The Oxford English Dictionary

Contents

Part One

✤

Green

Green

1

Although Muriel Ruznack was thirty-three years old and the mother of two children, her voice still, when she was upset, pitched itself childishly high. When she became indignant, as now she did over Mac Asher, her voice thinned to an even higher pitch and trembled. She did not like the sound of her voice and hoped for a change in it as she hoped for change in herself.

Her husband, Herb, spoke in a very different kind of voice, and she loved to hear it. Whereas Muriel's concern seemed to blow through her head like a fume and fly from her lips like vapor, Herb's settled in his chest, where it slowed his breath and deepened his tones. His large, dark eyes, behind natural-frame glasses, grew even larger and darker, his phrases hesitated, as if he searched out and tried for feel a point of view as far as possible from his own.

Sometimes, after that reach of imagination, a lightness, a bantering eagerness, overtook him. He was an artist, and did not like to shut much out of his appreciation. His judgments were broad and full of intelligence for the other side, lest it be misrepresented. Muriel's own judgments, she felt, were painful, sharp.

So that when Muriel said now, her voice high-pitched and quivering with emotion, "What does it *mean* about my sister Esther, that she can marry a man like that!" and Herb answered, "Say hooray! There must be good in him if Esther picked him," Muriel nodded, drinking in a deep breath.

"Be glad Esther has the capacity to be happy with a man like Mac," Herb went on. "Even if he is the opposite of the man she was married to before."

"I'm not so sure she *has* the capacity," Muriel said broodingly.

"That only means you'd rather she didn't have," Herb said.

Muriel nodded again, then burst out, "It's not just that he's opposite. He's awful."

Muriel spoke as quietly as she could, given the natural carrying quality of her tone. Janet, the baby, was down for the night, and their three-year-old, David, had stopped chanting to himself in bed his innocent parody of their kitchen conversation ("ma-ma-say-and-da-dy-say . . ."), which meant he was subsiding into sleep. Muriel had already swept the kitchen after dinner. Then, without realizing it, she had taken up the broom and was sweeping again. Esther and Mac were expected later for coffee.

"I don't know about awful," Herb said. "That's your bias speaking. If Mac weren't rich you probably wouldn't say awful."

"If I could ever hear about money without hearing awful things with it, I probably wouldn't have that bias." Muriel's voice shot up, shaky and shrill again. "We know how Mac got rich. Esther told us. There are probably babies in his horrible buildings that have been bitten by rats."

This time Herb said nothing, and Muriel, in the pause, grew alarmed by her lack of progress. "Every day I say to myself"— Muriel swept with slow, even strokes as if to show how every

4

day . . . *sweep* . . . she said to herself . . . *sweep*—"rela-
tionships mean more than principles. I say it" . . . *sweep*
. . . "and then I hurt my sister." She collected the sparse
sweepings in a dustpan and dumped them impatiently into the
garbage bag.

Herb still sat at the kitchen table. He rubbed his forehead
with broad, stained fingers. "Say to yourself when they come,
'Esther sees good in Mac.' "

"All right," Muriel said. "That's good. Thank you."

Herb got to his feet. "I'll clean up in the studio." He put his
hand on her arm. "You okay?"

She nodded. Once, much earlier in their relationship, before
marriage, they had mingled their ideas about "how life ought
to be lived" with perfect accord. Gradually, that accord had
dissolved. Herb had assumed the role of her reformer. Certain
revelations about herself had come as a blow. Not only that
they were true, but that Herb had seen them in her. Then the
blow had made itself bearable by giving rise to a series of images about her marriage.

"I know women who take tranquilizers to get through the
day," she said. She was leaning against the broom handle, sub-
dued, swaying a little with the give of the bristles. "I take your
insights and explanations instead. Sometimes I almost taste
them in my mouth. . . ."

"What, like medicine?"

"No—like food." She shrugged. "I can't explain."

"Anno Domini," Herb said in a sweet, priestly voice as he
bowed his way past her.

She blushed, delighted all the same that he had seen through
to what was behind all that.

"Herb?" she called after him.

He turned.

"I dreamed about Aunt Gertrude last night."

5

"Aha!"

"Yes, I know. How Aunt Gertrude would have loved Mac Asher!"

"Well, maybe . . ."

"In my dream she could still make me furious. But when I woke I was sorry. She's dead and I'm alive."

"You were angry at what she stood for, more than at her."

She bit at the broom-handle top and then asked, almost fearful of the challenge, "Can you explain Aunt Gertrude?"

Herb walked a few meditative steps back to the kitchen table, then turned and leaned against it, linking one leg over a chair. He took a deep breath and then began slowly, in a low voice, full of feeling.

"How much, really, was your Aunt Gertrude to blame? When she came to this country she was fourteen. Fourteen! When the big wave of immigrants came over, this country gave them every material thing that had been lacking. But then they had to learn to evaluate it from a value system that was shot to hell. I don't mean"—Herb interrupted himself because he wanted always to be fair—"I don't mean that things weren't a thousand times better for them here. I just mean"—his voice quickened—"what a wonderful opportunity missed! A whole generation transplanted young, eager to learn the best. If only the society that took them in had been more . . ." —he weighed something infinitely delicate in his hands— "more . . ."

Herb seemed to go off into a vision of better, of more. He saw Aunt Gertrude not meanly old, but in all her tender fourteen-year-old possibilities, and he grieved for what she might have become.

Muriel crept a little closer to his vision. "You aren't fed up with me, are you?" She meant she knew he was not, but she herself might be. "You see through me and past me," Muriel

6

said. "That's what gives me hope." She sat in the chair, under the arch of Herb's leg.

Herb untangled his leg and stood up to face her. "Your principles are great but you're too strict, Muriel. People just naturally stray from the course you mark out for them. At this moment you are flunking something like ninety per cent of humanity."

"It's not easy to give higher marks," Muriel said. She began to rub her legs as if reproaches tingled all along the skin. She had tried. She had tried to trick her sympathy. Someone who made a snotty remark about Puerto Ricans—well, she told herself, he must have been shamed by immigrant parents. A thieving storekeeper? He must have a driving wife. A housing official who took, a policeman who beat must be—well—sick.

She stood up, seized the broom she had left leaning against the table, and stuffed it into the overflowing broom closet.

"I try fitting everybody with an underdog skin," she said, "but it doesn't convince me. It's like a circus costume, two-piece, head and tail, with a sad expression at one end and a droop at the other."

She kept her back against the broom closet door as if the contents might spring out at her. "I can't even give myself high marks for my efforts. I'm suspect also. Everything and everybody is suspect. Except you."

"Wow!"

She nodded stubbornly. She persisted in her belief that a cloud hung in the atmosphere of her lifetime. Echoes bounced back from that cloud as if from a sounding board, like some queer *double-entendre* of human motives. And then there were the drops of acid that squeezed out of that cloud onto all the absolutes that still, somehow, survived, like ragged plants in abandoned gardens.

"Just look how badly the flowers of the spirit fare," she said. "What's one of the flowers of the spirit, Herb?"

7

"Can't think of any."

"Just give me one little flower of the spirit."

After a moment, with no trace of mockery, Herb said, "The meek shall inherit the earth."

"The meek shall inherit the earth," Muriel repeated. And then, with vicious sarcasm, "Oh, yes, the meek shall inherit the earth. And do you know why? Because under their meekness they conceal wolfish greed. See? Another, please."

Herb waved her away. "Can't think of any more."

"Well, but we know the kind of thing, don't we? Let's say some person scorns money. Someone, for instance, like me. Well, naturally, naturally, we know it's because that person *craves* money. The knowledge of easy opposites. My century's gift to me." She intended to say more. She wanted to put into words her suspicion that such crazy combinations were what kept her voice—her high, unsteady voice—from dropping into some more harmonious register.

But Herb, shaking his head, came and leaned against the broom closet beside her. "You get into such tangles. For a pretty girl, it's ridiculous!" He kissed her, then stroked her short-cropped, reddish-brown hair. Her face, with its pale skin, its small fleshy nose pricked by excitable nostrils, its full mouth, never lipsticked, seemed, like her voice, too young for her. Her figure, though, was full and womanly and had developed early. All during her growing up, while her mind was sorting through its pained refusals, her body had serenely gone on with its blossoming.

"I'm sick of tangles," she whispered into Herb's chest. "I'm sick of thinning out my love for my sister by judging what she does."

"If you're sick of it you'll stop." He gave her a final light kiss on the nose. "I'm off to clean up in the studio."

She clung a moment longer and then brightly pushed back. "I'll clean here, too."

"Easy about tonight, okay? Relax about Mac Asher and all the Mac Ashers in the world. The only way they do you harm is when you let them distort your own responses."

He moved off, and Muriel called after him, "Here's a riddle."

He turned again. "Speak, Sphinx."

"If courtship is a hall of mirrors . . ."

"Yes, yes."

". . . reflecting the image a person wants to see . . ."

"Go on. . . ."

". . . what's marriage?"

He pondered. "Mirrors . . . image . . . wants to see . . . Okay, here goes. Marriage is *through* the mirror? The upside-down world, the opposite of everything you thought it would be?" He looked at her teasingly. "But fascinating!"

"It's not what I meant."

"I give up then."

"Marriage is good ground glass," she began.

"The kind the wife puts in the husband's drink?"

She giggled, then said gravely, "No. The kind they make fine lenses from. It shows up the beetle in the rose—just in time to save the stock."

"I see you as roses, sweetheart," Herb said.

Very much moved and shaky-voiced, she went on, "I feel crawling with beetles sometimes. But I want to tell you that I'm glad you see what you see. I'm glad you say what you say."

"You'll do the same for me any day now."

She considered that. The shock of finding herself, through the lens of marriage, to be less, had long since been offset by the joy of finding Herb to be more.

She shook her head—"Un-unh. No chance"—and moved away from the broom closet. For a wonder, the door stayed shut.

9

2

Sweeping was not enough. There was still time to spare before Mac and Esther's visit. And so Muriel went over the whole kitchen, a box of scouring powder in one hand and a sink cloth in the other. Though this was Manhattan, she thought of it as her Brooklyn kitchen. Her wild, Brooklyn landscape. Because once, when she was a little girl, her father, explaining ancient history to her, said, "When we moved to Brooklyn it was around here all wild."

The big gray-and-black stove, which she now went over vigorously with the rag but without making much change, had started the fantasy. She saw it as an old streaked house on stilts. The range, with its four black burners, was the empty lot beside the narrow-faced, Brooklyn-style two-family house—oven upstairs, broiler downstairs. The other pieces fitted into the fantasy: the big, noisy refrigerator that every half hour gave a rattle and a shake as if the shelves were walking around inside; the deep double sink of white enamel on knobby-kneed heron legs; the broad back of the kitchen table that sloped with the floor. Distributed at random against various walls, they were wild beast shapes that had settled, mysteriously, in her yard. She curried them with her cloth and soothed them almost into

10

silence. The cupboards high up in the wall, beyond reach except by stepladder, were like treetop nests. Not long ago Herb had caught her dreaming. She had been standing on the kitchen ladder, her elbows on the bottom shelf of the cupboard, her face between her hands, staring in. Instead of crockery she had seen her sister Esther and Esther's husband, Sidney, who had died two years before. Something lovely played among the cups—Esther's children, Muriel's children, the whole glimpse once more of how their lives were supposed to have been.

Except for the neon ringworm of light that cast a blue shadow over the ceiling, the kitchen looked the same, Muriel thought, as it had probably looked when built fifty years before. An ancient metal drier with wooden clothespins hanging from its rods, no longer usable, still hugged the ceiling like an oversize grill. The rope by which it had been lowered and raised was twisted in eights over a double metal hook screwed in the wall.

They had lived in Brooklyn, when she was a girl, in just such a house of which her stove reminded her. They had lived downstairs and rented the upstairs. When she was fourteen, Mama had died (a picture rushed up from the grave: milky eyes, an exhausted beneficent face nodding its yes before the request, "Mama, can I have . . . ?" could be completed) and Aunt Gertrude, Papa's widowed sister, had moved in.

According to Herb, this was where trouble began. Some of Muriel's attitudes, he said, had stayed locked inside the mold she had forged to resist Aunt Gertrude. Muriel's older sisters, Esther and Sophie, were by that time past influence. But Aunt Gertrude tried. She considered that in a house with three unmarried daughters where no one troubled to point out the difference between marriage to a rich man and a poor, some crime had been committed. Poverty she had learned from life; wealth she studied faithfully in the newspapers. She would

11

spread the *News* and *Mirror* on the kitchen table and would draw the girls, twice her shrunken size, to the paper like puppies to learn their obligations. She rejoiced that the wealthy of the world should connive with her to win her point.

"You see what a smart girl does?" Rap! with an arthritic finger against the paper. "What was she? A ditchdigger's daughter, an *immigrant's* daughter, like you, Muriel, Esther, Sophie! Married to a millionaire! So he's on the stout side. But what homes she'll have, what clothes, what . . . what . . ." —Aunt Gertrude had groped for the opulent word—"what vacations!"

Esther and Sophie had shrugged. But Muriel, in her definite, high-pitched voice, had cried out, "Disgusting! His money's from pinching the poor. How could she!"

"She loves him!" Aunt Gertrude, determined, licked a finger and flapped over smeared pages. "Look!" A movie starlet and her aging oilman groom, smirking in mutual deceit. " 'This is for keeps,' " Aunt Gertrude read. "And look how cultured. A honeymoon cruise to Greece . . ."

"Disgusting!" Muriel's sturdy, child's voice would cry, while Sophie and Esther only made faces. Aunt Gertrude would clutch her hair. In America, she reminded them, women could improve their lot. If they didn't, if they picked crumbs from the floor instead of helping themselves to the feast . . . "Greenhorns!" she muttered. "Born right here and greenhorns."

The girls had married. Not as Aunt Gertrude wished, but as Mama would have understood. Sophie moved West with her schoolteacher husband, Esther married Sidney, a misplaced salesman who thought of going back to school and becoming a teacher as well, and Muriel had married Herbert, an art student and aspiring painter. Of all these choices, Muriel's fell into a special category of unripe greenness for which Aunt Gertrude reserved special scorn.

12

On one of their rare trips East to visit, Sophie and her husband had been killed in an automobile crash, dissolved away in their youth while the starlet and the ditchdigger's daughter, now richly divorced—Aunt Gertrude kept account—lolled through life. "If they could have afforded to buy a new car," Aunt Gertrude had said through bitter lips, "that *wouldn't* go out of control . . ."

The surviving sisters had drawn even closer together and had lived, with their husbands, close to each other and to Mama's and Papa's old house. Esther's second son was born and Sidney renounced his hope of returning to school. Muriel gave up her librarian's job when her first child was born, and Herb began teaching at an art school. Muriel limited him as to number of courses. "If you took on more, when would you paint?" she said. "And please don't start thinking up other ways to make money. There are already too many ways of making money. We'll manage fine."

When Papa died, and Aunt Gertrude shortly after, the thought of moving presented itself. Brooklyn was a cemetery, and now out, out to the City!

By wonderful fortune, the sisters managed to find in one old but solidly built house in the West Nineties two apartments coming vacant in the same month. They had been occupied by two related families, now making the leap to the suburbs together. The neighborhood people were a mixed lot—families, students, some infiltrating Negroes and Puerto Ricans—and the streets had a live, unexpected look that Herb, especially, found exciting. The house was not far from a park and from a public school noted for its high standards. Despite these attractions the landlord, who had previously had trouble with the rent commission, did not ask for anything under the table. Aside from the financial strain, such a demand would have been impossibly against the principles of the four.

13

Esther and Sidney had taken the larger apartment, and Muriel and Herb had taken the smaller one. Though it was for all of them more rent than they had paid in Brooklyn, it was not so bad by city standards. In fact, their finding the two apartments at all seemed almost miraculous. "It's a sign it's right for us, Muriel," Esther had said.

But as usual the signs had been more complicated than seemed. The landlord's old-time tenants drove him wild, deprived him of rent increase. For spite, he allowed his property to fall into decrepitude—the lobby stripped bare of every furnishing, all but a couple of dull bulbs snatched from the hall light fixtures. For paint or repair, the tenant had first to complain to a commission, after which a slow letter was sent to the landlord and a slow, nearly invisible, accommodation made.

The very walls were diseased. Their sores erupted in the surgical glare of wall fixtures—pieces of metal shaped like fat candles with hard drippings down their sides, magnetized for dust, and sockets at top for bulbs. There were doors and doors to every room, some with glass panes, some wooden, hinged swinging ones, some double or French, so that the place had an ajar, unfinished look, and in winter icy currents drove roadways through the warmer air. On a night of blizzard, Sidney had had his heart attack, a hammer blow that struck them all. Since then, Esther had for two years followed the hard schedule of her widowhood—cleaning, cooking for her boys, and working in a stocking store. Sidney, most loving and best-wishing father, not meaning to die, had left nothing.

Muriel cast a final look at her wild white kitchen herd, rinsed out the cloth, and felt how her own thoughts humiliated her. Mac Asher, owner of a large property from which the stocking store was leased, and which included, among other dwellings, a hotel where large welfare-supported families were crammed into apartments consisting of a single, over-priced room, had

14

come one day with a contractor to see about store alterations. Big operator that he was, accustomed to risking a deal on the speculation of his hunch, he had made his decision then and there. He fell in love, as he put it, "at first appraisal." Esther's rescue was assured. After the marriage, Esther would have a house and a maid and a car of her own besides the family car. These Mac had promised. Nice clothes, of course. But the main thing was the children. They came first. Childless from his first marriage and too old now, he said, for babies, Mac understood that. He even welcomed it—that the children should come first. It gave good meaning to a marriage, he had surprisingly said, that might otherwise shrink to selfishness on both sides.

Why, Muriel nagged herself, wasn't she happier for Esther's sake? It was frightful to be a poor widow with small sons. Granted, a thousand times, granted. Muriel had seen for herself. She could not hold it against her sister that she was marrying a rich man. But the trouble was that Mac was too close to what she and Esther had sneered at. Before Mac, Esther had shared her ridicule of such a man. This was a precious holdover from their childhood, when the villain was rich and cruel, or rich and ugly, or rich and old. The hero was poor and good. They had believed it, Mama and Papa had believed it, even Aunt Gertrude, without suspecting it, had believed it. "A rich man is looking for poor girls like you. Do you think among his own he'll find anybody who is so sincere?" It was a fairy tale that was fading. Soon it would be gone. Muriel thought there would one day be children who would not hear of it. Then, as they grew up and scrambled for money, there would be none of this nostalgia to prick them and make them miserable. There would be nothing but the scramble.

Between the sisters there was silence now on this subject. But Muriel could guess and suffer her sister's pangs. Esther's concealments she recognized as her own—the more stubborn, the

15

more afraid. Esther was nearly ten years older than Muriel, yet she seemed to wait, quiet and timid, for Muriel to approve of Mac. Muriel, of course, spoke the words of approval—"Mac's reliable, he's generous, he's really, I think, when you get to know him, warm. . . ." Esther's loneliness was painful to see, as if she felt estranged from the course of her own life. On the nights when she did not see Mac she came down the three flights to visit Herb and Muriel, losing herself in the events of their days, for which she felt an interest that was like a physical empathy. Or else she summoned the past while they all drank coffee. Memories of Mama, Papa and Aunt Gertrude sprang from their burial ground, green as spring, still full of life-giving juice and pain.

"You'll both feel better about things," Herb said to Muriel. "These reactions now are understandable. Give yourself time."

But Muriel nagged herself, "Where is my charity for my sister? Where?" till sometimes she mistook herself for Sidney's ghost that walked through the old rooms crying, "Gone, gone!"

3

That kitchen could talk. Words were groaned, whistled, snapped and ticked. But which words when? For instance, the refrigerator door, with its loose, jointed handle, made a double-knocking noise when you slammed it. It said a powerful something of two syllables. The day Muriel learned Esther was going to marry Mac she learned at last the meaning of that double syllable. The refrigerator door, when you slammed it, slammed "breakup." To clear her head and ease her throat before Mac and Esther's visit, Muriel took some grapefruit juice and the refrigerator door announced itself. Its tough, crackled hide swung heavily away from her hand. "Breakup."

"Don't forget the present," Herb called from his studio. It had originally been the utility room just off the kitchen, an architect's generosity of long ago. "I won't," she called back through the open door.

Go for eggs in the morning, "Breakup." Baby food in jars, "Breakup." "Breakup" with the chopped meat for Herb's supper, the American cheese for her own lunch. "Breakup" in the browning corsage of gardenias that Mac had brought her when he announced himself as Esther's intended.

The present for Esther was on top of the oven. Muriel fluffed

17

the bow and carried the box out of sight to the bedroom. Because she thought of it, Esther's wedding gift, as the "breakup" present, she carried it fearfully, as if it might live up to its name and slip from her hands. What was inside the box was delicate and breakable china.

And then, despite all her resolutions, she turned and marched back toward the living room exclaiming, "It's no use. I can't stomach Mac Asher!"

Then she froze, because over Herb's head, with its frantically staring eyes, she could see through the hallway to the door where Esther, mindful of the sleeping children, and having lightly rapped rather than rung, was standing with Mac.

It was odd how the strain of that moment—with its uncertainty as to whether anyone besides Herb had heard what she said, or even if he had heard or only divined what she intended to say—was neither greater nor less for Muriel than any of her other moments with Mac. Somehow they got through all the opening movements. Mac was shown the sleeping children. Herb carried in the present. Esther exclaimed and wept and held a dish against her bosom. Mac asked to see Herb's newest paintings and by the tilt of his head managed to show that he thought they were downside up. Esther remarked, quite calmly to Mac, that she had sat in this kitchen for two years and her whole life had passed before her. Mac, with equal calm, had remarked that it was a good thing to get away from bad memories. Then came the long pause.

Into the coffee-drinking silence Herb said, "Guess who I met today?"

It was Mac Asher, amiable guest, who finally asked, "Who?"

No storyteller, Herb cleared his throat once or twice. "I was carrying a couple of canvases along Third Avenue to the framer's and—there he was, Eliot Fantanucci!"

Esther's sad blue eyes looked disbelieving for a moment. She hesitated, then burst into a delighted laugh, and Muriel, re-

18

leased from her frozen silence, laughed, too. Even Mac Asher, who had never known Eliot, but for whom the difference between knowing and not knowing was small, it seemed, laughed amiably along.

"You didn't tell me," Muriel said.

"I saved it," Herb said. "Remember?" He looked at Esther, encouraging her. "Remember runny-nosed Eliot when he lived down the block from us? With his bag of marbles like a miser?"

"Eliot!" Esther said, her eyes moistening for those days.

Muriel felt her own tears prickle. "Fantan!" she said, and she and her sister laughed again and could look, first time all evening, warmly into each other's eyes.

"I was walking along with my eyes on the corner of the canvas to see it didn't get bumped, when I felt this hand slap my shoulder from behind. First, he said, he passed me coming from the opposite direction and then a second later he recognized me, you know how that is? But when I turned around I knew him right away. And then he told this friend he was with how we had grown up on the same block. And then he said, 'I never see anybody from there. I thought they were all dead. I even thought I was dead.' "

Herb explained to Mac. "We all knew each other, the girls and this fellow and I, when we were kids."

Mac polished off his cake with a cavernous "Uh-huh," swallowed, and then, "What does he do?"

"He runs his own advertising agency."

"Successful?" A question loaded with whipped cream.

"Yes. I think very."

Clear as yesterday Muriel could see that time, blue and hazy like the ceiling of a movie theater and pierced with lights. The blue Brooklyn evenings with the street lamps coming on, herself sitting snug at the top of the stoop, working away at her rattail horse rein. A gentle time, a gentle place. Mama and

19

Papa were peacefully drinking tea and reading newspapers in the house.

"I could tell he was really glad to see me," Herb said. "And I felt the same way. I felt almost overjoyed to see him. Isn't that funny? It was way back, from the past." He lifted his stained hands. "You see somebody and you feel, all of a sudden, how good that past was. I said, 'My God, Eliot Fantanucci!' " Under the table Herb grabbed Muriel's hand and pressed it tight. "And then he said, 'No, Fain.' "

In Muriel's vision, Mama and Papa were bent and small and perfect, like figures in a Chinese painting. She had to ask Herb to say again what Eliot had said.

"Honey, he said his name was Fain."

"What do you mean, Fain?" Muriel looked from Herb, who was beginning to frown at her, to Esther, who looked into her cup, her pretty soft mouth twisted to one side.

"What do you mean, Fain?" Muriel demanded again.

"Before you start . . ."

"Do you mean he changed his name?"

"Before you start judging—"

"Ooh, boy, your sister gets excited!" Mac Asher said.

"Muriel, he's an open, likable guy. Nobody suffers from what he did except maybe himself. We went for coffee. We talked quite a while. His wife is considerably older, and the agency was originally her father's. Eliot's trying to make something decent out of what maybe to begin with was not so decent. But he knows all that. He'd like us to come out and see his kids and meet his wife."

Muriel sighed. She made an effort to picture little Eliot Fantanucci goaded by life.

Mac began an enthusiastic account of the workings of fate in the business world. "Take Fantanucci. He's got a good business going. You meet him. Who knows what it leads to? Take me. My father left me some lousy real estate I couldn't unload. Sud-

denly rumors start. The El is coming down, the city is going to
do this and that, who knows what? Interested parties come to
talk to me about buying. But! If I know I got lemons and people start squeezing like they're Persian melons" (Mac's father
had, before buying real estate, been in wholesale produce)
"then I'm suspicious, right? So I let them talk, I let them
squeeze. Little by little, among themselves, they twist my property upwards till I got, thank God, something nice."

Then Herb remembered something more and broke into a
smile. "I told him, Muriel, a little about us. About"—his fingers waggled, plucked words from the air—"about our choice."
Herb hesitated. "He meant this good-naturedly, Muriel, if
you'd heard his voice—and I got a kick out of this—you know,
don't misunderstand—he said people like us ought to get
grants from the government because we're like Indians or some
other relics of other times and we ought to be preserved, a kind
of national treasure."

Mac Asher dared to laugh. But what was worse was that
Esther, watching him, was, even though guardedly, beginning
to smile.

"I hate, oh, I hate a sellout!" Muriel cried. "Why were we
getting sentimental over Fantanucci? He's not sentimental. He
couldn't wait to bury Fantanucci!"

Under the table, Herb squeezed her hand till it hurt. Esther's
smile died. Muriel pictured herself sticking not one, but two
knives into her own heart, and blood-red remorse running out.

One of the children gave out a sharp cry, as if injured by
waking. Mac Asher pushed his chair back. "It's late." He put
his hand on Esther's arm. Muriel said her good-nights and
made her escape to the children's room even before Mac and
Esther were out of the door.

There was nothing, of course, to say. But all the same, Muriel said, when she came back to the kitchen and company was
gone, "I know I was awful."

Herb lifted his arms and let them drop. "Let's leave discussion for tomorrow, okay? I'd like to finish up now in the studio."

Muriel checked again on the children and did a little ironing. Then she looked over the newspaper, in her own particular style (Housing Officials Take Bribe; Tenement Wall Collapses; Police Take Handout; Twenty Killed at Crossing). She switched resolutely to the ads, but there again: "Reign at home," she read out to Herb. "Make your hearth a throne." She banged her hand on the paper. "Who *buys* that!" she called out to him. "What kind of *person* buys a two-hundred-dollar housecoat! Why don't they give that money to war orphans instead?"

There was silence. Then Herb, muffle-voiced, answered, "In a minute, honey." It was like the patient put-off she sometimes had to use with her own children.

She felt nervous, thirsty, and again took some grapefruit juice. The refrigerator door, swinging away from her hand, again said, "Breakup." A moment later, she heard the light knock.

"I know it's late," Esther said, walking quickly by her at the door.

"She heard me," Muriel thought, and groped through her secret armory for a dagger, a knife. But also, stubbornly, she prepared with defenses ("I'm sorry, Esther, you weren't supposed to hear it, but I can't help my feelings." Or, at last, more honestly, "How could you, Esther, how could you?").

"It's what, now," Esther said, "two more weeks? It doesn't seem real."

Esther sat at the kitchen table, waved aside more coffee and rubbed her fingers over the corner of the table where the white enamel had chipped, showing its black underside. She looked down and rubbed carefully, as if polishing a thought.

"When Mac asked me to marry him, he put it almost like a business proposition. 'You're a widow with two children. I'm a widower with none. Let me be your provider. I want young blood around me.' " She looked up. "But fifty-two isn't old."

(Why, Muriel asked herself, am I waiting for her to mention what's so painful? Why can't I take it on myself to begin?)

"Afterward he told me—told me—he was in love with me but he thought I might not want to hear it because of, because of . . ."

("I'm sorry for what I said." That was not, Muriel thought, what she ought to say. But instead, "Bear with me. Until my judgments stretch a little wider. I'm working on it. I suffer from this narrowness, Esther, pinched in it. . . .")

Esther sighed and looked up at the drier on the ceiling. "They never fixed that."

"No."

"Mine either. Mac said you and Herb ought to come often and stay with the kids. When he says something he means it."

"We will," Muriel said. "That's thoughtful of him."

("Release me," she wanted to say, "from this narrowness. Show me I'm wrong.")

"He is thoughtful," Esther said. "The boys are getting fond of him."

"Very thoughtful. They should."

Esther pressed fingertips into the soft cleft of her navy crepe dress. "That dinner we had before we came. Mac likes to order and order. . . ."

("Release me," Muriel wanted to say. "Show some sign that you had at least to struggle to accept Mac, and I will, too.")

Suddenly Esther's hand slapped flat, fingertips extended over her heart. "Oh! Muriel! Remember! Remember what Aunt Gertrude said that time to Sophie?"

Instantly Muriel was all ears. Family lore remembered was

23

like the prodigal child, good because it came back, because it belonged to you, no matter what. Besides, in this remembering, Esther, she felt, would speak.

"I remember when she said it. Sophie had gone out to dinner with that fellow, what was his name?" Esther frowned, stared at something, shook her head, and raced on. "His family was rich. She thought he was awful. She was telling us about the dinner he bought her. And I remember, Sophie said they served appetizers from a little Ferris wheel with trays. . . ."

Muriel also frowned over the name of Sophie's young man and could not recall it. Nevertheless her skin prickled, the memories were so near.

"Anyway, anyway," Esther said. Her eyes stared into her vision, the eyeballs racing left-right, left-right, as if reading off something soon to be snatched away. "Anyway, Sophie thought he was awful, conceited, and I remember Aunt Gertrude said, 'Rich boys are always like that at first. It's shyness. They worry if girls want them for their money. Who is sincere today like you girls?' Remember?" Esther finished triumphantly.

Muriel waited a moment before she would allow the thought to sink in that Esther's memories were as sharp as her own, but they meant something different. For Esther, it must be, the transition from past to present was simple, from Sidney to Mac, simple. The explanation of Esther's behavior was that, for her, it required no explanation. There had been no lessons in Esther's past to gall the present. Muriel felt disappointment in her sister creep up from her feet like frostbite, but the next minute there was a thunderclap in her head.

"His name was Kenneth!" she cried. "Sophie's date's name was Kenneth!" Now thawed and getting hotter, she was off on a remembrance of her own, traveling fast, because that Sunday of Sophie's rich dinner had been the afternoon of her first date with Herb. "Herb came to see me loaded down with sketch pads, in an old army jacket. In brown shoes with worn crepe soles, thin as paper on the outside, Esther, and bunched and squished over on the inside—from walking over hard pavements, looking for things to sketch."

She stooped to duck her head under the table as if to look for Herb's shoes, and to trample with her chenille scuffs over the soft, scarred leather. She could picture the ones he wore now, in the studio.

"Didn't Herb remind you of Papa?"

"How of Papa?" Esther narrowed one eye critically. The sisters always challenged each other on claims of family resemblance.

"Because! How Papa walked with one shoulder up. And the brushes stuck out of his back pocket." Muriel had to hurry on, to keep up with the details of the picture that had suddenly appeared before her eyes. "How he'd walk slowly, as if he looked at everything. And Papa was a painter too—"

"A house painter."

"But he used to do little pictures for us when we were kids. He *might* have had talent."

"Papa!" Esther laughed. "All he wanted was to push his shoes off when he got home, eat, take a snooze. . . ."

"That's not true!" Muriel said. Then another picture sprang up. Almost in a whisper, Muriel said, "I see him sometimes in his grave, covered with paint—his hands, his hair, his eyes, his mouth." She pressed her fingertips against her lips. "Why was his life so hard?"

The sisters were silent. Then Esther put out a hand to touch Muriel's arm. "Suppose," she said. "Suppose Eliot offered Herb a job?"

She feels nothing for the past, Muriel thought. Neither hers, nor mine, nor ours. The thought took away the shock of the suggestion, but "What!" she forced herself to cry out. "What! What!"

"Shh, wait, Muriel. . . ." Esther was now alternately stroking and squeezing Muriel's arm. "Suppose, just suppose. Suppose Herb could still do mostly what he wants, only things would be so much better financially. . . ."

"Did Mac say that?"

"No, I say it."

"Why? What for?"

"You could leave this place—"

"Who wants to leave it?"

"You could rent or build, Muriel, out near us."

"Who wants to rent or build?"

"It's peeling here, Muriel. It's drafty. Where's the greenery so essential to children?"

"Don't knock it down just because you're leaving, Esther. It's got drawbacks, but you lived here with your kids and managed. I don't understand you, Esther. In fact, I'm beginning to think you're a very cold person. . . ." Muriel choked, swallowed, and suddenly jumped up and began smoothing and folding laundry from the pile in her basket. Tiny shirts and overalls. Most of the stuff had been worn first by Esther's boys and then carefully put away for Muriel's children. How could they quarrel with these things under their hands?

"I don't want to move!" Esther wailed. "I don't want to split up with you. I don't want to leave you here where it's old and move by myself to where it's new. How is it you don't understand me when what I say is so simple? I'm saying wouldn't it be wonderful to live close, out where it's beautiful?"

The double-pronged hook hopped from the wall and whirled up into the air on its string like some winged insect. The old grill drier shot down, one-sided, with a drawbridge clang. The sisters, in unison, gave out a panicked scream, Herb burst from his studio intent on rescue, and Muriel and Esther fell into each other's arms.

"Who's hurt? Who's hurt?" Herb yelled, seeing them drenched in tears.

26

4

Now at 4:00 A.M. it was a deep-sea kitchen. The tea kettle fumed soundlessly, its lid puffing up and down like the gills of a fish, the window breathed smoke on itself and washed itself down with drops of vapor, the neon ring on the ceiling swam round and round, flecked green and blue like an eel.

Muriel pieced together for Herb the dream that woke her. In the dream she had been walking along Amsterdam Avenue, wheeling the children in the big, battered carriage in which Esther had once wheeled hers. Finally she parked the carriage in the chilly sun outside a jeweler's store. Wearing her bulky storm coat, a wool scarf over her head, moccasins and socks, she went inside. She looked over the cases of merchandise. An old and ugly man came from the back to greet her. "You look tired. Sit down." She didn't want to sit. She preferred to walk and look.

"You like these things?" He waved his hand around the shop.

"Everything is beautiful," she answered.

"It's settled then."

He locked the door, pulled shades over the windows, turned up lights in the shop so that every jewel blazed. Muriel stared for a long time. Dimly at first, then like a noise growing louder

27

came the realization that her children were outside, that time had passed, maybe days, and they had not been fed or looked after. She rushed toward the door, slipped, rose in slow motion, ran some more, caught her coat on a nail, fumbled as if palsied, fell again and ran and fell and on and on, trapped in the wheel of nightmare.

"I know those dreams," Herb said. "They're torture." He touched her neck and found it ice cold. "Close your robe." He sounded stuffy-nosed. A possible cold.

"You don't think it matters? That I left the children? That I was panting over those diamonds?"

Herb hadn't stopped to put on his glasses. He squeezed his eyes with his fingers and assured her, "The opposition has a right to speak up now and then."

"That Aunt Gertrude"—Muriel insisted on her guilt—"came back to me disguised as Mac Asher? And after I settled all that? After I settled it?"

"You can't vacuum-clean your mind." Herb snuffed twice, to see if he could breathe. "Esther is married to Mac and has moved into a new life, that's settled." He bent close to her face, read there that she was still stricken. "Just so we know, so we do, so we live what we believe."

She took a relieved breath and stood up to embrace him. But he backed away. "Don't kiss me on the mouth, sweetheart, in case I do have a cold."

Two nights later, the dream was repeated.

Muriel, shaking in terror and sweat, woke Herb. He sat up groggily and sneezed. "Maybe it's not really a cold. I have no time for a cold."

"Herb, I dreamed it again."

"What?"

"That same dream. In the jewelry store. About leaving the babies."

28

"Well," Herb said, hunting for the box of tissues at the side of the bed, "dreams will be dreamed."

"I'll get you some aspirins," Muriel said. She came back with two tablets on her palm and a glass of water, and waited for Herb to drink them down. "In a dream, what would you read for babies?"

"I would read babies."

"But the babies were in Esther's old baby carriage, the worn scraped one, with the side buckles broken. It made me think of all other worn things—my father's sweaters with holes in the elbows, the house he lived in and where we live now, your shoes, my coat. . . ."

"Look, Muriel, everybody dreams. I dream, too. Suppose I dream I'm sitting at a brand-new rosewood desk with three-inch-deep carpets on the floor. I'm looking over a bunch of layouts and saying this is good, this is crap. I'm the new Art Director of a big advertising concern. What should I do? Kill myself over a dream?"

"Did you dream that, Herb?"

"Muriel." He rolled over and turned his face to her, keeping his germs a careful distance away. "There's no reason to call catastrophe on yourself because you're tempted. Because you're panting over those diamonds, the kids aren't really going to starve out there in the cold, are they? But your own self knocks you on the head for it. Bong! you're guilty, you fall down, the kids are screaming, you can't get out. The whole business."

Herb paused to get another tissue. Muriel was all ears, waiting for the continuation. She was, she recognized from the way Herb's voice was warming up, about to get a trouncing. But what did it matter? She felt exhilarated, delighted at the way Herb put things. Never in a million years would she have thought to look at things this way.

29

"How can you," Herb continued, "respect an attitude in yourself that wants to destroy you the minute there's a chance you may be claimed elsewhere? Wouldn't you call that nasty and mean of yourself? That's how you act toward your sister and toward Eliot. . . ."

She caught her breath. That was sharp.

"That's how hard you are on everybody, including you. Don't cater to that mood any more!"

Muriel sat motionless. It had been a bad blow. Stinging. Acid. Real dislike. She wanted to ask, like a child, "Don't you love me any more?" But she remembered with a little twist of self-mockery the answer for that. "We always love you. It's the naughtiness we don't like." Silently she let the rebuke be absorbed into her nerves and marrow. It was Herb's rebuke.

"All right," she said, "I know you're right. I'm trying to see it," and lay back quietly in the dark.

Herb reached for her hand. "Sweetheart, have some pity for struggling mortals. Admit there are alternatives. If there weren't any, we would never have to sweat out our choices, would we?"

At the end of the week, Herb called from downtown.

"How's your cold?" Muriel asked immediately.

"Well, it's not really a cold . . . ," he protested. "I had lunch with Eliot Fain, Muriel. He seemed to be hinting around at a job for me."

"Oh," Muriel said as quietly and neutrally as possible. "What did you say?"

"It was no offer, so there was nothing to say."

"What did you think, then?"

"I just thought"—Herb's voice was thickened by the cold that was not a cold—"I'll hear what he has to say. I'll listen. He made it pretty plain that the visit to the wife comes first. She's the not-so-silent partner. He wanted me to set up a date for a couple of weeks from now. I said I'd check with you."

30

It was strange to be asked to answer on the telephone a question Herb could have asked her at home tonight. Was he afraid of doing that? They couldn't see each other's eyes, and that was where the dishonesty lay.

"That's all right," Muriel said. "I'll ask the super's wife to stay with the children."

"It's just a chance for all of us to take a look at the possibility. Without commitment. If we all keep open minds."

"Yes, I see that," Muriel said.

"You haven't still got it in for Eliot or his wife? The visit wouldn't bother you? Because if you have got it in for them I guess there's no point."

She understood now that what Herb was hoping to keep at bay was that strict examiner in herself who might, despite her mild intentions, quaver out, "Zero! Expelled!" It was to keep from alerting that examiner, to approach off-handedly from a corner outside the classroom, so to speak, that he was telephoning her now. And he was right to show caution because she felt, to her shame, enraged. Open mind? Since when, on that particular subject, open? If she had not kept her mind proudly, determinedly shut on the importance of Herb's work over everything else would he have had any work?

"The only thing that bothers me," she answered shakily, "is if you'd still have enough time for your painting if you took that job. That's what we've always thought about, isn't it? When would you paint?"

"Weekends. Evenings," Herb answered with maddening lightness.

"Is that enough? How would you feel about that?"

"It's plenty, the way my work's been going. Look, Muriel, I'm not doing the best work I'm capable of. And I'm not earning us any of the goodies of life either."

"What goodies? Of what life?"

"All those things Esther's been talking about."

31

"Who *cares* about that!"

"Esther's got a point, Muriel. Your dreams know it, even if you don't."

"If you use my dreams against me I'll never tell you another one. Listen, Herb, it would be the irony of my life if you took Eliot's job for my sake. What I want is just the opposite."

"I know you do, Muriel. But damn it, I feel—I don't know—*guilty* sometimes. Why should I be spared having to sweat for a buck the way Eliot and Mac do? What's so special about me?"

"Am I supposed to answer that? Am I supposed to tell you what's so special? Am I supposed to remind you who you are?"

A pause.

"I can't say no to him out of hand, Muriel. I didn't ask for the job, but since Eliot may be offering me one, I have to follow up to see where it's leading. Maybe it will all fall through. That would be fine. But I couldn't live with myself if I just said no to something that would make things so much easier for you"— he corrected himself quickly—"us."

"Are you trying to torture me?"

She heard him taking deep breaths. "The job hasn't come to me yet. Not by a long shot. But when something falls into your life you can't just pretend it didn't. You have to pass through it."

She repeated, aghast, "Pass through it!"

The operator broke in. After Herb's second coin rang through the box, Muriel began again, quietly, "Herb, couldn't you just say you're not interested, and stop all this 'for my sake' business?"

"Okay, then not for your sake. Maybe I'd just like to have the pleasure, or the trouble, of having a job offered to me. Maybe I need to reinforce my own choice." He stopped for a moment, too. Then, in a slightly hurt tone, "Won't you trust me, Muriel?"

32

She fought against the lure of those words. He might just as well have said, "Won't you quit thinking, having instincts and hopes of your own?" Something rose up in rebellion for a moment, then quivered flat and went rushing toward the magnet.

"Oh, Herbie, I do trust you."

After she hung up, Muriel went into Herb's studio. It was something she liked to do by herself from time to time. She stood in the middle of the room and looked around at the propped canvases and felt, as always, astonished and proud. Her own efforts in art classes had been conscientiously realistic and detailed. She marveled at Herb's ability to paint in what seemed to her this free, pure way. No one, seeing the sweeps of color, could have taken Herb for a mild man. It was inconceivable to her that he was not already famous, that he could not yet, for instance, interest a gallery in a one-man show. But he had had glowing comments and encouragements. Part of her mind believed that he would be famous, and money would come. Another part of her mind believed that he would never be famous, only forever working, creating, filling their lives with color and with insight. Either way, she felt the prospect irresistibly enticing.

A job with Eliot now seemed crazy to her. It would only be a bird in the hand. She preferred, by far, the bright, elusive flashing of the birds in the bush.

5

"What will you get for the Fains?"

Esther had heard the hint of news on the phone and had come at once. On her first free morning she arrived to look after Muriel's children while Muriel, in turn, was supposed to shop for the present. The devout attention Esther gave to the question showed she thought the present, if rightly picked, might lend mystical powers to the whole project.

Muriel answered with impatience. "I don't know. Why must we get them anything? Or why not just candy or a box of nuts?"

"No, no," Esther said, frowning. "Let's see. What can you bring them?"

Esther twisted the new pearls in the neck of her new blue wool dress and ran her fingers through the new wave in her hair. Muriel guessed Esther's feelings about her new finery from the way Esther's new fur jacket was thrown over the back of Muriel's kitchen chair and her small hat, of iridescent blue and green feathers, had been dropped upside down on the seat. It was Mac, Muriel supposed, who enjoyed them most.

Yet even if her West Greenvale finery bored Esther, other things did not. She had spent most of the morning praising the schools. The children had learned more in two months than they had in a year in the city. And with hot lunches and buses and car pools you never worried, rain or snow.

"Something for their children?" Esther mused out loud when they were giving the children their lunch. "No, maybe something for the house is best—it's a new house, isn't it? Because the wife's reaction is so important."

"I tried to explain to you, Esther. Herb doesn't even want that job."

"Why not?" Esther demanded. "Doesn't he think about you?"

"Of course he does," Muriel said hotly. "The only reason he's considering it at all is for my sake—" Muriel broke off abruptly. In her pride, she had revealed too much.

Without comment, Esther went back to her musing. "A ceramic ash tray? A brass trivet for hot plates? A glass bowl for mints? She already has everything, so don't worry if you give her one more."

"It's disgusting to think of somebody having everything. Why should I clutter her house with one more thing? Candy, at least, the children could eat up. What's the matter with candy?" Muriel asked stubbornly. "What's the problem?"

"You can bring something—a little more than that." Esther's mouth was opening for the spoon with David's and shutting again when his did. "Eliot is a potential business associate as well as a friend. A gift for the house will please the wife. It can't hurt."

"I hate that kind of scheming."

Esther dragged her powerful empathy from David and turned it full force on Muriel. "It's what people do."

Before Esther's determined, self-doubting stare, Muriel dropped her challenge. "All right," she said softly, "then what?"

35

"It doesn't have to be big," Esther said. "In fact, the smaller the better." She pulled a wave out of shape over one narrowed eye. "Something—amusing."

Muriel was jarred again. "What's amusing? A fifty-dollar bill wrapped in toilet paper?"

Esther seemed not to have heard. "And it doesn't have to be expensive." She looked into the distance as if taking instructions from unseen voices who inhabited a better world. "But go to an expensive place. With a good name. A place that makes a good package." She extended a hand, palm up, as though proffering the good package. And in fact she had a name.

"Go to Tanner's," she said. "Mac bought me the salad bowl there, remember? Remember the silver box? The gold ribbon? Go there."

"But that *is* expensive!" Muriel protested. "And besides, too damn showy."

Esther sucked her tongue in exasperation. "Every good store sells low-priced things, too. Maybe they cost a little more, because of the good box, but still low-priced. That's how the rich buy presents. They go to expensive stores and buy cheap." She finished more assured than she began, and turned her attention to the children's milk.

Muriel also turned away. She felt pushed and watched herself for flare-up signals. Esther took pleasure in her new role of advisor on worldly matters. Muriel had no desire to rob her of it. But the more Esther talked, with her air of a medium getting messages from some spirit-world authority, about the importance of the right gift, the more Muriel felt the whole thing was a shameful fraud.

Muriel said as much when the children were down for their rest time and she and Esther were eating their own lunch. Esther answered that she saw nothing wrong in showing good will through extra effort, a gift that was more than run-of-the-mill.

36

But she did see something wrong, to tell the truth, in a show of indifference for reasons of pride. And all she could add to that was that when she came back to visit and saw the street, the dirt, the noise, her heart sank. In the country it was quiet, it was clean. The sun and air were like medicine for the children.

They dressed the children to go out. Esther threw on, without liking, her fur, and impatiently set on her head the hat whose feathers waved shiny blue and green. Muriel, also with indifference, buttoned on her old winter coat.

In the street they separated. Esther and the children headed for the nearest playground—Esther pushing uphill and into the wind the big black carriage with the booster seat on which David, stuffed into his snowsuit and his boots, swayed like a heat-dazed camel rider—and Muriel headed for the Fifth Avenue bus on Riverside Drive that would take her to Tanner's. But first, standing on the windy corner, Esther made a speech.

"I know what you thought," she said. "I thought the same. That a couple could work hard, live a quiet life, and be happy. Now it's changed. If you stand still you fall to the bottom. Look around and see who your neighbors are. They can't help themselves. They don't even speak the English language. It's the old story again. Maybe their children will stand on their shoulders and jump out. But you are back where Mama and Papa were when they came—in a slum. You fell down to the bottom of the ladder, Muriel. When you and Herbie weren't looking, it happened. And it's not fair to your children. That's what hurts me now. When I see how your kids look and I know that out there the sun and air are like medicine."

6

The woman next to Muriel in the elevator removed her gloves and revealed a diamond too big to shine. It glittered dully like a prism, a glassy corridor whose tilted planes went in and in and in. She wore a loose, yellowish-color fur coat, no hat, blue sunglasses with thick white elliptical rims. Beneath the sunglasses lay sad pads of flesh. Therefore she removed the gloves and left the sunglasses on. You fool, Muriel thought as she stepped briskly out at her floor. Next time marry for love.

But at the thought, Esther seemed to materialize at her elbow, reminding Muriel that she by now knew better than that, and claiming her remorse. For a while, Esther stayed to step round the showcases with Muriel and to whisper, "Something a little more is nice. Something—amusing."

It had turned into one of those cold dark afternoons that comes to the aid of shops just before Christmas, making everything in the stores look brighter and better than nature.

Gifts were on the third floor. But in fact, the whole store was one big gift shop, wrapped for Christmas. A yellow chair, thin and curved like a shell, held in its lap a lettered sign that said, "Give her a boudoir chair as delicate and costly as her own precious self." Muriel snorted. Esther said, "Don't laugh."

There were hundreds of smaller objects that could be tucked into the famous silver box and labeled gift. Hand-turned pottery, carved plates and bowls of teak, displayed on white shelves before sheer orange drapery. There were ceramic and stone animals. She paused to look at those, thinking how her children would love them, particularly a lion with its face flattened and fringed like a daisy, its features carved into the stone. Esther urged her to move on and keep looking. There were mobiles of all kinds, some hanging from the ceiling, some on stands. Gold and turquoise fishes swam through an arrangement of amber-beaded strings. Rectangles of colored silks, framed in silver, hung at different levels from thin silver wires, brushing the air and each other like those tinkling bits of glass she used to see in the doorways of stores in Chinatown.

So many of the wares renounced usefulness, as if that would have been too easy a thing for money to buy. Ceramic pots bellied to hold a gallon, but were sealed at the top. Carpets were tiny and jewel-like, and were hung on the walls. The silver bowls were too massive to lift.

The prices! Muriel could have worked up a wrath over the prices. "Never mind," Esther whispered. "Somewhere there's something."

Esther prompted her to look at the women. "Poor Aunt Gertrude. She never even saw for herself what she wanted to describe."

Muriel nodded with understanding. This was what Aunt Gertrude had, by sheer intuition, divined. This leisure, this coolness with the clerk among these treasures, these women dressed for a day of shopping as if for a celebration. "Don't say their lives are empty," Esther commanded. "Look!"

Muriel, pressed, admitted that she'd come prepared for gaudiness, grossness. She hadn't thought that the rich might live so much with beauty.

39

"Everything is beautiful," she said humbly, as she had said it to the jeweler in her dream.

Like a placated ghost, Esther withdrew. Muriel suddenly had the sense of being isolated in the room full of treasures. I'm an idiot, she thought. What am I doing here?

She turned and headed for the elevators, walking past a wall of glassware that shimmered like a mirage. A last, glass cabinet stood before the entrance to the elevator, and atop the cabinet stood a very small lion made of rope. Its body was made of braided rope and its tight little behind was a knot. At one end a mane of frazzled rope ends, at the other the bell-end of its tail in the air. It stood on four knot feet and stared at Muriel through black-thread eyes.

Muriel felt one corner of her mouth begin to turn up.

She stilled with a finger the minute price tag that spun from the tufted tail.

"Quite reasonable for a hand-crafted piece." A tall, fair man with a Scandinavian gaze and a salesclerk's book had suddenly appeared. Muriel stared when the young man added, "Our little lion makes an amusing gift." It was as if Esther had dybbuked her way into the salesclerk. The lion continued to regard Muriel with his strict, brave stare, and Muriel nodded, "Yes."

"Gift-wrap?" prodded the dybbuk.

"Yes."

Out through the perfumed entryway, out under the canopy of Christmas chimes, out past the nun sitting patiently with a wooden bowl, past the freezing, bell-ringing Santa Claus, the Salvation Army band, out into the singing, groaning world Muriel walked with her silver box. She had plucked a present from Tanner's.

7

"If I call this one a virus, too, Mrs. Ruznack," the pediatrician said, "you'll think I'm stalling till I see further developments. But it is a virus. Don't ask me what kind. It's a runny-nose, high-fever virus. It's new this season. Next year there'll be something else. Keep Janet in bed, give her fruit juice and aspirin. Try to keep David from getting too close, if possible. When it's over I'll be able to tell you how long it lasts."

Janet ran high fevers. That was her style in sickness: steadily high-fevered and somber, with big eyes staring from the bed. When the germ was transposed to David (as it was a week after Janet came down with the illness) it became erratic, producing rashes on the thin-skinned chest and back, and outbreaks of hectic energy followed by sudden collapses. In Janet's style she recognized Herb's approach; in David's, her own. There was unity even in sickness, and she was moved by it, even though she felt exhausted.

The date with the Fains was canceled, a further date was set in its place, and that was canceled as well. The second time Herb, speaking through a stuffed nose on the phone to Eliot (he had caught the germ back from David and it reverted again to Herb's style) had to leave things with an indefinite, "We'd better call you when we're all finished with this."

41

All through January, the lion in its silver box from Tanner's stayed up out of reach in a closet, where Muriel noticed it from time to time. She felt kinship for the lion, imprisoned in his box for as long as she and the children had been cooped in the house.

At last the month that was so hard on city kids and mothers was on its way out. Muriel put the children in the living room for their nap, shut several doors, and let a crisp wind blow through the bedrooms. Some of the dampness seemed to have left the air. The days seemed to be a little longer, the kids were definitely better, and Muriel, anticipating everyone's recovery, said cheerfully to Herb, "That was some siege."

But January, before it went, gave February a parting kiss on the mouth and infected it. Herb's cold settled in his sinuses and gave him headaches that made him dizzy. The kids came down with what acted like bronchitis, though the pediatrician said, "For all we know it's the same virus that just went underground for a while."

Except for the few mornings when Muriel ran down to do marketing while Herb stayed home stretching canvases and sneezing, she had not been out of the house for six weeks. Miraculously, she had not developed anything except a sore throat. There was no fever and she did not feel entitled to bed space during the day. At night she fell into exhausted sleep, broken by the children's calls and troubled dreams. The fragments of dreams, like far-off voices: "I'm coming, I'm coming," sank back quickly in the busy, bed-tending days. Finally, in the darkness of an early February morning, the voices collected themselves and announced, "We're here."

Muriel had been sitting in the kitchen across from Herb, each of them holding a fretful child. Muriel dozed, dreamed, and woke. Scanning the dim, receding landscape of her dream, she picked out a speeding car, a trudger on the road overtaken and passed. The memory persisted, "Who?" The trudger broke into toddling forms that dwindled into specks.

"I think they're both asleep," Herb whispered.

Whatever it meant, she was not going to tell Herb this dream. What could it mean? She was rushing toward, she was escaping from. Punishing herself, rewarding herself. Condemning, coveting. Just as if she were not already dizzy from the possibilities of her dreams and exhausted by the virus in her life, the artist below the decks, that tireless underground worker, was turning out fresh scenes and sending them up the dumbwaiter.

Herb whispered again, "They're both asleep." But at that moment Muriel was seized by a cramped laughter. She shook and gasped and the baby bounced on her lap.

"You'll wake her!"

"I know. S-s-stop me!"

"Ku Klux Klan," Herb said gravely. "Birch Society."

She bit her lips, squeezed her thigh with a free hand, and continued to shake and squeak.

"War profits," Herb said louder. "Pull with the Pentagon."

Muriel wrestled with herself. Pinched and bit and squeezed, while the tears ran down her cheeks.

Instead of quieting her, Herb, as weak as she from lack of sleep, caught her fit. "C-C-I-A," he sputtered. "Eh—eh—F-B-B-I."

"S-s-stop!" Muriel sputtered back.

The names they thought would sober them took on desperate clownishness instead. Warning, gasping, snorting, they writhed above the sleeping children, until they were too exhausted for more.

43

8

Esther had not come in several weeks, but she telephoned faithfully to check the course of the virus through Muriel's family. At the end of her conversations, confident that Muriel would not hold it against them, she gave glowing accounts of her own children's health, then more shyly, examples of Mac's thoughtfulness, and, finally, with amazement, reports of her own progress, the busy schedule that kept her from the visit she longed to make.

She had become a den mother. She had little use for the other mothers ("From the day the children are born the nurses and the maids take over") and spoke against them enthusiastically, appreciating in advance how heartily Muriel would agree with her. But she approved the results. "Anyway those mothers can't take away the good of it, the school and club outings, everything in the open air."

Also she, who had never been anything but a tense car passenger, imploring fellow riders to push down the locks on their doors, had taken driving lessons and astonished herself and everyone else by revealing a natural bent. She had passed her driver's test at the first go and was now passionately in love with driving. Her car was the adventure of her life and she spoke of it—of "taking off," of "hopping over"—as if it were a plane. Besides den mother, she had been made president of the "Safe Driving for Teen-Agers Club."

It was getting harder every week for her to get away to the city. Why couldn't Muriel come for a week with the children? "The air is marvelous, Muriel. When you come for just a few hours you don't get the benefit." Muriel and Herb had been out on a Sunday soon after Esther moved, but then after that there was always someone sick. "In the mornings," Esther went on, "and the early afternoons. The air is clean. Mac says in the city every mouthful of air has germs from eight million people in it. . . ."

Muriel, who had been thinking the same thing, heard herself protesting.

"Mac says you ought to come for a week at least," Esther said with a mixture of shyness and pride. "Just a minute, I'm putting Mac on."

"Why don't you come for a week, Muriel?" Even generosity could not take the bullying edge from Mac's loud, purposeful voice. "We'll be more than happy to have you. Space is no problem here. Whatever you need, you name it, we've got it or we'll get it." It was snappy sales talk, with a business-card slogan at the end.

"Thanks very much, Mac, we'll have to see how the children do." Muriel kept her thin voice resolute against the twinge of guilt for the children's sake.

What was it? Mac had come too close to the language of her dream: "It's settled then."

One snowy morning Esther rang their bell and surprised them. Muriel could have cried for joy. "But why, for heaven's sake, Esther, pick such a snowy day?"

"What's snow? Snow invigorates you. There was almost no traffic. My car practically flew here."

45

Esther had arrived like a Russian, a visitor from a more ro-
bust land. She stamped snow from her fur-lined boots and
tossed off her weatherproof coat with the sealskin lining. "You
should see the boys. Out in rain and snow and they don't get
colds. Come out now," she urged. "While the children for once
are well."

"That's not the point," Muriel said, uncomfortable. "They
can be sick and well and sick again overnight. And it's such a
big deal, packing everything I need for the kids. And then, I
don't know, the change might upset them, just after they've
been sick. They have their routine at home. It's probably better
to stick with it." She felt her excuses were overlong and she
added, "Much as I'd love to come."

Esther sipped coffee and kept her expression, Muriel
thought, private and quiet. But after a minute Esther raised her
head and said with simple directness, "You can have your routine in my house, too."

All Muriel could think of to say was, "That's not the point."

Esther bit her lip. "The point, it seems to me, is how your
children look. Those little faces are so pale they're almost
green! Is that how you like to see them?"

Esther turned to Muriel her own face that was suddenly haggard and sick, the eyes red-veined and pouched, the cheeks
gone slack.

"Are you doing too much, Esther?" Muriel asked in alarm.

"Nothing is too much in that air. In that sun and air which is
where your children should be."

That night Muriel asked Herb, "Green as a dollar. Did you
ever hear that expression?"

"No," Herb said.

"I hadn't thought of it in a long time. It was one of Aunt
Gertrude's. She might have invented it, but I used to think it
was an old saying. 'That woman is green,' she would say, 'like
the color of a dollar bill.' "

"Are you sure you don't want to go to Esther's?" Herb asked. "We could go up this weekend. I'd leave you there with the kids and pick you up next Saturday."

Muriel shook her head. "What a confusion of images. Green was innocence, and therefore to be despised. But green was also money and therefore"—she hesitated—"also to be despised? Well. Maybe at heart, by God, Aunt Gertrude only believed in having enough money so she could feel contempt for that, too."

"There's a lot of free-floating contempt in the world," Herb said. "More negative images than positive ones. It gets harder all the time to do any good work."

Startled, Muriel said, "That's a strange thing for you to say, isn't it? I thought the artist was supposed to—"

"The artist is supposed to keep his feet dry and not catch cold," Herb said. "And so is the artist's family."

By the middle of February Muriel was walking around with a chronic pharyngitis, and the pediatrician said, "Can't you get away at all? Can't you manage one week at least?"

"Look, no ifs or buts, Muriel," Herb said. "Esther's offer is the best plan we've got."

The next weekend he took Muriel and the kids to Esther's for one week's recuperation.

9

A vicious question popped from Muriel's lips her first day at Esther's.

"Is this the way," she asked, looking around, "his wife left everything?"

"This is the house she left to him," Esther said, "and these are the children that Sidney left to me. We're not stupid." Esther's head lifted proudly. "We don't expect life to be dreams."

All right, Muriel thought wearily. We've got that done at last. There was a coolness between the sisters for a day, but then it dissolved.

The weather was snowy and cold. The children slept well and ate well and napped on the sun porch under the supervision of the maid. The days passed slowly. Muriel slept late in the mornings. The maid did Muriel's laundry and mended her slip straps. In the afternoons Muriel and Esther sat in the quiet breakfast nook, drinking coffee, talking of the old days, without tears, like two chroniclers, noting everything. Esther's boys were out till dinnertime with club meetings and tennis lessons, and the whole family retired early. On weekends, Esther said, things were even quieter. The boys and their sports equipment vanished from the house.

By Thursday Esther had a suggestion. "When Herb calls tonight, tell him to make a date with the Fains. Now that you're resting up."

"Oh, I don't know, Esther. I feel too lazy." It seemed to Muriel, as she said it, that it was finally the true explanation. She was feeling rested and indolent. She no longer had any opinion of the Fains. Certainly she no longer felt angry at poor Eliot for the circumcision of his name. Only she felt it would be silly to go. It had nothing to do with their lives.

She heard, through a fog of laziness, Esther making the suggestion herself, when Herb called.

But late that night Muriel had to rouse herself. Little David developed a fever of 102° and showed a spotty throat.

"It's the poisons coming out," Esther said. "It shows he needs another week."

Esther brought Muriel a pad of grained paper and some pastels. "How long since you've done any drawing?" she asked. One evening after dinner Muriel did heads of Esther's boys and was strangely touched to see the results of her own efforts. She said timidly to Esther, "Not too bad, I guess, for a first try after so many years," and prepared to throw them away. But Esther snatched the drawings from her hands and carried them with reverence to be framed.

On Saturday, Muriel left the children playing on the sun porch, watched by the maid (David was well and lively as a puppy) and went with Esther to the hairdresser's where her scalp was massaged, hosed with water, and rubbed with warm oil. Stretched out in the scented, busy room, Muriel fell asleep.

"You're tired to the marrow of your bones," Esther said, like a doctor diagnosing. "If you'd gone home this weekend it would have been the same as if you hadn't come at all."

When Herb came up later in the day and told her she looked marvelous, Muriel had a feeling of injustice. "It's only that you haven't seen me with my hair set in so long."

Early the following week, the sun came out, the air cleared

and grew balmy. "At last spring is coming!" Esther clasped her hands and looked off into the bare trees.

"In the spring is when it first begins," Esther said. "That's when the children should be here, in the spring, when every breath they take, every bit of sun is like a vitamin pill that keeps them healthy all the next winter."

Yet healthy noonday sun, for all she extolled it, seemed with its shadowless bright fortune to eat at Esther's soul. She was haggard, exhausted, as if worn out with searching for shadows she had lost.

"In the spring what thoughts come back to a person," Esther said to Muriel when they were alone.

Esther grew quiet and sad, no longer hovering over Muriel. It was Muriel who now suggested things to soothe and distract. "Should we take the children to the animal farm? Do you want to shop?" Except for Esther's haunted spring, there was nothing now to stop Muriel from going home.

"We have to go," Muriel said gently. "This weekend Herb will come up and get us. It's been wonderful. We're all bursting with health."

"Give it another week," Esther said. "To make sure."

"It's not fair to Herb," Muriel said.

"He's getting a lot of work done in the peace and quiet. He told me so."

But then Herb telephoned to say Eliot had suggested the coming Saturday evening for their visit.

"Wonderful!" Esther said, with revived spirits. "You can go from here. I'll be the baby sitter. You won't have to worry about that." She added, "They're anxious to have you. They probably canceled another date just so you could come up."

Muriel's irritation melted. The ruses of love. She felt weak, agreeable. A weak sister—how apt! Why not, why not go? She had nothing against going. Only the feeling persisted that it was silly.

50

"Isn't this silly?" she said to Herb on the phone. "It was all started so long ago."

Herb laughed good-humoredly. "Maybe silly. Only let's not cancel out if we can help it. Let's go through with it and not wonder later what if."

It was all good-humored and, by now, unreal-seeming. Only Esther stuck to her practical enthusiasms, reminding Herb to bring from home Muriel's good blue wool dress and the present from Tanner's.

Muriel sniggered. "The present by now has probably fallen apart in the box."

To which Esther calmly replied, "Then you can give them the pieces."

10

The start of the visit to the Fains had an eerie turn to it, because it resembled a dream Muriel had had of stumbling, during a night of pouring rain, into a strange house where every light blazed, but no one lived.

The Fains' house, large and dominating a well-treed rise of land, was lit up welcomingly when Muriel and Herb arrived. But the Fains were not at home.

A slender Negro woman with butterscotch skin and glossy black hair pulled tight back to a bun swung the door wide and smiled at them. Muriel's first thought was, what if that were the surprise Herb had hinted at. That the lady of the house was a Negress. "You *may* be surprised," Herb had said. "You may find something pretty different from what you think you'll find."

They followed the maid (her uniform was a black silky dress buttoned high at the neck, with a tiny black fluted apron attached in front) down a cheerful, skylighted walk to the living room. Muriel could hardly believe that a room could be so enormous and so warm at the same time. The walls glowed with paintings (Ah, so Eliot's wife painted—well, she had seen enough of that surprise) and sunlight. Everything in the room,

from the wood of the tables to the deep red wools of the chairs
was lit up by the dying sun that struck up a fiery blaze at the
edge of the meadow and the woods beyond the windows.

The maid explained that the Fains had gone for cocktails in
the afternoon, expecting to be back in good time. But they had
just phoned. They had been the tiniest bit delayed and were on
their way over now. "It's a shame it's too early for the dogwood," she added. "It's just a mass of blossoms in the spring."
She pointed all around the edge of the meadow.

A piercing voice called, "Who's that?"

The maid lifted her soft voice slightly. "Friends of your
mommy's and daddy's."

A tall blond boy of about nine, wearing jeans and a sweat-
shirt with a Y on it came into the room followed by two other
children—a blond boy of about seven and a slightly younger
girl.

"They went out," the oldest boy said, staring at the silver
box Muriel still held in her hands.

"This is Jimmy, Tommy and Debby," said the maid.

"How do you do," the oldest boy said. "Do you live in the
city?"

"Yes, we do," Herb said.

Tommy clapped his hand to his head and let out a
"Whooooo! An hour and a half coming and an hour and a half
back. For nothing! Wow!"

"It's not for nothing," the maid said. "Your father and
mother are a little late, that's all."

The little girl moved closer to the silver box. "Which one of
us is the present for?" she asked.

"Be quiet, you stupe," the oldest boy said. "It's not for anybody. It's a house present. Can't you tell that yet? When it's
just one like that it's always a house present."

"Is it?" the little girl asked Muriel. She moved an inch

53

nearer. Her hair caught a shaft of sunlight and a gold fire burst
out.

"That's right, Debby," Muriel answered.

"What is it?"

"Well, actually," Muriel said, "it's kind of a playmate, too.
Very brave. And he'll stand guard. Do you know who's called
the King of the Beasts because he's so brave?"

The children exchanged glances. "Let's see," the younger
boy said.

Muriel untied the ribbon with one hand, lifted the silver lid,
and put it underneath the box. The children gathered around
and looked in.

"He might still be sleeping, from his long trip," Muriel whispered to the little girl.

She opened the tissue paper and tipped the box for them to
see. "There he is! He's wide awake!"

The children backed away. "That's it," said the oldest.

"Yeah," said the middle one.

The little girl tossed back her gold mane and stared at Muriel. "We already have one."

"Do you?" said Muriel. Not knowing what else to do, she
began to replace the tissue paper.

"Well, my goodness," the maid said. "What difference does
that make? You know how you love that lion. You're always
fighting over it. Now you can have two."

"Yeah, that's right, maybe *they'll* fight, maybe they'll tear
each other to pieces!" Tommy shouted.

"Get the other one," the little girl said.

"Where is it?" One of the boys dropped to crawl under a
table. "It must have fallen under. There it is."

He grabbed the little lion that was twin to Muriel's, gave its
slender braided body a savage pull, said "Raaah!" and then
said to Muriel, "May I please have our second one?"

Muriel handed it over.

"Raaah!" he yelled again, smashing the lions head on, then circling them around each other while gnashing his teeth and growling in his throat.

"Let's take them to Daddy's den—that's the place for lions, in the den," shouted the other boy.

"Hey!" Jimmy yelled. "I have the greatest idea. We can play martyrs. Martyrs!"

"Yeah!" Tommy shouted.

"What's that?" the little girl screamed.

"Come on, come on, you'll see!" Jimmy led the way at a run.

"Well, what do you *say?*" the maid asked.

The three children stopped in their tracks, wheeled, and composed their faces into a respect-for-the-dead look.

"Thank you very much," they chanted.

Jimmy stepped forward very tall to shake hands and added, "I hope you'll come soon again."

They watched the children go out and then together they turned their heads toward the front door.

A tall, handsome, sandy-haired man, with a boy's grin she recognized, came striding toward Muriel. He lifted her up, whirled her around and then kissed her on the mouth. "How's the best marble-player this side of the Williamsburg Bridge?" Then he draped one arm around Muriel's shoulder and the other around Herb's and said sentimentally to his wife, "Helen, these are my two oldest friends."

Eliot's wife was also tall, with a good, lithe figure, a composed, handsome face, and an active manner that seemed to swirl protectively about her. She looked younger than Eliot. She stepped forward to shake hands and said, with a directness of manner that vanished as soon as she finished speaking, "Rediscovering old friends is such a joy."

55

Eliot then demanded to know why the hell they hadn't fixed themselves some drinks, why they hadn't looked around the house, why they hadn't made themselves at home. God damn it, his oldest friends!

Helen moved quickly around the room, stopping once to point to the blue silk wrapped around her left forearm, fastened with a gold pin. "This silly thing," she said to them, "that looks as if I'm being initiated into something, is just because I gave myself a gash with a trowel while I was gardening." She apologized again for their lateness, remarked it was a pity the dogwood wasn't out yet, then warned her husband he'd better make their guests double drinks so they could catch up. Eliot obliged and Muriel, thirsty in her nervousness as always, took several deep swallows of the icy whiskey. Her tongue seemed first to shrink and then to swell.

"Good girl," Eliot said, offering her salted nuts. Then Eliot and Herb walked down to the far end of the living room, to the bar.

Helen hurried out to see her children, then hurried in again to thank Muriel for the delightful gift. Muriel conscientiously drank from her drink, catching up. Eliot's wife, in her great joy at the rediscovery of old friends, seemed unable either to stand or to sit. But when at last Helen did sit with a drink in her hand, Muriel felt herself rouse as if from a sleep. Not for the world could she have suppressed those words, those true words that were rushing upon her.

"The children already have a lion like that." Muriel thought it strange to hear her voice come out high and trembly, when she otherwise felt so heavily calm, both chilled and burned, and shriveled and swelled.

Eliot's wife smiled over to the sideboard. "But they love it." She began to adjust the blue silk bandage and tugged, one-handed, at the little gold pin.

56

Muriel got up to help with the pin. She apologized first for her cold fingers and then announced to Helen, "Innocent things are sometimes transformed. They turn into moral issues, without a person even wanting them to."

"It's true," Helen said agreeably, if somewhat absently. "Who on earth would want them to?"

Helen was watching her lifted arm with interest. Muriel was bungling the wrapping job.

"The children love having another lion," Helen repeated absently, as she watched.

"They had to make up some destructive game," Muriel said, "or they'd be bored with it. I blame myself. I should have suggested something else."

"Children are bored and destructive most of the time," Helen said. She gave a little laugh and reached out her free hand to help with the tugging of the scarf. "Thank goodness they have the lions to take it out on. And guns."

Muriel's hands suspended themselves over the scarf. "But they have at least as much desire for constructive things as destructive ones, don't you believe that?"

"I'm not sure I do," Helen said. Then she added, coolly polite, "I'm not sure it matters whether I do or not."

"I think it matters," Muriel said passionately. "I think it matters very much how such things are channeled."

Eliot's laugh crackled out behind her.

"Terrific, Muriel. You haven't changed," he said. "She once told me I cheated, and I punched her in the nose," he said to his wife. "Remember, Muriel?"

Eliot was squatting by the liquor cabinet and grinning, the way he had grinned when they were little and he was winning most of the marbles. Was he grinning at his wife's discomfort or at Muriel's?

"Didn't I tell you, Helen? She's got integrity!" Now, Muriel decided, he was laughing at both of them, his wife and herself, linked together by the scarf.

Thinking of the scarf may have made her tug too hard. Suddenly the blue silk slipped away, revealing beneath a perfectly adequate Band-Aid on Helen's arm.

Helen murmured, "We don't need this camouflage any more, do we?"

"A toast to Muriel," Eliot announced. "Wife, mother, childhood companion, guardian of the early, early American way of life . . ." He stopped to think. ". . . and what else?"

"Shall we drink to the transformation of the innocent thing?" Helen asked softly.

"That's good, Helen," Eliot said. "But not quite good enough. Here's to that Early Jewish-American-Indian heritage. You can't beat it."

The maid announced dinner, of which, afterward, Muriel could remember nothing except that it was delicious, rich, copiously washed with wine, and some of it had found its way onto her dress. Neither could she, to Esther's frustration later, remember much of what was said. Eliot had recalled the characters in the old neighborhood—he could still imitate the short-tempered storekeepers, the neighborhood queer ones and cranks—and though all of them had protested he was cruel, they had laughed in spite of themselves throughout the meal.

On the ride back to Esther's, her head lolling heavily against the seat, Muriel murmured, "I wouldn't want David and Janet to have two lions, would you?"

Herb shook his head. "Or a den or martyrs either."

"We must be unnatural parents."

She said again, "I wouldn't want you to drink as much as Eliot. . . ."

"I wouldn't want you to garden as much as Helen."

"Selfish of us."

She waited, then began softly, "Couldn't you just tell Eliot no, you're not interested? Tell him before he tells you?"

"You think he's going to tell me no?"

"I think he's going to tell you yes."

He laughed. "Because you've got integrity?"

"Because you have. He can't stand it that you're a holdout instead of a sellout."

"Maybe you're right. Although it's not exactly a flattering explanation of Eliot's interest in me."

"Oh, Herb!" she wailed. "I thought it was supposed to be some kind of a game. I thought you always knew you would say no."

He stopped for a light—turned to her and explained patiently, "I still think people can improve the way they live, Muriel, and they don't have to get drunk and they don't have to slash themselves with a trowel or whatever it is, and the children don't have to feed martyrs to the lions. I'd like to make that point, regardless of what happens, because I believe it."

"When would you paint?" she demanded for the umpteenth time.

"I'd use all that time I wouldn't be using up getting drunk, sweetheart. Don't worry."

She shook her head. "I can't believe it. I can't believe we'd get away with it."

"We would," Herb said.

"We'd be the same as we are?"

"The same," he said. "You're so distrustful of human nature."

She looked at Herb's face after he turned back to driving. He appeared perfectly peaceful about what he had just said. She was a coward, of course. That was something she and Herb had already discussed. There were lessons to be learned there, too.

She let her head flop back again and closed her eyes. "I still think Eliot is jealous of us, just as we are now. Or anyway," she added, "I would be if I were Eliot."

11

On Sunday morning, Muriel was the first in the household to rise. She sat alone in the sunny breakfast nook, finishing her coffee, waiting for Herb, and planning to look at the papers. But instead, in the warmth, she went dazed and loose, and in that unprotected state was sent up a message and a corrected sketch of the image by the tireless underground worker.

Their ancient car had finally fallen apart, when her daydream began, and she and Herb were being driven to the station by the Fains' chauffeur. He was a colored man, possibly the husband of the maid, as short, ugly, and awkward as the maid was poised and handsome. It was late springtime, everything in bloom, and the chauffeur was taking them on a tour of houses owned by the Fains' neighbors.

At the first house, a uniformed maid stepped onto the flagstoned terrace and looked toward them. The house was sparkling white, like a Mediterranean house, and full of openings, in which pots of something like fuchsia bloomed. One house was all shimmering glass, another was set back in a park with boxwood cut into the shapes of animals, still another seemed to hang over a waterfall.

Wherever they arrived, the servants stood outside the house, watching.

"Is this all right?" Muriel asked. "Nobody minds?"

"There's nobody to mind," the chauffeur said. "I told you. They all at the party."

"Anyway, that's enough," Muriel said. "I've seen enough."

The chauffeur's eyes were glinting; he was short of breath and perspiring freely. The glory of the houses had taken hold of him and the hand with which he mopped his face trembled.

Muriel also felt herself trembling and perspiring from her efforts. She had been decorating the interior of each house they came to. Rugs, chairs, pottery, glassware, linen, silk, and wool from Tanner's. She set the pieces in the rooms, arranged and rearranged them. The chauffeur had built, and she had furnished, a county of homes. Their eyes glittered at each other in a lust of collaboration. "That's enough," Muriel said.

But the chauffeur had one more house to show.

Before a monstrous pile of stones and cement, the chauffeur stopped the car one last time. "This one yours," he said. Then the chauffeur got down on all fours and Muriel rode him up the graveled drive. They moved slowly, sweatingly, toward the monstrous door.

In Aesop's fable the poor country girl, on her way to market, tosses her head in her haughty fantasy and smashes the eggs that are to begin her fortune.

Muriel, to wrench herself from her daydream, pushed her chin resolutely off her palm—"Disgusting!" she cried out loud, as in the old days with Aunt Gertrude—and let her fist slam on the table. The china cup hopped from its saucer and smashed itself on the brown-veined marble tiles.

Esther's maid came in to clean the mess, and Muriel, abashed, watched while the maid crouched and wiped. The thought came to Muriel that what she ought to do was speak to Eliot. To see to it that the haughty smashed fantasies would not be repaired. To see that the goose would not lay the golden egg. At least not at her doorstep. Golden egg indeed!

You're not to be trusted, any more than the next person, with a golden egg, she said severely to herself. And to Herb's admonition, repeating itself in her head, that she was being hard on herself, she replied, That's right, I am. If it's to be this contest between high ideals and low cravings, let me at least pick my side.

Esther was delighted when Muriel said she would stay on another week with the children. Muriel murmured vaguely about wanting to take care of some things in the city, and how it would be a help if the children could be here with Esther. Muriel congratulated herself. For once she, the blurter, had not revealed what was on her mind.

12

This was the office of Herb's dream, the one he had described to Muriel the night that now seemed so long ago. Carpets. Monstrous plants dormant under artificial lights. Dark walls joined onto smashingly bright-colored walls, where abstractions, mostly running to vertical panels, were pinned like oversize campaign ribbons.

"You like them?" Eliot asked, coming up behind her.

"They don't hold a candle to Herb's work." Muriel braced herself for the crackling laugh. It came. Muriel recognized, belatedly, a painting by Eliot's wife—a small landscape of the meadow behind the Fains' house.

"Well, we won't stay here with them," Eliot said. He took her hand and led her through a door into a sitting room beyond his office.

"This looks very comfortable," Muriel said. "Almost like an apartment."

"It is an apartment. Mine."

"Why do you need it?" Muriel asked.

"I play marbles with pretty girls."

"You don't, Eliot!"

"No, that's right, I don't. Sometimes we have late conferences and it's simpler for me to stay here than catch the last train out. But anyway"—Eliot kissed her lightly on the lips— "you don't mind me doing that? I felt I had to. You restore my faith. The purest of puries and the realest of realies."

He drew her to the sofa. "I asked you to come at five-thirty instead of lunch, because I thought it would be so pleasant for us to relax here. Isn't it?"

"It is, Eliot, but as I mentioned on the phone, I'm here on business."

"I understand," Eliot said. He stood up. "I'll do the businesslike thing. I'll make us a drink."

"Don't make my drink as strong as you did at your house."

"Why not? I thought you were delightful under the influence of drink."

"I blabbed stupidly. Although," she added thoughtfully, "I'm apt to do that even without a drink."

Smiling, he handed her her drink and sat beside her on the sofa. His purposeful face was all attention. "You don't mind if I sit next to you, do you my dear?" He smilingly mocked the courtesy.

"I don't know if I can say what I have to say . . ."

"By all means." Eliot slid an inch or two away. "Businesslike."

Muriel wrapped both hands around her glass. "It's about the job you're thinking of offering Herb, Eliot."

"Yes," Eliot said, in a deep, encouraging voice.

"I'd like to ask you a favor about that."

"Go ahead, Muriel. Feel free to ask anything." Eliot's tone now took on a sentimental tinge. His hand went lightly over to her lap.

"Please don't offer it to him."

Eliot's hand withdrew. "Let me get this straight."

Muriel repeated, "I'm asking you please not to—"

"Okay, okay," Eliot interrupted. "I heard you. But why?"

"Because Herb doesn't really want it. It's not right for him. He has other things to do."

"In that case why wouldn't he turn it down?"

"He wouldn't."

"Let me get *that* straight."

"He wouldn't for my sake."

Eliot got up and mixed himself another drink. "Have I read this in a short story somewhere?" he said musingly. "The husband sacrifices himself for the wife by taking a job and the wife sacrifices herself for the husband by queering the job."

"I'm not queering it, Eliot. I'm asking you to not offer it."

"But the husband," Eliot went on, "already sold his watch—that's it—and the wife already cut her hair. That's it. Story by O. Henry. So they both, by the way, lose."

"They both win," Muriel protested.

" 'The Hairless Watch' "—Eliot made a frame of his hands, through which he looked at her—"or, 'The Fobless Chignon.' Painting by S. Dali."

"I asked you for a favor, Eliot," Muriel said reproachfully.

Eliot sipped his drink, grinned, and sat down again on the sofa.

"I've heard of young ladies in Hollywood sleeping with the producer to get the job," he said in a lisping, gossipy tone, "but I never heard of them sleeping with the producer to not get the job. Of course, the advertising business isn't the movies."

Muriel's drink chilled her fingers. Her tongue froze and burned again. "Don't be funny," she said thickly.

Eliot slid closer. "We're old friends, Muriel. I know you as long as Herb does—well, all right, I didn't see you for a few years after my family moved. . . ."

"Sixteen."

65

"But at least you'll admit I know you from as far *back* as Herb does." His arm moved around her shoulders, his fingers dangled near her breast.

"We've played marbles before," he whispered, laughing. "We even played doctor once or twice. You liked me when I was nine. You flirted with me. I remember that. Am I so different now?"

"Yes."

"I'm older. So are you. And I'm rich. People who were poor can feel how sexy money can be. Money is sex. Can't you feel it, Muriel?"

She caught her breath. She began, in her own particular style, to read headlines: "Money Is Sex: Housewife Offers Bribe"; "Sex Is Money: Executive Pays Off Housewife." She said severely, "I have to catch a train."

Eliot drew back. His face had the hard handsome glint to it again, like a man who has been on a bender and then gone for a workout and a suntan. One minute loosely spilling over, the next minute corseted up. She began to suspect that none of it was involuntary, that each mood was deliberately set out like a piece on a chessboard. Every feeling was recognized and put down to the level of a work horse, harnessed to its appropriate goal. Even Eliot's cynicism was something he used to inspire some kind of intimacy.

"You're on the wrong track, you know, Muriel," he said. "Herb isn't the great talent you think he is."

"Don't speak about it!" she said hotly. "You wouldn't know how to judge."

"Oh, but I would know. And I'll tell you frankly. He's a damn good photographer. He has a good design sense and a natural flair for the mechanics—layout, typography. But a painter? An Orozco? A Braque? Even a de Kooning? No, you have to be blinded by love to think that."

66

"I never compare," she said. "Herb is Herb."

Eliot's look relented a little. "Wonderful," he said softly.

She did not relax her glaring. She waited stiffly, forewarned by her intuition of Eliot's nature, for the next attack.

Eliot continued mildly, musingly. "Herb is a lucky man. He has a wife who overestimates him, and that's rare. Most American wives don't err in that direction."

"I don't know about most," Muriel said. "I don't know whether they underestimate or overestimate. I know that I appreciate Herb for what he is."

"Muriel," Eliot said, almost cajolingly. "I would like to suggest one thing to you. I've had a good number of years of analysis, and although I clown around sometimes, I think I do know a thing or two about motivation."

"I'll be surprised if you can surprise me," she said, "but go ahead."

"You seem very afraid of any open discussion between you and Herb about the job. You want it to be settled before it's discussed. Don't you think you might be afraid of your own reaction? Maybe a part of you would like Herb to have that job. Only that doesn't fit your image of yourself." He scrutinized her face, to catch any signs of discomfort. "Do you think I can possibly be right?"

"You are right."

"So then"—his voice, which a moment before had been so tender, now dumped a ton on her head—"you're suppressing it!"

"Of course I suppress it. Or rather, I don't suppress it. I see it's there. But I don't let it lead me by the nose. Look, I'll tell you my daydream. . . ."

So she told him—about the chauffeur she had created for him, Eliot, and the grand houses they had inspected, and how she had built for herself the biggest, grandest house of all, and

how she had ridden up to the door on the black man's back, as
if he were an animal. . . .

"So you see!" Eliot said.

"Of course it's there. But that doesn't mean I give in to it.
You have to suppress things in yourself—if you want to call
not doing an immoral thing suppressing. You don't commit
murder every time you feel murderous. You don't beat your
children just because you've had a frustrating day and they're
weaker than you are."

"Yes, but you . . ." Eliot started to wave his hand, to dis-
parage.

"No, it's the same," Muriel said excitedly. "People expect of
their statesmen, their political leaders, that they won't allow
themselves to acquire more power than they can fairly use.
They're expected not to become tyrants or dictators or financial
manipulators. Why shouldn't individuals demand the same of
themselves? Not to acquire the things that would separate them
from their best feelings?"

"You must have a damn low corrupting point. I don't consider myself corrupted. I don't ride on any backs. Politically
I'm as liberal as you and Herb. Maybe more so."

She refused to meet his look.

"Furthermore," he continued angrily, "I'd say your ideas—
if I were being polite—are utopian. Otherwise, I'd just call
them comical."

"Then laugh."

"Self-deluding."

"No, no," she said firmly. "That they're not."

"Because you are banking on Herb's being an artist."

"Well—yes—I'll admit that. But be careful about the word
banking. Not banking for money or for fame. As a way of life,
yes."

Eliot set his glass down. "It used to be," he began in a large, ruminating way, "in the time of your parents and mine, everybody wanted to be in on the American way. Now everybody wants to escape from the trap. Everybody wants to be an artist. That's a good way to pursue—what was that phrase the Germans used to account for themselves during the war?—inner immigration. I myself wanted to be a poet. I was a poet, in college. I wrote poems, not bad, they all got published in *The Luau*. It was the happiest time of my life. God, when I think what that feeling was like. It was like holding onto a ledge inside a volcano. If you could turn the trick you could climb out. The trick was something, some talent. Could you write poems, stories, a novel, a song? Could you act? Or paint? Maybe you had perfect pitch. If not, then it was waiting for you. Drop! Down into the cauldron of big business. The smelter of souls. I thought to myself, Now, great! I've got myself a one-way ticket out of the whole mess. I saw myself writing, publishing, getting grants. Now and then, as I saw it, I'd give an evening's reading at the Ninety-second Street Y. The only trouble was once I got out of college I stopped being a poet, as far as the outside world was concerned. Nobody wanted my poems, and nobody was willing to feed me just because I liked writing poems."

She listened to him, unmoved. She thought it was the cheapest kind of comparison for him to make, between himself and Herb. She contented herself with saying, "You chose one particular life and you didn't choose another."

"That's right. I made, you might say, the old-fashioned choice. To become rich in America."

"I don't hold it against you, Eliot," she said sincerely. "I try to see that in people's lives, forces drive them on. It happened to my sister. Only for Herb and me, it's something different."

"Yes, it used to be," Eliot said, still speaking in that large manner, "everyone wanted to be in on the American way. It was the land of female emancipation and equality, right? Now

69

every woman wants a patriarch for a husband. A wise daddy. With or without mustache and side whiskers."

She blushed.

"Am I right?" he demanded.

"Why did you change your name?" she demanded in turn. "Speaking of the American way."

Eliot laughed appreciatively. "Why the hell not? It was ugly. A leftover. It hung down behind me like a tail."

"It meant something."

"In the old country, you mean?" he said sneeringly. "What the hell did it mean? 'Old-falling-down-hut-where-beggars-sleep?' Who knows? Who cares?"

She shook her head disapprovingly.

"Don't you know America is the land of the free? You can be free of what you were yesterday. And tomorrow you can be free of what you are today. You can be a refugee from yourself forever. It's the land of eternal escape. Plastic surgery for the face, acid for the fingertips, dye for the hair, a court order to change your name, psychoanalyst to change your psyche, and a public relations man to change your public image. Don't you see, Muriel? The irony? You don't even come close to the ambiguity of the thing. You sentimentalize morals and you moralize about feelings. Wow! What a mess. Don't set yourself up as a thinker, Muriel. It's laughable."

"I don't. I don't. You're dragging in everything but the kitchen sink just so you can knock down everything."

"Changed my name? God!" He struck himself on the forehead. "Don't you know the colored people are shucking their good old American names altogether? They don't want those slave names. They're calling themselves X."

"That's different. Who oppressed you?"

"Life! Life oppressed me."

"All the same," Muriel said stubbornly, "you violated something of yourself." She didn't want to say anything about his wife, his marriage, but she reflected that they certainly were, as Eliot had said, old friends. If not old friends, then old enemies. How else could they be having this weirdly intimate conversation? She had wondered, before coming, how she would be able to say what she wanted to say. But already they had disposed of that and plunged into other things.

"Oh, do you think so?" Eliot was now assuming a mock contrition. "Well, at first I didn't see it that way, Comrade, but now, yes, Comrade, I do see that you are right and I was wrong to do as I did. I see now, Comrade, that I have been guilty of bourgeois decadence."

One of the things that was unnerving about conversation with Eliot was his quick changes of tone and mood. His quick, clever changes. His image about hanging inside a volcano seemed to apply here, too. And the turning of tricks. He seemed to fling himself through a whole circus of acts, imitations of every tone and stance, as if to see which kept him aloft. Without all this rigging he might drop down—into what?

"I'll tell you something I sense about Herb." Eliot was again suddenly crisp and direct. "Something you may not suspect yourself. I don't think he's half as interested in being an artist as you are for him. I think he'd like a job. But not for your sake. For the job's sake. For the tightness of it. For the structure. The poor guy's tired of wandering back and forth between being nursemaid and painter in that back room of yours."

She gasped. "You're making it up. Herb never told you that."

"I'm telling *you*," he said. "I sense it."

"He's a painter, not a businessman. Even during the times when things aren't going well. A painter. Not a salesman for . . . for . . ."

"What's the matter, Muriel," Eliot said calmly, "don't you

71

like our accounts? That's really neither here nor there. The question for now is, how much painting, really, can Herb get done? How much has he got done? Between his hours of teaching and nose-wiping at home? It's just an interlude of pretty colors, isn't it? Squeezed in between the acts."

"You have a nerve!" she shouted. "You don't know anything about it. He's a painter. He turned the trick!"

"Okay, Muriel, have it your way. It's just that I'm usually good at sensing things. And what I sense is that Herb doesn't have the heart to tell you. You're set on one thing. You locked him in a mold and you won't let him out. It's as if he signed a contract with you—he's got to be Michelangelo or bust."

"He's perfectly free to choose his own life."

"And that's why you're here, isn't it? To make sure of his freedom?"

It took her breath away. The cynicism of it. The pure, destructive strength of such an argument.

"You can't have any idea of our lives." She tried to keep her voice from flying up like a kite. "The cynicism, the hardness of your own life—you have no way to measure ours." She was thinking of how he had married a woman he did not love, how he kept this apartment for other women—it didn't even matter whether he had told the truth about that or not. There was something in the feeling of how he had said it.

"You can't judge what we do," she said shakily, proudly. "You've forgotten about a whole range of motives. They've been out of your life for so long. . . ."

To her shame, tears were running from her eyes. She fumbled in her purse for a tissue and while she was wiping her nose she heard Eliot's voice, the tone again abruptly changed. "Is it time to confess?"

She looked around at him in bewilderment. He had closed his eyes and his voice was a whisper. "I've struggled since

72

those days. Wrenched myself out of shape. I don't know myself any more."

"For heaven's sake, Eliot."

He opened both eyes and said, with what sounded like perfect sincerity, "Tell me where time has gone." He stretched his hand out to her. "Come near. You restore me. I feel close to my innocent childhood when I'm close to you. My fobless watch. Sundial in my childhood Garden of Eden."

In spite of herself, he had caught her by surprise. She leaned toward him, breathing through half-open lips.

He was quiet for so long she thought he might have lost hold of his verbal ledge.

"Eliot?" she called softly. "Eliot dear, don't be hurt by anything I've said. What do I know about anyone's life, after all?"

His hand, when she took it, was limp, but it strengthened. The other hand braced itself strongly at her back.

"Anyway"—Muriel wriggled up, retrieved her coat, clutched it into a bundle, and muffled her face in it—"I said what I came to say. I asked you the favor that I came to ask you."

She stood half-turned to the door, listening for Eliot's answer. He still seemed to have no words, so she turned to look at him. When he saw her turning, he lit a cigarette and leaned back, silently smiling.

As she passed through the empty anteroom, Eliot's voice carried after her. The ledge Eliot had caught hold of this time was fairly far down, but anyway, he had caught hold. Piercing, singsong, Eliot's words pursued with a nine-year-old's vindictiveness modified by an adult's grammatical correction.

"We'll see, Muriel Ruznack, who does whom any favors!"

13

Locked into suburban isolation, Muriel worried about the possibilities. But what, after all, could Eliot do? He could say yes out of spite or no out of remorse. Or else he could say no out of spite and yes out of remorse.

"If I were a Catholic," Muriel thought, "or in analysis, or even in group therapy, I could confess what I did, how I interfered. A breach of trust between husband and wife." She told herself that she worried less about the breach of trust than about whether Eliot would tell Herb yes or no, no matter if from spite or remorse. Then she worried about the breach of trust again.

Esther, sensing restlessness, said, "I know you don't care for such things any more than I do, but if you like we can go to the Temple on Friday night. There's a coffee hour afterward and you can meet the rabbi and see what things are like."

"Why not?" Muriel agreed, thinking, if priests can set up confessionals in the street, why not a rabbi in a coffee hour?

And so on Friday night, Esther and Mac took Muriel to see the splendid new Jewish Center. There was an enormous thermometer at the door—Mac joked, "It's a reform mezuzah"—to show how, like a rising fever, the fund for the new social service department of the Synagogue grew.

"They are planning wonderful things," Esther said. "For the old, for the sick, for mental health, for the poor."

"Who is poor?" Muriel asked, looking around.

"Maybe not right here, but someplace," Esther said.

The rabbi was an impassioned liberal. In his sermon he spoke with enthusiasm of pending federal legislation to aid the poor and underprivileged. Housing, medical care, job training programs, education, were high on his list. He said it was the duty of every Jew to participate in the great effort to bring each man to his rightful dignity. He quoted from the Talmud. "The Talmud says the poor man is like a dead man, and we should raise him up. If he is without the earth's bounty, he is like a dead man."

After the service, there was a coffee hour. Muriel, for reasons of her own, let herself be led, unprotesting, to meet the rabbi.

"My sister, Muriel Ruznack," Esther said. "She's still living in the city with her small children, but I think, one of these days, she'll be moving out here too."

Rabbi Goodson, a handsome, middle-aged man, tall and athletic-looking, was balancing his coffee cup and shaking hands when Muriel said to him, "May I speak to you privately for a moment, Rabbi?"

"Certainly," he said warmly, and before the eyes of an astonished Esther they walked a little apart.

Muriel took a deep breath, to help dislodge what she intended to say: "I broke faith with my husband, Rabbi, with another man. That is, I didn't commit adultery, although in fact this particular man says sex is money. I discussed money with somebody I was not supposed to talk about it to."

But she was ashamed to let out such a flood in the rabbi's

75

concerned, intelligent face. So instead she said, "When the Bible speaks of the fruits of the earth, everyone can see that's a good thing. To work for the fruits of the earth. But that was long ago. Things are much more complex now."

"It's all symbolic language," Rabbi Goodson said.

"Yes, I know," Muriel said. "But for a long time now people haven't been getting rich by honest labor. They've been getting rich by dishonest labor."

"Sometimes," Rabbi Goodson admitted.

"By dishonest"—Muriel was suddenly fearful that the rabbi might be more courteous than understanding—"I don't mean robbing a bank or stealing from stores. You understand I don't mean that?"

"I understand."

"I mean manipulating people, their minds, I mean, selling out principles, making any means do to get to the ends."

"I understand you," Rabbi Goodson repeated.

"Well, in that case, wouldn't it be better sometimes to choose poverty? Hasn't the Talmud foreseen anything like that?"

"The choice isn't that extreme. If one path is unethical, we can choose another."

"But suppose there aren't other paths. It's poverty or—or prostitution, let's say."

The rabbi shook his head. "Not in America. Not, at least, since this new social awakening. No one consciously chooses poverty. After all, as Emerson said, man is an expensive animal. Not only for one's self, but there are also children to be cared for, to be educated. The whole point is that everyone is entitled to earn for himself the fruits of the earth, symbolically speaking, in some dignified, self-respecting labor."

"But that's the fruits-of-the-earth simplicity again. Labor isn't always dignified. More and more it's undignified. What's dignified about the advertising business?"

"Well, some people manage to keep it so. I can't condemn a

whole profession, or one-third of my congregation, for that matter." He smiled.

"But isn't there anything?" She hesitated, then blurted out, "Isn't there anything, at least as much as in Christianity, of the value of poverty, of doing without?"

For the first time since their exchange began, Rabbi Goodson bristled. "Where is poverty of value in Christianity?"

"Well—some nuns, some priests, take vows of poverty . . ." She felt stymied by ignorance, she wasn't sure of her ground, and rallied herself with an improvised, "It's considered at least as close to godliness as chastity."

"Who is poor?" Rabbi Goodson demanded. "The Pope? He can only command the Church's wealth till he dies. The richest man in the world can't keep anything longer than that. And have you ever seen priests dine? And do you suppose nuns go hungry?"

"Well, then, Quakers," Muriel said. "There are Quakers . . ."

Rabbi Goodson gave a heavily sarcastic nod. "Indeed there are Quakers and there are Quakers. There's Mr. Richard Nixon, now he's a Quaker. . . ." Muriel bit her lip. The rabbi added kindly, "I'm only trying to point out that flesh is flesh and spirit is spirit."

"I don't seem to be saying what I intended to say." Desperately, from the corner of her eye, Muriel spied a woman with a bowl of fruit, bearing down on the rabbi. A man carrying a coffee urn had already jostled Muriel and the rabbi a few steps apart. A little to one side, a smiling couple were waiting to seize the rabbi's hand. And Esther, nervously standing by, seemed to be waiting only for a third party to intervene in order to make her own re-entrance. The distance between Muriel and the rabbi was now great enough so that by error a young man carrying a plate of cake passed, with an "Excuse me," between them.

Across the gulf, Muriel called out, "What about Jesus?"

"What about him?"

"The meek shall inherit the earth! The last shall be first!"

"But not here! That's in heaven. That's pie in the sky. Do you know how many generations were sold into slavery by that concept? No, ours is a here-and-now religion. Make *this* world better. Make *this* God's world."

"How?"

"The Golden Rule. That was the heart of Judaism long before the Christians took it over—although, God knows, they didn't take it over—and wire your congressman that you are in favor of the legislation I've described—"

"But the quality," Muriel cried out, "the quality . . . !"

The rabbi, encircled, was borne away.

14

Herb did not get out to Esther's until late Saturday afternoon. Muriel kissed and hugged him—how terrible not to be able to confess to the one she had always confessed to—scrutinized his face for hints of what Eliot might have told him, and at the same time tried to conceal her own. Right up till dinnertime, Herb said nothing about Eliot, and Muriel thought, "So that's it. Eliot's going to make us sweat." But during dinner, Esther brought up the subject herself. Attempting casualness, she asked, "Did you hear anything from Eliot?"

"No, not yet," Herb said. It seemed to Muriel that Herb looked evasive, but it was possible she was suffering from her own concealments.

Esther's disappointment burst out. "What's keeping him? How long does he think people can dangle?"

"It hasn't been that long, Esther," Herb said.

Mac entered his own opinion. "Look, he's a businessman. He hasn't only got Herb and Muriel on his mind."

Esther gave them both an irritated look and said to Muriel, "You said yourself it was long enough for the present to fall apart in the box."

"But that wasn't their fault."

79

Irritation was in the air. When they were alone in the guest bedroom Muriel said to Herb, "Tomorrow it will be time, and more than time to go home."

"Good," Herb said. "And when we get home will be time enough for us to talk about Eliot's offer."

She stared. "But I heard you tell Esther . . ."

"I know. I hated to lie to her. But I just didn't think it would be fair or right for the thing to come up like that in front of Esther and Mac. We've got to go over the ground ourselves first. So I told a white lie."

"Eliot offered you the job," she repeated stupidly. She felt suddenly weak and sat down heavily on the near bed. "Oh, I think I'm—" She lowered her head quickly between her knees.

"Muriel! Hey! You're scaring me," Herb said, embracing her bent back.

"I feel better," Muriel said. She cautiously raised her head.

"We'll just weigh everything, sweetheart, that's all," Herb said. "And the decision we both come up with, that will be our answer. I told Eliot that—"

"What did he say?" she asked quickly.

"He said that was just fine with him."

Herb went into the guest bathroom. Muriel lay flat on the bed a while and then got up and put on her nightgown. She began to pace up and down the guest room, bumping into one or the other of the twin beds as she turned. She was trying to pace away the transposing of Eliot's words into Herb's mouth and hers. "Are you so afraid of a discussion?"—this from Herb. "You must be afraid of your own desires, then." And from her, "It's you that's afraid of your freedom. You'd rather have your chains, be shackled to a desk and an office and a structure. All of that is very attractive—right?—compared to what you've had."

"The job is only to be considered," Herb protested, "it's not a foregone conclusion. . . ."

"But it should have been foregone. Foregone the other way."

"We've been through that." Herb was exasperated.

"When would you paint?" Muriel could hear how she was threatening him with it now instead of showing him how much she needed it for him. "You're an artist, not a businessman."

"I'm not in a mold. That's how I came to be an artist in the first place."

"The flexibility of your mind"—at last the vibrations in her chest, the silent speaking, had shaken loose a few sobs—"a thing I used to admire, just now terrifies me!"

The shout came back at her, "I never signed a contract with you to be Michelangelo!"

Herb came out of the bathroom and Muriel fell on his neck. "I'm sorry," she said. "If we had a dollar for every time I've said I'm sorry, we'd be millionaires and we could give it all away."

"Sorry for what, sweetheart?"

"For not saying congratulations. Whether you accept the job or not."

In the narrow, unaccommodating guest-room twin of a bed they embraced, grabbed hold of each other as if to restore themselves to some wholeness that had been broken.

In the very midst of lovemaking, Muriel was overcome by a nostalgia for love. What was gone were the familiar colors of her marriage, never clearly stated to herself, but sensed—a pairing of the heroic blue of heaven with a clear sunlike yellow. They had given way, merged into a duplicitous blend, and sunk toward an older, murkier part of the marriage spectrum.

"Darling," she whispered, from the depths of duplicity, "whatever you want, is what we'll do."

15

In the morning, as Muriel bent over her suitcase, she saw, from the corner of her eye, Esther come into the doorway and stand with hands on hips. Herb was downstairs. They had had an early breakfast with the children, quietly, so as not to wake the house.

"Good morning," Muriel said with a half-guilty smile.

Esther glanced at the suitcase, said nothing, and folded her arms. She looked as if she had been hurled from her bed by nightmares. After throwing on her red wool robe she had come rushing in with hair disheveled, eyes bloodshot and protruding.

Finally she said, "I've been thinking about it all night. I thought to myself in bed last night that something must have happened. You made something happen. Am I right?" Esther demanded. "What was it?"

Muriel dumbly shook her head.

"Something changed the picture. Something you said or did. Wasn't that it?"

"What did I do?" Muriel finally asked, in a bare whisper.

"Eliot's wife! Wasn't it something you said to her? And on purpose, too, if I know you, to make sure they wouldn't offer the job. Because there's something that's really so *off* in your thinking about this, about everything. . . ."

Muriel broke in before Esther could go on. "I don't remember any more what I did or didn't say, Esther. And what does it matter. . . ."

"What did you do," Esther asked, in a low voice, "flaunt something? How honest you are? How high-principled? How much in love with your husband? Some people—you'd be surprised—don't appreciate it if you rub their noses into something."

Muriel stared at the unaccustomed harshness of Esther's voice.

"Each person has a life," Esther went on. "You know that? To each person what he has is precious." Muriel lowered her eyes. "Everybody was young." Esther's voice was suppressed and breaking. She strode around the room. "Everybody was in love. Life! Life! Marches on!"

"Esther, please don't." Muriel leaned toward her sister, but Esther drew back.

"It's time to grow up. It's past time."

Esther grasped her own arms, her shoulders. She ran her hands over her breasts and her stomach, as if these places gave her pain.

"Esther." Muriel placed her words carefully, tenderly, so they would have little power to bruise. "It just doesn't matter that much about the job. Herb and I will get along. We'll be happy"—but her words were falling dully, they were becoming her own clichés—"with or without it."

"Of course Herb will be happy without it," Esther said unjustly. "He'll go on exactly the same as before."

"I'll be happy, too," Muriel said.

"No. Herb will go on. What does it matter to him? He'll stay young. But not you. A wife can't. Didn't you see what happened to me? Didn't you learn anything? Still dreaming, even though you're a grown woman with children of your own to protect?"

The reproach through her children pricked Muriel.

"How am I dreaming?" she demanded. "What am I supposed to be dreaming of?"

"How do I know what you're dreaming? You're dreaming you're living in the world the way it once existed, and maybe it never existed even then. Only your stubbornness believes it. And on top of that you think it's *right* to be so—so green!"

"What way was that? What way?" Muriel was exasperated, pushed beyond patience—it was too much, this shoving and knocking from all sides. Because I admitted I was dissatisfied with myself, Muriel thought, and hoped for changes, everyone thinks they can hammer pieces off me and it won't matter.

"How should I know what way?" Esther countered. "God sits in heaven with his eyes on you. Maybe that's the way."

"That's utterly ridiculous," Muriel said. But at the same moment her mind sifted and revised Esther's words: Herbie sits in heaven with his eyes on me.

"Please let's not start all this," she said to Esther, "just when I'm going."

"Going where?" Esther demanded. At last she allowed herself to look at the suitcase.

"I have to go, Esther. We wanted to get an early start, maybe have a cup of coffee with you and Mac and then go."

Esther advanced some silent steps. "Go where?" She spread her hands wide and said, "To that slum?" She turned her face from one palm to the other as if following a journey.

Muriel traveled the distance with her. Carrying a weight of tombstones, she arrived in the city and met more stones. She came to her street, that effort-wracked, broken Stonehenge of the poor.

She smiled at Esther. "I live there."

Esther's hands dropped to her sides. "At least stay a little longer. Now that it's coming to spring. And you know how welcome you are."

"Esther, I have to go."

"In the spring?"

Muriel smiled again and said, "Come on, come on." She bent again over her packing.

"Are you crazy?"

Muriel looked up to see Esther staring at her like a madwoman. Her body was tightening itself as if it knew better than she that Esther might come at her. "Not yet," she said quietly.

Esther advanced again while Muriel stood perfectly still.

"Now?" Esther put a red-tinted thumb and forefinger on the hem of the little nightshirt Muriel held. "Now?" She tugged. "Now? In the spring?"

Without a word, Muriel held it tight.

Esther stared and gripped the nightshirt with the nails of her fingers, and the shirt, with a rending sound, burst the interlocked arms of its tiny stitches. Esther let out a cry. Mac and Herb strolled in, as if by accident.

Mac clucked his tongue at the shirt. "What a shame that tore."

Esther stroked the gashed garment with her hand and carried it with her out of the room. Muriel hid her red eyes from Mac by pretending to search for something under the bed.

After Mac left the room, Muriel got up and began to rummage in the closet and at the back of the dresser drawers. "I can't find the insulated bag for the baby's bottles."

Herb was stowing a few last things in a shopping bag. He looked up briefly and then said, "We can go without it."

"I can't," Muriel said. "I need it."

Herb straightened slowly. "All right. Let's look downstairs."

Mac sat in the living room holding a newspaper.

"Sorry to disturb you, Mac," Herb said. "We're looking for the baby's insulated bag."

"You're not disturbing me," Mac said. He at once began peering behind the sofa.

Muriel went out to the sun porch and sat down. After a while she stopped feeling like crying and held her face up to the warm sun.

Herb stuck his head through the doorway and she said to him, "I'll be up in a minute to get the children ready."

But she somehow didn't rouse herself. Her head was tilted back against the top of the high wicker chair. She almost began to doze. When she opened her eyes about half an hour later, Herb was back, looking at her. She looked back stupidly, her vision marred by black images of the sun.

"The car is packed," Herb said, "and the kids are ready."

She jumped up immediately and followed him from the porch. As they entered the hallway, Esther was coming downstairs. She was dressed in her new maroon plaid dress and she was wearing her pearls. Her hair was neatly combed and pinned, her face pale with powder. Esther held up the baby's plastic bag. "I found this, of all places, in the upstairs hall closet." The lipsticked bow of her mouth went askew as she smiled.

They walked in silence through the snow-clotted yard to Herb's car. Herb carried David and Esther held the baby. Mac and Muriel walked side by side. Everyone kissed at the car. Herb settled the children in the back seat with Muriel, then warmed the motor. Muriel turned to stare through the rear window at Mac, who was enthusiastically waving now, and at Esther, standing quiet.

As the car sped along the straight road, Muriel continued to stare back. She was shocked to recognize the dwindling figures of her dreams. Esther, Mac, the house, the trees, all were dwindling, receding, shrinking to specks, and would soon be buried in the ground.

She cried out, "They're gone! They're gone now."

"We'll see them," Herb said.

"Not that, but gone from our lives."

86

The pain seemed unbearable, and she cried out, "My mistakes! I never learn!"

"It's nothing so terrible, Muriel," Herb said.

"How, not terrible?" she pleaded.

But Herb was busy with his driving, watching for the turnoff to the highway.

She was silent. The car sped on past fences, stubble meadows, frozen trees, and vast, shut houses whose windows gleamed with sunlight. She began, out of loneliness, to people the houses. Mama and Papa in that lovely house, all on one floor, so no steps to climb. Esther and Sidney and the boys in the next house, a meadow and a stream away. Like the boxwood trimmed into forms, the countryside took the shapes of the old affections which now, under the light of this spacious sky, went hurtling past.

Herb asked quietly, "Are the children asleep?"

"Yes."

"We could discuss a little bit now—if you want to—in the car."

"Yes," she said wonderingly, "in the car." She looked at the back of his head, tried to picture the expression on his face, tried to shift a little without waking the children, to catch his face in the mirror.

"How long before you have to tell Eliot?" she asked.

"He said to take two weeks to decide. He said to think about it from all sides, weigh everything. . . ."

"Oh, my God," she said faintly, "weigh everything. . . ."

"Hey," Herb said. "Let's wait till we get home before we discuss, okay? Otherwise you'll be talking behind my back."

They carried the sleeping children into the house, took off their snowsuits and laid them in their beds. The car nap had merged with the afternoon nap, and the children did not stir. The house was quiet, sanctified by the children's sleep.

Muriel unpacked and wandered through the run-on rooms

till she came to the kitchen. There it was, all the ill-assorted lot, ticking, snorting, settling, as if still trying to find its harmony.

"Home!" She stretched out her arms. "Every bump in the wall belongs to me."

Herb was standing nearby, watching her.

"We're not going to start weighing everything now?" she asked nervously.

He shook his head. They both seemed at a loss.

"I could get a little work in now," he said. "While it's quiet."

"I could get going on this kitchen. Poor Herb. How did I stay away so long?"

She heard a crashing from the studio. For one shocked moment she believed Herb was kicking at the canvases.

Herb's head poked out of the door. "Remember that mosaic table we started to make a while back? I was going to finish it and surprise you. Except I didn't finish it and I surprised myself, because I forgot I stowed it away in here."

"I'm glad you didn't finish it. I wanted to do it with you."

"Now?" Herb peered at her from the doorway.

"Well—it's quiet."

Herb carried the table to the middle of the kitchen floor and set up two chairs at opposite ends. Then he brought out the box of mosaics, the cement, and the tools. They took their seats.

"I like working on mosaics," Muriel said. "All these little bits and pieces are going to be fitted into a pattern."

"But the mosaics don't know anything about it," Herb said, zestfully shaking up the box. "They're saying to each other, 'What's going on here? What's going on?'"

"Right, that's right!" Muriel said, delighted. She put her hand in the box and began to rummage. "They're saying— poor little bits—'What in God's name is going on here!'"

The refrigerator clicked on. The floor began to vibrate, the fragile table to shake, and the mosaics to jump around in the box as if hoping to move themselves to some spot of greater safety.

Herb cleared his throat and Muriel responded nervously. Was he going to begin, now, to weigh everything? Her hand trembled, hovered over a blue piece, a red piece, a black.

Herb cemented in a row. Another row. Another. Patterns took shape. He began a small humming sound. He frowned, concentrated. She held her breath, waiting to hear if he would begin. But no, eyes on the table, he was engrossed.

Still another sound. Herb blew out through his lips, a small, repeated, popping sound. She sat alert, waiting.

But why was she waiting for Herb to begin? Why—out of habit—waiting for the next hard lesson? Watching his deft hands, it was difficult not to believe again that Herb knew not only the next lesson, but its solutions as well—in the strength of his strength and the goodness of his goodness, he had simply not wished to tell her yet.

Herbie sits in heaven with his eyes on me. She had believed in her husband the way some people believed in God. It's all for the best. Trust Him. He's working something out. Some kind of advanced, advanced, advanced calculus. Sundial in my childhood Garden of Eden. (And if Esther is right, and I've been dreaming? But my life in that dream is as real to me as hers is in her dream.)

All the same, something had changed. She believed in her husband still. But sitting there, in the quietly clicking kitchen in which every ancient motor was running down, she felt that she believed differently. Just as she believed differently in herself.

She could see that the answer to the question, "How should we live?" had always eluded her, except in its one, perfect, dreamlike form—"We ought to live with love, and no other desires"—and that this perfect, dreamlike answer was not enough, even, to get her to her sister's house and back with honor, much less through the world. Still, who could get through the world with honor if they did *not* honor such dreams? She was, like everyone else, a virtuoso of flawed accomplishments—a parent, a wife, a daughter, a sister, a dreamer. And the power that had pushed her, stumbling, from the jeweler's shop, that had knocked her off the Negro's back was, likewise, torn, split, harried, and nightmare-choked. The answer to the question, "How should we live?" eluded her. But there could be worse, she told herself. If the question, so stubborn and yielding so little, were lost.

All the same, another question was being asked now. "Shall we begin to weigh everything?" The question mounted itself in silence against a background of assorted sounds—her muttering kitchen, the quiet breaths of her sleeping children, her sister's whispers of loneliness, her husband's unspoken plea to be released, if he should require it, from her expectations, her own quavering, lifelong cry—"Disgusting!"

"How shall we live?" Although the answer eluded them, the question had in it an upwardness, a lightness of breath and aspiration. The other, the "Shall we begin to weigh everything?" was heavy, deadly heavy, a stammering wrenched from the here and now. She was not, by nature, a weigher of anything. Loves and hates blew through her heart like strong winds, and she had, truthfully speaking, liked it that way. She had hoped, truthfully, to avoid this wisdom of weighing that brought with it compromise and loss. It was the practicalness of weighing that led people to choose from among choices that were neither beautiful, nor desirable, nor good. It was the destructiveness of weighing that led them to these things, despite the revulsion of their hearts.

Herb sat hunched over the table, frowning at the jagged bits of his intentions. She felt a strong surge of love or compassion, and it didn't matter which. He seemed a fallen king.

She reached over and touched his fingers. He looked up, still frowning.

"The question is," he said, "how could we begin to weigh everything?"

"And how could we begin"—she leaned forward like a supplicant—"to speak of how we should live?"

Part Two

✣

Green in Love

✤

Apples

Larry, awaking, heard his chin stubble rasp the satin ribbon of their white blanket.

"Oh, you lucky bum!" he said to himself, as a small doubt hit him. "Oh, you no-good lucky bum!" Finnegan had said to him on Larry's wedding day. Larry said it to himself now as, stifling the doubt, he stretched between fine percale sheeting and turned to his wife.

To where his wife should have been.

"Where is she?" he asked himself. She was always beside him, nuzzling close till he was ready to get up, just as she always waited for him at night, no matter how late he sat over his books. And last night had been a late night. He had sat in his study, reading and rereading what he had already written of his dissertation, asking himself if he would ever be able to finish.

Larry twisted his neck to see the gold wedding-present clock on the bed table. A little past one. The blinds were drawn, but he could see enough gray light to know it was a cold, gloomy day, a wonderful afternoon for sleeping. He remembered now that his father was coming for dinner, and after that, Finnegan. But that was later.

"Then where is she?" he asked himself again. At the same moment he was telling himself, "Don't panic. For God's sake, why the panic?" It came to him at times when the unreasonable panic rose up that on the reverse of the coin of his lucky-gold-piece life was engraved a shipwreck. Somebody, someday, might flip that coin.

He strained to hear sounds. He flung back the blanket and, in his pajama bottoms only, he went down the short hall, through the dining room and to the kitchen.

He watched her first from the doorway. Tall, long-legged, slender—the baby hardly showed yet—Penny stood at the table, furiously whipping some gray stuff in a bowl. He admired all over again those long, fine legs, that silky blond hair that she let go just any which way. All of her body was fine and long-boned and tennis-y, even to the elegant stoop of her shoulders. ("Wings, Penny!" he had heard her mother say, on the very day Penny and he were married.) Now and then dabs of the gray stuff flew out of the bowl and spattered her shorts.

"Penny?" he said. "You didn't wake me."

She continued whipping for a moment in silence. Then she turned her young, unsure face to him and answered, "I got up early." She picked up their cat, Maxine, and rubbing her face against Max's ear, she continued, "I'm making things your father likes." She moved away for him to see.

Larry peered into dishes and pots to see the careful replicas, like waxworks in a museum, that Penny was making of the contents of the old-time meal. On a plate, chopped liver in a mound surrounded by slices of white radish. In the huge pot, yellow soup, bubbling and breaking like a turbulent sea. Upon its surface, round matzo-meal balls, yellow and smooth, bouncing like buoys; a faggot of greens, neatly tied with white thread, sailed and steamed and gave off its crisp, acrid odor.

Deep in the pot, the long thick slices of breast meat, each with three flat marrow bones protruding from their slippery envelopes of gristle.

"Well, it's perfect, wonderful," Larry said. "It smells like home, which is—you know—good and bad. But you've done it all wonderfully. Where did you learn it?"

"From a book," Penny answered. "I had to get a book. You know. There was no one I could ask."

He put his arm around her and made her sit down, because she hadn't yet had breakfast. He took her answer as a reference to the death of her parents, and also as a sad little complaint about other things, too.

Six months before, suddenly and nightmarishly, Penny's parents had been killed in an auto crash. For a year before that—part of it was over him—Penny and her mother had not communicated. And with her father the connection had been mainly money, because he was a man who converted love obligations into money ones, and discharging those, cleared the books. Their death had left Penny and him rich enough so that he need never finish his dissertation and begin to teach, except that if he didn't live out his old dream, what would he do?

Penny did her best to feel grief. What wasn't grief was guilt and confusion, and they worked as well, bringing tears to the mourning, and a sadness and sense of loss thereafter.

"Penny," he said. "Penny Benny."

He made coffee for them and poured it into two big mugs. He toasted coffee cake and buttered it and put it on a big plate between them. Penny held her mug in her two hands and sipped from it dreamily. Though she was tall, a little taller than he, she huddled down small when she sat.

"Eat, Penny dear," he said. "Eat coffee cake. Get fat."

"For the kill?" she asked absent-mindedly.

He said nothing. His wife was given to extravagant sayings

97

and doings. He felt satisfied when she took a piece of coffee cake and began licking the butter off the top.

"Let him come live with us," she said.

"I'd ask him, Pen, you know," he answered, "but what's the good?"

"He'd want to come."

"Maybe. Maybe he would, if I could ask him a right way, a welcoming way. I'm willing to do whatever duty I owe to him, but I can't put in feeling if I don't feel it, can I?"

"Just ask him."

"But I know him. He won't come that way."

"He looks so lost every time he leaves," Penny said.

"I know," Larry answered.

"He looks so frail."

"I know."

"I wonder, how does he shop for food and make his meals?"

"You don't have to wonder. When my mother was alive, she had to yell to him to get out of the pots." Larry said this with more assurance than he felt. His father had been a different man then.

As suddenly as it began, the conversation stopped.

They dressed and settled in the living room. It was Sunday. The *Times* lay on the table, a challenge to Larry's nerve and will. He picked three sections to read in order of his duty as he saw it: first, "News of the Week"—caring for a world that might reciprocate by blowing him up; second, books—his profession, if he had one; and last, music—his love.

Larry offered Penny a piece of the paper, but she refused. She had settled awkwardly on the sofa. Though her belly hardly showed anything, she had already started to move with the deliberateness of a pregnant woman. In her lap was Max, who at the first sign of disturbance was ready to plunge off. She gave her a few soothing strokes, and Max purred.

The "News" was full of horrors. But the cat purred, good if disturbing smells came from the kitchen, the room was filled with Brahms, his wife sat content. . . . Or did she? He looked up, just in time.

"Cigarette, cigarette!" he yelled wildly, pointing to where her cigarette had toppled to the cushion from the ash tray balanced on the sofa arm.

Penny thrashed the cushion and poured coffee from her cup on it. Larry went to examine it. Not quite burnt through, but a brown scar on the beige-and-yellow tweed within the brown coffee stain.

He couldn't help then looking back at the coffee table at older scars there, and thinking of chips or mars or scars throughout the house.

"Penny," he said, "Penny, for God's sake, don't be tearing up the playground."

"I don't do it on purpose," she said.

He put his hand on her head. "Of course you don't. Any more than I care about it on purpose."

She smiled at him then. "You didn't fall so far from that tree."

He smiled back. "We are what we are?" he asked.

"But we're changing every minute?" she asked back.

"Falling from the tree is easy; it's rolling away that's hard," Larry concluded, and with it finished their ceremony of repentance, their restatement of their situation in life.

"If I hadn't met you then, I could have met you now," Larry said. He was referring to the night he had dropped his ping-pong paddle at the USO and dashed across the room yelling, "Listen, your skirt's on fire!"

It had been her expression he had noticed first. He liked it. A kind of naked look about her face, despite a childish stubborn set to the mouth that he could see too. But naked the way the forehead was smoothed tight back, the way all the skin of her face lay tight against its bones, something the way a dog looks when it lays its ears flat—naïve and scared and hopeful. She had been staring ahead, not talking to anyone, one hand lying across the edge of her lap, holding a cigarette. He had kept one eye on her—she seemed to be falling into a daydream. And then he thought he saw the live end of her cigarette nestle into the fold of her tweed skirt. It wasn't exactly on fire, of course, but there was a fair-sized scorch in it that, as she worried it with her fingernail, became a hole.

At first, without much interest, she had looked down, poured a little coke into her lap, and thanked him. As he continued to stare, she had added, "Don't worry, it was bound to happen. It always does. I guess I like things to be worn and torn." Then she had looked at him with sudden clear interest and said, "Your forehead has wrinkles. That's nice."

He had sat down and that very night had begun to tell Penny about himself, his mother, his father, the store. About how his mother and father had told him that the apple doesn't fall far from the tree, and how he had vowed it would. That night and the nights after, as he said much and Penny said little, he learned, out of the corner of his eye, about her too. Not only did she burn; she cut, scratched, and bumped herself, and never remembered how or when. She also lost purses, containing a good deal of money. The naked watchful look was not for that, but instead for the many interrupted scenes where the mother and father had stood silent and glaring, the unspoken words hanging in the air like blimps.

He had told Penny how he had had so much energy as a boy that he could not sit still. He sometimes even read or wrote standing up. When he ate supper, he used to shake one leg under the table until his father and mother, who wanted a deathlike stillness in which to ease their aching bones that they said felt broken, declared, "Did you ever see? Such a crazy kid? Stop with the shaking!" But he was like a runner, warming up, ready for the sprint, to be gone.

He had tried to tell his father about his dreams. "Not for me, Papa. Not the store. Something I'll be happy with. Here the son doesn't have to follow the father. The son can do new things. . . ."

Larry knew he should keep the excitement out of his voice. He should be grave, to show he understood life was hard. But he got swept up. And his father was a choleric man. With a way of moving his glance furiously up and down the length of a person as if to include every bit, from crown to toe, in his contempt.

"Did the parents struggle so the son could be a failure?" he shouted. "Who gives up a store for a nothing—a maybe?"

And his mother, who had it in for him because he dated girls who weren't Jewish (he had to admit they had a fatal attraction for him—the pale, quiet ones with freckles and sandy eyebrows and a shy admiration for the way he talked, incessantly, about his work), said, "You think if you read your eyes out and run around till all hours you'll stop being my son and Abe Goldstein's son? Never! It was already too late twenty years ago. You should have talked to God before you were born."

When everything else lost its sting they even—anything to stop his flight—sacrificed the image of their own self-esteem. "The apple doesn't fall far from the tree," they said wearily.

It seemed that all during his growing up, for one reason or another, his parents were angry with him. And he, too, mixed with his pity, felt angry and choked.

Knowing he should leave, but unable to get the power, he had sweated it out at home, working in the store days, at night grinding his way through a dreary B.A., a dreary M.A., and at last starting on his Ph.D. This was to be the dove that would bring him back in its mouth a piece of the green growing life at some university far from the East Bronx.

But before that could happen, the army had taken him. Then he had met and married Penny (she had put her hand on his sleeve once after they kissed good night and said in her whispery voice, "I want to be new too. But not alone. I can't make it alone") and they had gone to live in a good but not flashy apartment house in downtown Manhattan where he was to finish—finally finish—his dissertation.

They had seen his parents infrequently. Penny had seen hers not at all since the wedding—though there the excuse was that they lived in Cleveland. When Larry's mother was dying, his father did not summon him until she was far gone, and her mind in confusion. She took Larry's hand and said, "Promise me. . . . Promise me you'll find a nice girl and settle down," even though Penny was there the whole time.

"Put Max in the kitchen," Larry said to Penny now. It was getting near the time—it was always near evening—when the cat's digestive system went to pieces.

Ignoring that, Penny said, "You don't have to be afraid of your father any more, if that's it. A television set, a warm room, and some food is all he needs now. He's changed."

It was true. Although it never made the elderly stranger seem less a stranger, he could see that his father had changed.

After his mother died, his father had shut up shop. He had taken Larry aside and said, "I have to be a different person now. The world has changed. I spent too many years in the store—in the dark."

He then sold out the store, moved to a smaller apartment in the Bronx, and bought a television set.

"Look, look how people live," was all his cry.

He saw with his own eyes that people had more rooms in their houses than they could live in. That they burned lights for the joy of warm, beautiful light, that they ate from uncracked plates on clean white tablecloths. He peered inside the set at "Person to Person," his neck stretched forward, his mouth open as if he would take a bite out of the fruit that was just standing around in a bowl, getting rotten.

He learned that people who read and wrote books and talked about them were not sunk in the river with their feet in cement, but were actually paid. Scholars and scientists became his heroes. "Brilliant mind!" he said, whenever one appeared. All the same, he squinted in perplexity, searching the screen. Where was the aggressiveness, the loud voice, the smooth brag of the success? Vanished. Gone from this new, well-lighted world. He hesitated, confusion peeping out from under his wrinkled, straining lids. Then he gave up, leaned back, and pronounced the benediction, "Brilliant mind."

Penny had told Larry his father was proud of him. But Larry thought rather that his father looked upon him as a straggler who had fallen to the rear of his own parade. "Larry!" his father would say, tearing his eyes from the screen for a moment. "You read more than him. Why don't you get up there?"

The new and the modern was wonderful. His father was determined not to be a back number, and to go along with all of it. When Penny burned a cigarette hole, threw out a piece of sterling with the garbage, or when the cat, whose diarrhea was chronic, did it on the sofa pillow, Larry's father sat stunned for a moment. Then he leaned back, gave himself up to the new and the modern and, nodding his head, dumbly smiled.

"I'm nervous," Penny said. "What are you thinking about? The past? Then you won't ask him."

"I would if I could," said Larry. "If I can I will. Can I help it if I don't feel it yet? If I just don't feel it?"

"All right," said Penny. "But please. I can't bear to see him walk out into the cold another night without some offer from you."

"I'll try. I'll try. I'll try," said Larry.

103

The doorbell rang. Penny gave him one full glance before she went to the door.

The next moment Larry's father stood before him. Not, as he still thought of him from his childhood—a heavy, powerful man. But as he had been for years now—shrunken, frail. The soft yellow sports shirt was buttoned at his throat and he had made a careful knot in his navy-blue-and-red flowered tie—a big, loose, slippery knot, and the collar and the knot fell away from his wasting neck. He stood rubbing his hands uncertainly, searching for a joke.

"Well, professor, did you get your TV contract yet?"

"Not yet, Papa, not yet. Sit down."

"I'll put everything on the table," Penny said. "We'll eat soon." She hurried out to the kitchen.

His father sat down on the sofa. In the old days he would certainly have first shooed off the cat that was curled in a deep cup on the pillow beside him. The dog he had brought to the store to catch rats when Larry was a boy he had forbidden Larry to take home. And the dog had—so Larry had thought— died of loneliness and starvation in the first few months. But now his father sat with his hands in his lap, meekly sharing the sofa with the cat.

Larry reached for the whiskey bottle. "A little schnapps, Papa?"

"All right. I will. For the appetite."

He knocked his back neat. Larry did the same, and they sat silent for a moment.

"Tell me the truth, Larry," his father began. "You're a married man, almost a father, you could tell me." He said it with a smile and a wink, now that the mother was safely underground, and nodded in the direction of the kitchen. "She's really a *shiksa,* no?"

It was a two-year-old joke between them. And each time Larry answered with a shrug and a laugh, "Could be."

"How's your apartment, Papa?" he asked.

"Fine, fine," his father answered, looking into his shot glass.

"They give you enough heat?"

"Oh, sure."

Larry couldn't go on with it. Reaching for the whiskey bottle again, he asked, "A little more, Pop?"

His father raised his palm vertically. "No."

Larry let his hand fall from the bottle. His father gazed through the window where snow was beginning to fall. Suddenly he said, "All right, yes, I will, a little more."

As they finished their seconds, Penny called them to the dining room. "It looks good," said Larry's father politely. Penny's face brightened. Then his father, about to sit in his accustomed chair, seemed to remember something. Taking Penny's arm he said, "Let me look at you. I hardly saw you before. You look good. But tell me, where you keeping it, in your handbag?"

Penny's face broke into a delighted smile. "Oh, Papa!" she said. "Just a few more months and you'll be complaining that the crying keeps you up. You'll . . ." she stopped abruptly.

"Let's eat," said Larry.

They sat down and Larry felt grateful, as he always did at such meals, that his father was not intimidated by the Jensen silver candlesticks, tarnished as they were, or the white Museum of Modern Art dishes—wedding presents from Penny's side. None of these things could disguise from his father the real purpose of such a sitting down. It was to eat, and he did. They had little conversation.

Larry thought of another "dining room" that had been no more than a bulged passageway between two other rooms, without windows, where they had sat under the six-bulbed chandelier with little brown paper lampshades—his mother's extravagance. But his father kept three of the bulbs twisted loose so that they did not light. "Who sees us here?" he had asked.

When the meal was over, Penny, Larry, and his father seated

themselves in the living room. Larry looked at them all now in the moonlight of television. His wife, nervously reaching for a cigarette with one hand, rubbing the cat down with the other; the cat, looking to him to be dangerously near her hour; his father, open-mouthed as at the creation of the world. All his straggly, limping household. The next move was his. He couldn't make it.

He jumped up. "Papa, I still have work to do on my dissertation tonight. I'm going inside for a while."

His eyes glued to the screen, Larry's father waved him away. "Sure, sure. Go, Larry."

He went to his study and found Penny close behind him. "Get back inside," he said.

"Are you going to ask him in here?" she demanded.

"Leave me alone. I don't know. Go watch television."

He wanted very badly to go to sleep. But he sat at his desk, gazing at the index cards, the card-file boxes, the library reserve slips with catalog numbers written on them, his half-written first chapter, "Roots of the Present Dilemma in Antiquity," and tried to think. But nothing came to his mind except that he wanted to crawl under the blankets and sleep.

He took a packet of cards from the file box, rolled off the rubber band, and idly began turning the cards face down on the desk in a kind of mosaic arrangement. One by one he faced each card up, looked at it, replaced it face down in another spot. It came to him what he was doing: dealing out the cards for a game of "Concentration" that he had played as a kid. All the cards in the deck were laid face down on the table and you tried, when your turn came, to make a pair with two picks. You had to show your cards when you picked, and if they were unpaired, you turned them face down again, but changed their locations so that only you, you hoped, would remember where they were when your turn came again.

Soon it came to him also why he had been playing "Concentration," because he had begun to think about an incident from the store. He had come to the store after his classes one day to help, and a woman had walked in after him and asked his mother for a blue slip, size 44. His mother had looked first on one shelf, then another, bending down to the bottom, standing on the little stepladder to peer at the top of a column of shelves. She had come down, her face flushed.

"I don't think if they make that size in such a color," she had said to the woman. "Take a black."

"What's the matter," his father had roared out from the back of the store. "You don't want to sell your customers? Or you don't know your own stock?" He had ducked under the counter and pulled out a dusty box—blue slip, size 44.

Larry had tried on many Saturday nights and Sundays when the store was closed, to arrange the stock. But it was hopeless. Soon everything would be a jumble again, because they would shove merchandise back in the bins any old way in their eagerness to please a customer.

Or was it only that? Sometimes he thought there was something else too. That they really *wanted* to trick each other, like in "Concentration."

He picked up the cards quickly and put them into the file box again. He didn't like to think about the charades in the store. It still made him feel sick, even at this distance.

Through the half-open door of his study, Larry heard, mixed with the television voices, the voice of his father, in his new wisdom, explaining the commercial to Penny.

"You think that's the cake from the recipe they tell you they put in the oven? No! It's a different cake entirely."

"You said it, Papa," Penny answered. "They're all *goniffs*."

Something Penny picked up from Larry's father was this old-time Yiddish word for thief. In Penny's family no flick of the oll sorrowful-comical tongue had been allowed to touch the children. But like the princess in *Sleeping Beauty*, Penny wandered through all the rooms of her young life till she came to what was forbidden.

"My father," his father was saying, "what did he know of such things? Never a kind word to us, never a sweet look to his wife. Can you imagine *I* should have had such a father like in the play? *I* should go to school, my father should buy *me* a car, give *me* money to travel and see the world? He was as mean as could be, to prepare us for later on. So we wouldn't be disappointed in life."

There was silence. Then Larry's father sighed deeply. "Aah, what's the good? I lived in the dark. Now it's almost over for me."

Larry had never heard his father speak this way before, and his face grew hot. What kind of parody was this? Then he thought better of it. No, it was sincere. His father's own wail for his own sorrows. He never saw the connection between Larry's and his. The generations could only project backwards, on a bridge of grievances. How ludicrous that was. When you came down to it, just ludicrous.

Larry stood up. "Papa!" He went to the doorway of the living room.

"Federal Man" was on. The scene was the inside of a bank vault. Thieves were packing in dynamite.

"Papa," he said.

"It's going to go off before they get away," his father said.

Larry waited. There was a tremendous explosion. Martial music came up loud, and a strong male voice told how many years everybody was getting.

"How do you like the way they figured out where the money was?" his father said. "Brilliant men, aren't they?"

Larry wasn't sure whether his father meant the crooks or the cops, but what the hell did it matter?

"Papa," Larry said, "come into my room. There's something I want to show you."

"Oh yeah?" said his father in surprise. Meekly, he got up and followed.

In his room, Larry pointed to the stack of papers on his desk. "This is how far I am in my dissertation."

"Wonderful, wonderful," said his father. "When it's all through how many stacks like this will you have?"

"About five."

"Don't say! So big? That's wonderful."

"Papa," Larry said abruptly, thinking it would be over soon, "Why don't you come live with us?"

"You mean I should move in?"

"Sure. Why not? We have the room." He didn't say any of the little lubricating things needed at such a time—about how much they wanted him, how they worried about his being alone, about how he could be company for Penny and the baby. He kept it plain fare. Not very nourishing maybe, but all he had to set before him—a hard-boiled egg in a cracked soup-plate.

"I should stay here with you and your wife? That's what you're saying?"

"Yes."

He looked Larry soberly and steadily in the eye and shook his head up and down a few times. Larry had no idea what it meant. He knew it was not an answer. A reflection of some kind.

Suddenly his father's face cleared. He laughed a formal little deprecating laugh. A Jewish-type laugh. Or maybe it was Japanese.

"Then where would I visit?" his father asked. "You know I like to visit. If I lived with you, where would I visit?"

"You're sure, Papa?" Larry asked.

"I'm sure," his father answered.

This time it was Larry's turn to give his father a heavy look and to nod his head. "All right, Papa," he said.

They returned to the living room and his father announced that he was leaving.

"Must you, Papa?" Penny asked sorrowfully.

And Larry added, "Stay a while, Papa, and meet a friend who's coming. In fact you know him. Finnegan, remember? Then I'll drive you home."

"No. It's enough," his father said.

Larry helped him on with his coat, a shabby brown herringbone. His father pulled out of the pocket the beige cashmere muffler Penny had knitted for him, looped it around his neck, and crossed it carefully over his chest.

He went out, refusing, as usual, Larry's offer of a lift or of company on the walk to the subway.

Larry leaned against the window looking down, waiting to see his father come out into the street, and watched him walk in the lamplit snow.

"Did you ask him?" Penny asked.

"He refused," Larry answered.

He turned from the window to look at her. Her eyes were intently on him, very full and unhappy. She was stroking Max, who looked at him once, and yawned.

Larry sat next to them. "Some things," he said, "just can't be made new."

He stuck out his little finger. "Fins?" he asked softly. Slowly she hooked her little finger around his and answered, "Fins."

Finnegan, of course, came early. Loneliness beat him from his furnished apartment the way hunters in Africa beat small animals from the bush.

He tore off his overcoat, kicked off his shoes, pulled off his wet socks and draped them on the radiator, gave Penny a resounding kiss, and sank into an armchair.

110

"Aah," he said, "aah, comfort, aah, companionship. Oh, people, people, you'll have to give thanks for your blessings when I tell you what my life has been like."

"Poor Finny," said Penny. "What's the matter?"

"Everything. All of it. You two probably don't even notice— what does it matter when there's someone to come home to?"

"What's eating you, Finn?" Larry asked.

"Have you noticed how early it's getting dark lately?"

"It happens every year," Larry said.

"I thought you'd take that insensitive tone," said Finnegan. "Sure, it's bad enough ordinarily. You step into the street after work. Bingo, it's already dark. You go straight home because tonight you're going to work. You're going to be somebody. You eat your supper fast, just to get through with it. You want to know what I eat?"

"No," said Larry.

"I do," said Penny.

"Never mind," said Finnegan. "It's not appetizing. So there you are, the whole evening ahead. Do you work? I give you half an hour, myself forty-five minutes because of strong character and self-discipline. Then, brrp, brrp, brrp!" In quick, agile movements, Finn pantomimed picking up the receiver, dialing, drumming his fingers on his knee. "Hello, hello. Help, save me."

Penny leaned over and put her hand on Finnegan's arm. "It will be spring before you know, Finny. In the meantime, you can come live with us."

Finn looked at her blankly. "That's what I mean, though. It's not just winter solstice—that crap. It's not going to lighten up. It's THE DARK. Inching up, creeping in, taking hold. Every day a little darker. It's like leprosy. You don't know it's got you until one day your nose falls off, splash! into the soup."

He leaped onto his bare feet. "Oh, my children. The time of the great darkness is coming. You must cleave unto one another." He sat down moodily again, his feet on the chair, hugging his knees. "Everyone's got someone to cleave to but me."

Larry heard Penny saying gravely, "I know what you mean, Finny. My nose doesn't have to drop off before I know what's coming. I know the dark is coming, too." He was already heading toward the kitchen and called to Finnegan to help him dig the ice cubes out of the trays.

"I'll do it, I'll do it," said Penny, dumping Max to the floor. Larry watched their progress into the kitchen, Penny slow and listing, Max following closely, high-tailed and suspect.

Larry took hold of Finnegan's arm. "I want to talk to you." Instead of taking him to the study, which was too close to the kitchen, he led him to the bedroom. Both he and Penny had been back to the room several times, but it struck him now for the first time that the bed was still unmade. The big white fleecy blanket with its satin ribbon binding—more trousseau—dragged to the floor on the side of the bed nearest the door. Someone, maybe Penny, maybe he, had walked on it and left shoe marks. He looked at it as though it were an injured child. A beautiful blanket. How many people had white blankets on their bed? Why did they have to walk over it? At the same time he cursed himself for a covetous bastard. He was houseproud on his wife's father's money.

Finnegan flopped on the bed and Larry turned away, pretending to examine his chin in the mirror. "I need a shave," he said. On the dresser top were Penny's toilet articles—bottles and jars—set at odd intervals and angles, like chessmen in a suddenly interrupted game.

"Nothing in this house is in one piece," he burst out to Finn. "Everything's broken, chipped, cracked, crocked, or burned. Us too, Finn."

"Why you silly bastard. You fell in so lucky you don't even have a complaint."

112

"Things aren't right, Finn."

"Sure, I told you. It's the dark. It's closing in."

The glum insistence of Finn's joke was making itself felt. It crept along Larry's skin like a draft.

"Penny wants my father to come live with us," he said.

Finnegan had been letting his shoes dangle off the edge of the bed. Now he hoisted himself back so that his heels rested on the blanket, and he folded his arms under his head. "If I were you, and Penny was my wife, and your father my father, I'd make a strong stand. I remember him from the old days."

"He's changed a lot, Finn. You haven't seen him since my mother died."

"They get old they get feeble. That's justice."

Larry didn't answer. Instead, he looked at his face in the mirror. He was the picture of his father as he used to be. He had the same deep-set black eyes, the same long, down-curving nose, the same large, soft cheeks that he knew from watching his father's old age would one day sag lower than his chin. His beard, like his father's, was tough and very black, and grew high up under his eyes. When he had dressed his best to appear on the City College debating team his mother had said with pride to his father, "Did you ever think you would see yourself dressed up in a tweed jacket so handsome?" But when he wore his tuxedo and took his date (who wasn't Jewish) to the prom, his mother shrieked with bitter laughter and said, "Look, look at that face, how it thinks it's going to stop being Abe Goldstein's son!"

Finn sat up on the bed. "Why all of a sudden does Penny want your father to live with you?" Without waiting for an answer he went on. "Maybe because of impending motherhood. She wants to consolidate her world into one big cozy crib. Then of course she couldn't stand her own parents, so by some crazy logic it all fits."

113

"Maybe she should have married someone else," Larry said slowly, scaring himself as he said it. "Why don't mothers see to it that their daughters marry the right men? I know, it's too square. Besides, the daughters aren't even speaking to the mothers."

"Penny couldn't be married to anyone else," Finn said. "She's positively your woman." Then he added glumly, "Everyone's got somebody to cleave to but me."

"Then tell me why is it things are so wrong? Penny gets more and more eccentric. And then there's me and my dissertation. It doesn't get done. It just doesn't get done. I work on it. But I also don't work on it. I'm so much better suddenly at everything else. I practice my recorder. I read the papers, three a day—do I have to read three a day? Why do I have to be so perverse? And I clip things. My filing consumes hours. And talk. And dream. Waking and sleeping, I dream. I daydream sometimes that I'm giving a lecture at the Sorbonne in French, and there's my mother in the audience, wearing a cockade hat and knitting, and shrieking above the applause, 'Look at that face!' "

"You think your father living here would bring a benediction?"

"I don't know. But how do you think it would be, just once, to be able to do a right thing?"

Finn thought a moment. "First straighten yourself out about what's right. Every story, you know, every situation, has its own right ending. The right ending is finally what everything adds up to. Not what you wish it did, but what it does."

"Life is arithmetic, you think?"

"Certainly. Every relationship a long column of additions and subtractions. In your case, with your father, sum it up, you get zero. Don't try to make it a passing grade and don't blame yourself. Zero is the right answer. Look, if I read in the paper that a boy kills his mother, I'm not filled with horror. I read on. He babbles things: his mother burned his hand with a candle when he was seven, punished him by making him stay in bed for a week, and so on. By the time I've finished the article I've seen the beautiful mathematics of life shine through. We see the right answer because the poor mad boy is incapable of juggling the figures the way the rest of us do. The mad boy doesn't conceal his right answer from us any more than Einstein tried to fool us about the speed of light."

Larry's attention had not stayed with Finnegan's argument. It had wandered back to his father, and now he said, "He's so stiff-necked. For him to agree to it, I'd have to go out to him in a way that's just not in me to do."

"How could it be in you?" Finn said impatiently. "He never put it there."

Larry lifted the perfume bottle, removed the stopper, and sniffed. A sweet, flowery scent filled his nostrils. He was startled to find that it conjured up all of Penny—her face, body, and voice, as well as her smell. He felt a stab in his heart as he recalled what he had said about her marrying someone else. As if to atone, he turned his back on Finn and kissed the bottle before putting it down. But in doing so he noticed again that the stopper was chipped and he said sadly to Finnegan, "I don't know. It seems as if everything has started to smash or warp or crack."

Finn stood up, walked on the blanket, clapped his hand on Larry's shoulder as he passed through the door and said, "It's the dark."

Larry began making the bed. He had opened something in his mind to Finn and now he couldn't shut it down again. A welter of images to describe his state was forming in his brain. To calm himself, he smoothed the bedclothes with care. "Out, chaos!" he cried, shaking a sheet.

Never, he reflected, since he had been old enough to read a book, had he ever done a thing with undivided attention. While he read he would make double images—one from the book, one from his fantasy world of the future. He had done well in school because—why? Because he was bright. Wasn't he bright? Didn't all the IQ tests testify and hadn't his teachers wrung his hand and told him so? And then the competition. And the challenge of a particular class to crack, a particular exam or paper to hurl himself through in a mad frenetic sweat of particular goal and achievement.

But here, now, finished with classes and conferences and seminars, adrift on his own, where was his brilliance? Shattered into a hundred shining points, scattered over a swelling surface like glitter on the ocean. And he couldn't—God!—couldn't drop anchor and sink into a subject. Just as it seemed the bright pieces might, in a lull, come together, up rose the thought of his father like a wave, humping the water, sending the points of light dancing again.

He asked now the question he had ignored when Finnegan asked it. Did he think his father's coming, if he could go so far as to believe in his father's coming, would bring a benediction? For him, not. A too-late closing of the barn door was all. With the horse already galloping over the plain (he threw away the water image and saw the heaving, panting horse, frantic, unguided, what a shame, what a shame) without shoes, or saddle or bridle, all unprepared. He would run till he stumbled, and if he was able, pick himself up and run some more. He hadn't grown up slow and easy and sure. No, the barn door had opened a crack and he had streaked out, thundering hoofs and flying mane, and his teachers, and he with his mirror eye, had watched his frenzy and sweat and said, "There's what it takes to get there." But time to graze, boy, family and sweet home tethers, and flying horses write no theses, boy. The unshod hoofs were tender from too many stony paths, and the legs were gamey, and the early diet of brambles and bitter herbs marred the digestion forever.

For Penny it was different. She wanted, needed this father. And looked to him to somehow make it right. But suppose he couldn't make it or anything else right, what then? Why then, she was just mixed up enough herself to take it without quite knowing why or what was wrong. It wasn't for nothing he had picked for wife a girl just this side of the loony bin. She would never hate him for failing.

She knew the feel of a right thing, though, he'd say that. She had a child or an idiot's feeling for home and warm things and nice smells and "Oh! to be able to do a right thing," he ended saying to himself as he had said to Finn. The sheer, refreshing, sweet springtime rain and therapy of a right move.

"But not alone, I can't do it alone." He readdressed to his father the echo of Penny's long-past appeal. "And you won't help me. Let's blame it all on your father, Pop. I never knew him so let's blame him. Let's give the old bastard a kick. It's not in us because—we have Finn's word for it—he never put it there."

Larry gave the two pillows a final caress ("You at least can lie easy till we get here") and headed for the living room.

Penny and Finn had already started their drinks, sitting friendly and silent across the coffee table.

"I've just been telling Penny," Finnegan said to Larry, "maybe I'll take her up on the invitation to move in. Paying boarder, of course. At first. Later I'll take advantage. Become indispensable—you won't hear of my leaving. And of course, I'll never go."

Larry thought of having their very own herald of the dark, night and day in the bosom of the family, and shuddered. "Where's my sense of humor gone?" he wondered. "I used to enjoy old Finn's idea of a joke."

"Up to Penny," he said, moving nearer her chair. "I can't

117

stand the thought myself." He saw his chance to lift the cat off Penny's lap and said quickly, in a low voice, "I'll put Max in the kitchen."

"No," said Penny. "She'll be lonely there. Just put her on the floor. She'll be all right."

Penny watched him deposit Max gently on the floor, beyond the rug, and then said in her serious way, "Finny certainly can't go out in all this snow. No one should go out in all this snow."

Finnegan put down his glass and made a humble Hindu bow.

"But not the extra room, Finny, I'm sorry, it would have to be the sofa. We have to leave the extra room open for a little while longer."

"You're not still thinking of it for my father!" Larry burst out in spite of himself.

Penny's face flushed. "No," she said, looking away. She dived suddenly out of her chair, scooped up Max like a sea gull skimming a fish out of the sea and ran for the kitchen. Larry looked at the floor and saw three little dots like melted chocolate, while Penny's voice, suddenly brave, called from the kitchen, "I meant for a while. In general."

"This calls for a reduction in my rent," said Finnegan. "How often does it happen? At, say, a dollar-fifty per episode?"

"Well, Penny takes care of it," Larry said nervously. Raising his voice a little he added, "She's wonderful with animals. She has a lot of patience."

In a few minutes Penny returned and sat down. With one hand she held Max, towelled like a wine bottle, in her lap, with the other hand she lifted Max's little pointed face, which drooped. "Poor Max," she whispered.

"Time for refills," Larry said, setting up a clatter with the ice cubes and bottles. "Penny, refill? Finnegan? A touch?"

Finnegan was leaning forward to extend his glass, when he sounded a piercing whistle that shattered Larry's ear. Larry's nerveless fingers let fall the jigger glass, spilling whiskey and sending a glass chip, naturally, skittering across the table. He followed Finnegan's stare to Penny's blouse. Max's droopy head peeped out from between the middle buttons.

"Good old Penny," said Finnegan, leaning back and hugging his knee.

Under Penny's blouse the body of the cat spread grotesquely.

"It's too much," Larry thought. He wanted to stand up and say, to whatever devils gathered, leering, in the four corners of his house, "Begone. . . ." He wanted to say to his old friend Finn, "Dear buddy of my childhood, go home. My wife is not well. I am not well. Our cat, Maxine, also . . ." In fact, he did stand up and opened his mouth, but he never found out what it was he was about to say because just then the doorbell rang.

Larry went shakily to the door, expecting to see a ghost— Banquo or Ichabod Crane maybe—and threw it open.

Bareheaded, soaked, his few strands of hair plastered to his scalp, tiny ice-crystal flowers abloom on the ridges of his muffler—there stood his father. He was carrying his old black suitcase in one hand. The other hand he extended formally for a handshake.

"Papa, my God!" was all Larry could say as he pulled his father inside with the handshake.

"I was thinking, thinking, all the time in the train," his father began calmly. "My son asked me something and I refused. Why should I refuse? Because I didn't believe a person should say yes. That's the old way. From the old days. From the dark. I came back to tell you that if you want me to stay, I'll stay. Why should I say no? I even brought a few things, for a start."

"That's fine, Papa. Very good. I'm glad you did it. Yes,"

119

Larry said, while he helped his father off with his things. And the whole time he asked himself, How do I feel? How do I feel? How do I feel?

The truth was that, aside from the shock, he didn't know.

But one thing he could do was call into the living room and say, "Penny, Papa's here!"

He heard the cat's short yowl as she got dumped to the rug, and then Penny's heels clattering on the bare parts of the floor. In the doorway to the hall where they stood she stopped, suddenly shy or scared. A smile curved her lips, her eyes widened, she stared entranced, as if some prophetic stranger out of Biblical days had stepped across her threshold. So at least for the time being, Larry had that for a guide.

✦

The Open Window

"Change your mind and go with us," Evelyn's mother said, coming into her room for the tenth time that morning.

"Good-by. Have a good vacation," Evelyn replied. "I have projects this week. Projects. Of my own."

"Such a busy person," her mother said, wide-eyed, in a way that chilled Evelyn's marrow and put her on her mark for the counterspring.

Say nothing, she advised herself. Conserve energy. She'll try something.

All week it had been like this, the three of them foxing and being foxed. And now, on the day of her parents' departure, Evelyn was exhausted but still holding on. She hadn't known there could be so much energy for connivance in her old parents. She was eighteen and determined to outmaneuver.

"I'm not going if Evelyn's not, that's all," her mother had said. But the owners of the little farm-hotel where her mother and father had vacationed one week every summer since Evelyn's birth had called, finally, to inquire, and her father had sent a deposit. "She'll change her mind," he had said soothingly to her mother. "Or we'll lose the deposit," said her mother. Then her father had picked up a new summer-weight topcoat on sale, and in fairness had sent her mother out to buy something new. One step had followed the next until now they were packing their bags and, for the first time, Evelyn was the holdout.

"It's done all the time," Evelyn had told her mother. "There's nothing to it. In regular American families the parents do things by themselves, and when the children are my age they do their own things."

"So we're not a regular American family. Report us to the FBI," her mother said.

"You and Papa were born here, first generation," Evelyn said. "Fine thing, still greenhorns."

"So you're second generation. Be a Yankee. Go march in a parade. But first get married."

Again that morning, her mother burst into Evelyn's room with, "Well, Yankee-Doodle? Change your mind yet?"

"I'm thinking what color to paint my room. I'll paint while you're gone. That's one of my projects."

"Why not red, white and blue?" her mother said. "With flags. And a big banner saying, 'Born here—one-hundred-percent experienced American.'"

And another time her mother asked: "Will you see Isadore?"

"Maybe," Evelyn said evasively. "Why? I thought you liked him."

"Did I say I don't? He's a sweet boy. He's fine. I trust him one hundred per cent."

"But you don't trust me?"

"What will Isadore think of you, staying here alone?" her mother said. "Don't you think a smart boy like him knows the difference between right and wrong? How does it look? What can he think of you?"

Evelyn glanced wearily out of the window. "That's all

changed, Mamma. Nowadays boys don't respect girls if they stay tied to their mother's apron strings."

"Since when?"

"Since years, Mamma."

"It's news to me."

"What isn't news to you?"

Her mother began to pace the room. "Get married, then I'll stop worrying." She paced energetically. "How many years have I got? Give me grandchildren. Will I live to see it?"

"I have to live my own life, Mamma."

"She has to live her own life, doesn't she?" her father echoed, sticking his head in the doorway to see.

"I know it," said her mother. "Don't I know that? Of course I know it. But I worry," she said, kneading her hands together. "Oh, I worry. I worry."

"What's to worry?" her father said soothingly.

"Oh, big shot! Somebody gave you a tranquilizer? You don't worry no more? For thirty years side by side we worried about the same things. Don't tell me."

"I have a new outlook," her father said.

"The inside of his stomach is like a potato grater," her mother said. "Full of holes from worry. The doctor said so."

"It's true," her father said sadly. "How we worried all the years foolishly, about nothing. There were things you wanted to do, we said no. You wanted to ride a bicycle downstairs when your mother did housework and we said no. We were afraid of the traffic. Sometimes a wild driver goes up on the sidewalk. You wanted to play upstairs with another little girl, we said no. We were afraid of measles, whooping cough, chicken pox, whatever it was. But it seems whatever we did, you understood we loved you. That's a wonderful thing, a blessing on the parents. Sometimes they don't know themselves how to show it.

123

"We didn't even go to the beach. We'd sit in the kitchen and discuss it. The crowds, the germs, polio, kidnapers. She'd scare me and I'd scare her and in the end we wouldn't go. We'd sit here and sweat—except for the one week in the country—and sometimes we'd go up on the roof to catch a breeze and I held you in my lap."

"Tell, tell about that summer, big shot," her mother said.

"All right. I have a new outlook, so I'll tell. That summer—do I have to say?—it was so hot the sweat poured down our backs. There wasn't a breeze. It was a pity to see you burning like a fever; you were six. So one Sunday we looked at each other and said: 'Why are we different? We'll go to the beach like everybody else.'

"There were a thousand people, a million people. If you put out your foot you stepped on somebody's head. We turned our backs one second to put down our things, and you were gone. We ran to the lifeguard like crazy people. He told us not to get excited, we should stay by the stand and not run around, they would bring in hundreds of kids, we could take our pick. That's what he said, for a joke. We stood there for one hour in the sun. With one hand I held up your mother, with the other I held myself up, hanging from the lifeguard stand. They didn't find you for a long time because you weren't crying. You were having a good time, playing with kids beaches away."

"And after, big shot?" her mother said. "You're gonna leave out about after?"

"And after was, when we got home I was afraid your mother would pass out, instead it was me. Something came over me like, I don't know, a weakness."

"A heart attack," said her mother.

"From heat."

"From worry, you mean."

"Papa, believe me, I'm so sorry," Evelyn said. "But is it my fault you worry like that?"

"No. Absolutely not. It was foolishness. I have a new outlook."

"Oh, big shot," her mother said, unable to endure any more and leaving the room.

Evelyn herself wondered about the new outlook. Where had it come from, and why now. She hoped, in atonement for the heart attack, that her own new stand was maybe responsible, partly.

Her father glanced into the hall to be sure her mother was not listening and said in a low voice: "I want you to know that I appreciate, Evelyn, what you're doing. Independence is a wonderful thing. I don't make myself out to be such a wonderful father. I have selfish reasons. When you get free, I'll get free."

He sat on her window sill, as if suddenly tired, and looked out.

"It's not that I begrudge it," he said. "A child needs care—warning, watching. But enough is enough. The children do what they want anyway, in the end. A pair of policemen, that's how we spent our lives. What enjoyment did we have? What new thing did we try? For twenty-six years I'm a salesman for Friedman—a mean man, I hope you never know such a person—and why? At least with Friedman we had security, we knew our child would eat. But for twenty-six years I had to eat dirt with Friedman.

"If your mother could stop worrying, I think I'd take her and we'd go . . ." He swung his arm around half the globe. "I don't know where we'd go, but someplace far away, new."

Somehow, the packing got done. When her mother found Evelyn's father in the bedroom she chased him out. "Is that how you pack? Hopping around like a rabbit?"

And when her father found her mother there he said: "You're packing or worrying? Which?"

Once during the morning when her mother came in to say,

125

"Change your mind!" Evelyn took courage to ask: "Why didn't you have other children besides me? You're always saying a son would take your side. Why didn't you have one?"

"You're curious about life? You want to know everything?" her mother said. "Get married. You'll find out."

And once during the morning she asked her father: "What made you such worriers?" More than one teacher had thought she was the child of immigrant parents because permission slips came back unsigned, and her sixth-grade teacher, Miss Malone, had taken a gentle interest and given her pamphlets printed in different foreign languages to take home. "Sometimes the children of immigrant parents can do a great deal toward educating them," she had said. "My parents aren't immigrants, Miss Malone," Evelyn had said. "No?" had come the doubtful, disappointed answer. "Well, it's no shame either way, Evelyn."

At last, today, she had to ask: "What made you such worriers?"

"What *made?*" her father answered. "It was only your mother made it like that. Who knows why? It's in the nature of some people that if they read in the paper somebody died in a fire, they wake up in the middle of the night and smell smoke. Personally, it's in my own nature to be a modern person. To be cheerful. By myself I wouldn't worry. You ever saw how a fire spreads? That's the same with worry. Thirty years ago your mother read there was a fire, and ever since I'm choking from smoke."

Evelyn found time during the day to phone Isadore and invite him to come that evening.

When she returned to her room she found her mother leaning far out of the open window that gave onto a fire escape, looking down. Below was the haphazard Brooklyn view: steep-gabled frame private houses, the newer but already more old-fashioned-looking flat-topped two-family ones, lots, the tops of maple trees. Theirs was the only apartment house for several blocks. In a day when almost everyone lived in a private house, her parents had felt advanced when they moved into an apartment. Moreover they feared burglars and fire in a single-family house. "At least in an apartment house," Evelyn recalled her father saying, "somebody has a dog that barks. Or you hear a yell if something happens."

Her mother drew back from the window and turned with a guilty flush on her face. "What's that look?" she demanded. "That look, that squinty look?"

"I don't trust you," said Evelyn.

"Me you don't trust? Of course. Strangers yes, me not."

"Maybe you're planning to come up the fire escape and scare me?"

"I tell you one thing. I don't go anywhere till you promise to keep this window locked the whole time."

"But it's hot!"

"Never mind. You don't know what degenerates roam around at night, just looking for an open window on a fire escape."

Her father stuck his head in the doorway, waiting.

Evelyn felt again the rough jerking of her mother's cold hand that held her own childish one, pulling her past car accidents ("See what happens when people aren't careful?"), elderly men having heart attacks on sidewalks, covered with coats ("Look away, Evelyn, the poor man is sick. See what happens when you don't take care of yourself?"), and once they saw a man urinating in the street, in a high arc over the top of a car ("He's crazy, he's a degenerate. See why you mustn't ever go out at night alone?").

"I can't do it," said Evelyn. "Aside from the heat, there are other things."

127

"What other things?" her father asked with interest.

Evelyn looked at him and said earnestly, as to a fellow student of experience: "Papa, a locked window says no to life."

Her father widened his eyes. "Look at that," he said to her mother. "Isn't it wonderful to get so much out of a plain window?"

Her mother sat abruptly on the bed. "Then I won't go!"

"Again!" her father shouted.

"Why did we ever take an apartment with a fire escape in the child's bedroom?" her mother said. "It was a mistake from the beginning."

"Did I know eighteen years ago we would have a child who wants to leave a window open to let in life?" He turned in desperation to Evelyn. "Respectable life comes in the front door, Evelyn. Besides, look what you're doing. Your mother's health will break down."

"All right," Evelyn said. "All right. I promise." But as her mother was leaving the room she called: "But your enjoyment this week will be at my expense."

"So this week you'll take care of the bill," her mother said from the doorway. "Next week it will be our turn. And it was also our turn when you brought into the house this hunk of wood full of bugs—"

"My driftwood—" said Evelyn.

". . . and put up these what you consider fine pictures—"

"My Matisse—"

". . . so that I actually have to turn away my eyes every time I come into the room."

"We agreed," said Evelyn stiffly, "that this is my room in every sense of the word."

"Absolutely!" her father broke in, holding up his hand. "We agreed. I gave my word and I keep it. My customers know and my family should know that I do not renege."

He glanced into the hall to be sure her mother was out of

earshot and said in a low voice: "Don't worry, Evelyn. So you give in a little bit now. I see change in her already. Did you dream she'd go? I didn't. It's like a miracle. Believe me, I didn't sleep the last few nights, worrying she wouldn't go. Never too late to change, hah, Evelyn?" he said joyfully, giving her shoulder a squeeze. "Isn't it a wonderful thing?" He gestured at the books in her room. "If there's something here, or something you learn in college, don't pass us by. Tell us about it. Never too late to learn. They still teach that in school, don't they?"

At last they were leaving, their bags waiting in the hall, their summer coats over their arms. Evelyn's mother went to the bedroom window and closed it with a bang.

"Just a minute," said Evelyn. "That's for me to do."

"Let her close her window," said her father. "She'll close it. She'll lock it. She knows."

"I'm finished," said her mother, and walked out.

Her father gave Evelyn a hasty kiss and hurried after. "Remember everything," he said vaguely and urgently.

A few moments later the doorbell rang and Evelyn ran to answer, flinging the door wide.

"See?" her mother said to her father. "See that? No chain, no 'Who's there?' Nothing."

"Oh, for heaven's sake," said Evelyn. "I knew it was you."

Her father stood shamefaced before Evelyn's scornful stare. "You don't know," said her mother. "You never know."

"Good-by!" said Evelyn.

"Go and have children," said her mother to her father as they turned away.

Several minutes after that her mother called her name from the street.

Leaning out of her bedroom window, Evelyn called down: "What did you forget?"

"Change your mind," her mother called.

129

"Good-by. Have a good time."

"Lock that window *now*," her mother called.

"Okay. Don't worry about anything," said Evelyn. She lowered the window and locked it with five locks: one swivel, two snap, two screw. Then she looked out the shut window through the fire escape bars and waited for Isadore.

Isadore was two years older than Evelyn but a hundred years more than that, she guessed, in wisdom and courage. It was Isadore who had given her courage to make this stand, Isadore who had told her that in every family there had to be one who teaches, driving it forward like a motor. "Some people think this is the function of the parents," he had said, "but like as not it's the child." That phrase had taken hold of her and she had jumped up when he said it. "Like as not!" she had repeated joyfully. "Why not? Like as not!"

He had gone on. "Listen, Evelyn, did you ever think why it was the princess in *Sleeping Beauty* had to have a spindle? Why, with everything else, a spindle? And go and prick her finger, and fulfill the curse? Only then was she kissed by the prince and her life began. Did Eve," he asked, "need the fruit? Or Lucifer the power? Or Faust the knowledge? It's clear they did need. And also clear that with all of them their real lives began only after disobedience. Danger and daring are the windows to life, Evelyn. If you let the fears of your parents infect you you'll never get through the windows, just like them. But if you do get through maybe you can pull them after too."

Half her mind had listened in fascination, saying: It's true. How beautiful and true. But the other half had filled with suspicion. Oh you, Mr. Isadore, she had thought, what are you leading around to with your speeches? What window have you got in your mind? She had been fed on doses, like cod-liver oil, of her father's warnings—before his new outlook—that began,

130

"Listen, Evelyn, a girl has to be smart. Some men don't care. There are things . . ."

But Isadore had seemed to care. He had given her books and records and sweet good-night kisses and all he asked was that she should be brave and resist the infection of her parents' fears. Isadore was a born teacher.

Barely visible in the heat-haze distance, if you knew where to look, was the scaffolding of Coney Island. Delicately filigreed, it turned and looped, a weird fascination. On still, hot nights they could sometimes hear the screams of the tortured, catapulting over the crest of the Cyclone, sliding around the topmost rim of the Giant Ferris Wheel or plummeting from the Parachute Drop as from an eagle's claw. There, nightly, thousands challenged their ancient fears of heights, of depths, of dark, of sudden drops. Now and then someone riding the screeching cars on the mountainous rails of the Tornado went mad with fear, stood up and was fired to his death as if by slingshot. Evelyn and her parents lived within rumor of Coney Island and the echoes of screams sharpened their sense of danger. When they saw the dainty scrolls of light against the black sky they were not deceived.

The doorbell rang again and Evelyn ran eagerly, but just in case she put on the chain and hissed through the door crack: "Who is it?"

"Hard to say," came Isadore's answer.

When she opened, he said in quiet reproof: "I see you've adopted your mother's door technique. Better watch that." And then, small and swift, he strode into her room, carrying records.

Isadore sat in her desk chair and looked at her through wise spectacles. "So you're on your own. That's nice progress for your family," he said. "I'm glad." He stared gravely down at the floor and sighed. "You may have better luck than me."

"What's happened?"

"No. Nothing. I was just thinking about progress, my father."

Evelyn was shocked to see, suddenly, his grieved eyes.

"You know how small my father and mother are. Evelyn. I'm exactly my father's height. But he acts like it's my fault I'm not taller. Even when he's bragging about me he says: 'The only thing is, he should be a little taller.' "

"That's silly," Evelyn said. "Whose genes are they, after all?"

"He's going to have an educated son, so he says, a professional. Not only that, but with a scholarship—he didn't think such things happened to Jews. He feels now that everything is possible. And that I could somehow have been tall, if I put my mind to it."

"You look fine the way you are, Isadore," Evelyn said, feeling how strong she was becoming, able first to send her parents away and then to comfort Isadore.

Isadore ignored her comfort. "So I gave him a book on Mendelian biology to read. A simplified one, a cram book."

"Did he read it?"

"He flipped through, looked at the pictures, put it away and didn't say a word. Then last night at supper he asked me, kind of offhand: 'You know about mutations, Isadore?' 'Sure,' I said. 'Definition, please?' he said. 'It's a difference that springs up all of a sudden in a generation, a real departure from the parent generation,' I said. Then he looked kind of triumphant and sad at the same time and turned to my kid brother Saul and said: 'That's you, Saulie, my mutation. You did very good, Saulie.' "

"That was mean of him!" said Evelyn heatedly.

Isadore smiled wanly. "It *is* funny, you know. Saul is three years younger than I am and already he's bigger. He's going to be a lot bigger yet. You can see it in him. He's got confident bones. They're not afraid to reach out." He hesitated. Then he said slowly: "I guess the oldest bears the brunt. The brunt that stunts."

"Isadore, are you giving up? I don't know what I'll do if you give up."

"Oh, no, no, no," said Isadore. "Just recognizing something. Reformers have to be realists. And I can't blame my father. I wanted him to learn what I wanted to prove. He wanted to learn what he wanted to prove. Still, it's a beginning. Who knows what he may learn next?

"But meanwhile I know," said Isadore, with his air of plunging bravely into whatever was most painful, "girls like big men, don't they? That's something that will never change."

"Isadore, I want you to know I consider myself practically deformed."

"You?" said Isadore in astonishment. "Where? How?"

Evelyn stood up. "Don't you see my hip—higher than the other? My mother tries to tell herself it's because I sit on one leg while I read. But it's more than that. I can tell from her voice when she tells me to stand up straight that she knows it too."

Isadore looked at her hips in silence.

"Maybe you're fooled because of my skirt," said Evelyn. "I wear a full skirt to hide it."

Isadore squeezed his eyes critically and considered a moment. "Yes, I see it. It's not a big thing, but it's there."

"Yes," said Evelyn.

"Evelyn, that's good. I mean your telling me like that. Whatever handicap a person starts with in life is only important in the overcoming of it. I mean, if you had a wart on your nose that would be good too, because then you could overcome it. It's great. You're on the right track. I admire you for it." Isadore gave her an earnest stare full of emotion and then a swift fervent kiss on the lips.

He turned to get the records. Evelyn, flushed with success at overcoming and with Isadore's rare admiration, rushed to the window and hastily unlocked, unswiveled, unscrewed the five fastenings. Raising one finger, she declared: "My customers know, my family should know, I renege!"

She watched Isadore's face as he bent intently over the machine, first carefully wiping the needle free of dust, then placing his fingers precisely on the rim of the disc to lower it on the spoke. So much attention stirred her. Suppose he were to peer down at her with all that tender concern? Suppose he placed his hands on her with so much worried love?

"It's the new music, Evelyn," Isadore said as they listened to the Bartók. "What a departure. What a stepping-out. It took guts to write that, didn't it? Courage and beauty, Evelyn. That's what life asks of us. Courage and beauty."

He lay on her bed, his shoes dangling off the coverlet. For all his talk of danger and chance he was a careful boy.

Evelyn sat in her chair and looked about her room. Hadn't it taken courage—Matisse and driftwood, crazy pictures and bugs, her symbols of beauty? Now what was supposed to happen? If they were her symbols, why didn't they ignite and burst into flame? Were they her symbols? She looked through the open window into the blue air of early evening. The lights were coming on in Coney Island. Strung over the Tornado, the Whip, the Parachute Jump, the Cyclone.

"Isadore, do you want a drink?"

"Sure. Pepsi?"

"I don't mean that. I mean my father has some Three-Star Hennessy."

Isadore sat up, straightened up, grew formal. "Yes, I do."

The white gauze dining room curtains her mother had sewed

hung innocent and reproachful. Turning her back on them, she poured out the heavy liquid into two little maroon glasses with onion-bulb bases and brought them to her room.

"To Life," Isadore toasted.

"To the Tornado and the Hurricane and the Whip," Evelyn replied. "More?" she asked.

Isadore thought a moment and then put down his glass and said gravely: "No. In case we want to make love later, I don't want us to think it was because of the liquor."

"Will we want to make love later?" she asked. Once, with a boy from school, she had gone on the Caterpillar Ride, terrified, lying back between the legs of the boy, body twisting wildly, some powerful force holding it down, rushing through black tunnels, the drop, helpless. Had Isadore taken that ride? Did he know about all that?

Isadore had small hands and small agile fingers that curved backward slightly, Oriental fashion, when he stretched them. Now his hand trembled as he stroked her hair. He kissed her with full, warm lips. "I love you. That is, I want to be honest, I like you so much. I almost love you, Evelyn."

Through the open window she saw the starry steeps of the Tornado. Did she imagine? She thought she could hear its roar and feel the floor tremble as it rushed for the drop. There! Down! She hung from Isadore's neck.

"Can we lie down?" he asked.

"I don't want—anything to happen," she said, and wondered how she came to say such a thing.

"Nothing will happen," Isadore said, kissing her cheek and removing his glasses. "We'll lie on top of the covers."

But as she lay there she thought: I do want something to happen. But she didn't know how it could be told.

"I'm taking off my shoes," Isadore said. "So we won't dirty the covers."

135

"Yes," she answered, and they took off their shoes and lay down again.

"It's so warm," he said. "I'm taking off my shirt."

"Yes," she answered, watching as he stood up.

"Evelyn, your dress. You're creasing it."

"Yes," she said, and stood up and was in her slip and stockinged feet.

They lay in a quiet embrace. The Coney Island breeze cooled her skin and she trembled on the coverlet. And with the shudder came a notion of the new language and she tried it. She said complainingly: "I'm cold. Under the cover."

So they were under the cover and Isadore's arm reached out —so thin, so bony and frail, across her face to the light. In the dark the warmth burst through suddenly between them and he kissed her and said, "I'll be back," and went bumping his way in the dark to the bathroom and she heard the medicine chest door squeak and slam with a shaking of the loose mirror, and several things fell at once into the washbasin and water ran and something metallic clattered to the tile floor and went *rinnnn-nnnng* as it rolled, and Isadore bumped his way back in the dark and his cooled skin touched hers, but he kissed her with lips warm as before and she smelled tooth paste on his breath and soap on his hands and she thought: Oh, Isadore! For me?

The thin curtains blew in gently like mist. Evelyn gazed over Isadore's shoulder. The bars and steeply running stairs of the fire escape stood out black and stark like objects in a surrealist painting, their clarity so intense they seemed about to speak. But what? Isadore was murmuring into her ear: "I don't want you to do anything you don't want to do. But oh, Evelyn, oh, Evelyn!"

What else was speaking? What other voice was murmuring, somewhere inside her head, cautioning, warning?

What will Isadore think of me? she thought sadly. "Isadore

136

dear," she whispered, "I like you so much too. But I'm afraid."

Isadore lifted his head slightly. In his eyes glowed reflections of the devil's lights at Coney Island. His face was changed. She didn't know him. Who was he after all, a stranger?

She sat up violently. "I can't!"

Slowly Isadore's face came back to him. He looked at her. He was listening. Waiting to understand. She was ashamed and looked away.

"It's natural," said Isadore. "I understand."

"I can't be a new woman in one night."

"Of course not," said Isadore.

"Then why do I feel so bad about it?" Evelyn asked.

"Here." Isadore jumped out of bed and pulled Evelyn out too. "Let's dress, then we'll be able to talk about it." They handed each other things from the chair and silently dressed.

When they were dressed, they lay down again on their stomachs, in the dark, across Evelyn's bed.

"I feel better," said Evelyn.

"Good," said Isadore.

"I don't want to discuss anything."

"That's good too," said Isadore.

They gazed through the open window at the lights of Coney.

The front door softly slammed. Isadore and Evelyn lifted their heads and froze.

Isadore started up. Evelyn put out a hand. "I think it's my parents," she whispered. "It must be them." She called: "Who's there?" There was no answer.

"It couldn't be robbers. It must be them." She called again, "Who's there?" and there was no answer. "They're trying to scare me," she said. But Evelyn thought she heard a faint creaking of floor boards as whoever it was came closer to the bedroom.

137

"It can't be robbers," she whispered. "Things can't happen that way. It must be them. Oh, God!" she whispered as fear drew the skin on her arms and damped the palms of her hands.

"Courage!" whispered Isadore. "Whoever it is, they don't know *I'm* here." He seized the small bronze sculpture that stood on the night table, crept off the bed, tiptoed to the door of the room and crouched to the floor just inside the doorway.

"Who's there?" Evelyn demanded once more in a voice that rose suddenly at the end to a shriek. If it's you, she thought, and you're trying to frighten me, then I don't care what happens.

The creaking seemed nearer, and then Evelyn recognized the shapes of two heads in the doorway. The lights from the window lit the faces of her mother and of her father behind her, just enough for Evelyn to see them peering into the dark. She and Isadore had grown accustomed to the dark (he must see who it was!) but her parents had not, yet, and her mother was feeling with one hand along the wall to get her bearings. She fumbled past the light switch, felt along the elbowed piece of driftwood that stood next to the doorway and began to inch her way into the bedroom when Isadore, with a tremendous yell, jumped into the air almost before her face, flapping his arms like wings.

With a piercing scream Evelyn's mother grabbed the stick of wood and swung it like a baseball bat over Isadore's head just as he crashed down from his second leap in the air. Isadore crumpled to the floor like dead, his head twisted to one side.

Evelyn rushed for the wall light. But her father had already found the switch and he and her mother were staring down at Isadore in amazement.

"What's Isadore doing here?" her father asked weakly.

Evelyn, crouched beside Isadore, shot back through clenched teeth: "What are *you* doing here!"

138

"I? I?" asked her father. He opened his palms as if to read a message there, but Evelyn cut him off. "Is this how I can trust you? Is this the way for a father to behave? Look what you've done!"

Her father rocked his big head from side to side and blinked dumbly. "I don't know. I can't think. We were on our way, your mother wouldn't go farther, we had to turn around and drive by the house to see if your window was really closed. When she saw it was open she wouldn't rest, she had to come up, just to give you a scare. What could I do? Who has the strength? Now look—look at poor Isadore, whatever he was doing here, does he deserve to be hit on the head and maybe killed like this?"

Her mother let out a sob. She was standing with her hands clasped under her chin, her face screwed into an expression of wincing pain. "Call the police. Send me to jail. Kill me," she said in a breaking voice. "Little Isadore, so sweet. Why should I hurt him? Why am I punished?"

"Because you're stupid!" Evelyn yelled into her face.

At the moment her mother buried her face in her hands and began to cry, Evelyn felt a cold touch on her ankle. She looked down into Isadore's bright-eyed gaze and, unmistakably, he closed one eye in a wink, opened it again, then shut his eyes and let his head roll to one side.

Her father, too, had seen, and he was gazing down, open-mouthed.

"Go and get some cloths soaked in water for Isadore's head," Evelyn told her mother in a voice of authority.

Gratefully, her mother nodded and padded out.

Isadore jumped to his feet. "Mr. Applebaum," he said in a hasty whisper, "my word of honor, nothing happened between Evelyn and me that shouldn't have happened."

Evelyn's father shook Isadore's hand warmly. "You're a fine

139

boy, Isadore. I always thought so. Doesn't your head hurt?"

"She missed me. But what an opportunity for a lesson," Isadore said excitedly, "if we use her own system, and give her a good scare now."

"What do you mean, a scare?" asked Evelyn's father. "She's already shaking. Let's tell her the good news; it's a pity. Why are you whispering?" Her father, in his astonishment, was also whispering.

"A lesson, a small but powerful lesson. She thinks she hurt me, let her think it. Listen, we'll disappear for a while. Tell her, Evelyn, we went to the hospital. Later we'll come back, and I'll be better. At the very least she'll feel confused, she won't interfere so quickly, she'll wonder first about consequences. If she learns that, she'll learn a lot."

"You think so?" Evelyn's father said doubtfully. "She shouldn't get a heart attack."

"Papa," said Evelyn, "don't you want to be free?"

Her father pressed his lips together. His eyes sharpened, he weighed. He nodded.

"We'll go down the fire escape. Careful. I'll go first," said Isadore.

Evelyn sat down, her heart triple-hammering, to wait for her mother.

Panting, drenched with perspiration and tap water, holding the dripping cloths extended in both hands like an offering, Evelyn's mother came in and looked wildly around the room.

"Where?" she asked.

"Papa carried him to a cab and took him to the hospital. You'd better sit down. We can only wait."

"He's living?"

"Yes," Evelyn admitted, "but unconscious."

Her mother sat on the edge of the bed, while the cloths dripped into her lap. "Maybe when he wakes up he'll be out of his mind altogether," she said dreamily. "Like poor Mrs. Friedlander's son after the accident. Maybe he won't remember his name, or how to talk or how to eat. He'll be a helpless baby." She brooded for a moment, then said: "In that case, if I know his mother, a selfish woman who goes every week to the beauty parlor, she won't have the patience to feed him and teach him all over from the beginning. It will have to be me. I'll do it. I'll take him to live with me and I'll be to him like a mother with a baby." She sighed, not unhappily.

After a moment she said: "What did you and Isadore do here in the dark?"

"We made love," said Evelyn.

Her mother looked up sharply. "Who makes love before a wedding?"

"Anybody who wants to."

"Only tramps."

"Anybody, Mamma."

Her mother transferred the wet cloths from one hand to the other. "That's the new way?"

"That's right."

"Do people also get married from the new way?"

"Yes."

"So then, if Isadore is all right, and he doesn't turn out like poor Mrs. Friedlander's son, you'll get married?"

"Oh, God, Mamma, you've got such a one-track mind, how can anybody tell you anything?"

"I'm wrong this time also?"

"Yes. Wrong. Wrong."

"So what's right? Let me learn."

"People have to choose, and decide, and see, and try."

"Uh-hah, uh-hah," said her mother faintly, nodding.

Evelyn was suddenly cut by pity for the gray head, the drooplidded eyes, the wattle of loose flesh beneath her mother's chin.

It's terrible to force her like this, she thought, but it's for her, and for Papa, and for me. For all of us, so we can breathe.

"You'd like that, wouldn't you?" she began, biting her lips and searching for words that would pour guilt on her mother's head. "That part about Isadore becoming a helpless baby and you'd be his mother. You always wanted a son. You didn't want me. That's why you were so protective." Her voice rose, she found she believed what she was saying. "It was guilt all the time."

Her mother looked up, patient. "When you're married you'll also find a woman wants sons. It's natural. And you'll love a daughter too. The only thing is," she looked away sadly, "a daughter never loves you like a son does."

"What are you comparing with? What sons?"

"Didn't I see?" her mother said, now beginning to be out of patience. "Didn't I have brothers to see how they took their mother's side? And Papa. You don't remember any more your father's mother, how can such a woman rest in peace? Peace she never gave her son. Every day a new complaint. She would tell your father everything—she had pains, she needed a coat, her married daughters didn't treat her right. Me she didn't like. So your father went himself to visit her. The money he gave her that I never saw, I don't care. Only that she made him a sick man. And at the funeral he cried more than all the married daughters put together. That's what a son is."

Evelyn felt that a key, ice-cold from the cellar where it had lain, had been thrust into her hand. "You're jealous!" she cried with a combined fear and triumph. "Jealous all these years! Jealous of your mother! Of your mother-in-law!"

"Bite your tongue!" her mother said fiercely. "They should rest in peace! What does it mean now? Who remembers? For them it's over!" She stopped to breathe heavily. "That's what you'll remember of me? That your mother was jealous? That

142

she didn't let you do what you wanted? That's what it boils down to? That's all there is?"

"Did I ever say I knew what anything boiled down to?" said Evelyn in fright. "I only said let me learn."

Her mother excitedly threw the wet cloths onto the dresser top. "You see who has the one-track mind? How can I tell you anything? You take and make something of it that isn't there."

The doorbell rang.

"That's your father!" Evelyn's mother jumped up, one hand over her heart. "Oh, what's gonna be?" she moaned. "Let's have good news for once."

They went together to the door, and her mother, with a cry of joy, fell on Isadore's neck. Isadore had a large square of gauze against his temple, stuck with court plaster, which her mother kissed and gently stroked.

"I hurt you, Isadore? I should hurt myself better, a thousand times."

To her husband she said: "Come, let's go."

"Go where?" he asked, his complicated story of what the doctor had said still untold.

"Go where we're going. You forgot already we're going away? A week's vacation we waited for all year?"

"You want to go now? So late?"

"What's late?" her mother said. "Tomorrow is late. Tonight is not late. The car is packed."

"Well," said her father, his smile coming and going as he struggled with his astonishment, "every minute here is progress, nobody can deny."

"Is it motor trouble, Mr. Applebaum?" Isadore asked politely as Evelyn and he stood downstairs waving at her mother and father in the car that would not start.

"Not exactly," Evelyn's father said, looking sidewise at her

143

mother, who gazed silently ahead. "I just thought . . ." He hesitated and broke in on himself to lean out the window at Evelyn. "Evelyn, when you go upstairs you'll lock the door good, because Isadore is going home now—hah, Isadore, it's so late?"

Her mother rapped her father's arm sharply with her knuckles. "What's with the instructions, instructions? We're going or not going?"

Her father said in astonishment: "You won't even remind her to lock her window on the fire escape?"

"I can see with my own eyes," her mother answered scornfully, "that the fire escape comes down the front of the house on a street where cars and people pass by all night. It's hot. Do you see one window closed?"

Her father said in a fury: "So where were your eyes all the years that you made me crazy till now?" He lifted his right fist from the steering wheel and pounded it against his chest.

"My eyes were in the ground. In the cemetery. But tonight I learned a lesson. My eyes are in my head. No more!" her mother shouted, striking in turn her own heart.

Isadore, who had looked puzzled till now, heard the word "lesson" and his face brightened. Crouching to bring his face level with theirs through the window, he said emotionally: "That's wonderful, Mrs. Applebaum. Then it was worth everything. You're a very intelligent—"

There was a roar from the engine, her father yelled at them, "Good-by and good luck!" and pulled away from the curb, the engine exploding and the car bucking for the first few seconds.

Isadore squeezed Evelyn's arm and whispered tensely, "There they go! There they go!" as the car smoothed out, turned a corner, and was gone.

Evelyn nodded. The long day and night hung on her. She was sleeping on her feet, and everything had ended sadly. So

144

far as she could see, her father and mother were only driving to a poor week's rest from a life of wrong moves. And she was left alone to make hard choices. Open the window, close the window, it was all the same to them. Her parents had worn themselves out, given up and gone off. They had taken with them their ridiculous collection of signs and posters done in the elaborate lettering of fifty years ago, but they were all she had to go by: a fist with index finger pointing—*This way;* bold yellow on black—*Do not bump head—In case of fire—Ladies are requested.* As long as the signs were up her direction was clear: the opposite. But what when there were no signs?

She was startled to hear from Isadore an "Oh!" that was something between a groan and a cry. He tilted his head back and lifted his fist to the sky. "Parents! Children!" he said fervently. "Let us pull and push each other toward the light!" As Evelyn watched, dumbstruck, Isadore removed his glasses and wiped them with his handkerchief. When he replaced them and looked at her, the street light made dazzling sparklers in his glasses and wet eyes.

"This whole evening has been very beautiful for me," Isadore said.

Was it possible? Did he believe it?

Everything she had dismissed a moment ago as sad failure reformed itself in her mind now clothed in Isadore's word. Over the disordered freight-yard shapes of her childhood "beautiful" sifted like new snow.

❖

Pack My Bag

First thing this morning, as every morning, Dr. Joseph Bart's assistant, Mrs. Sternberg, comes into the main dental room to recite through her malocclusion from his appointment-book. He doesn't require such orderliness. But orderliness for Mrs. Sternberg is a tranquilizer pill, soothing down the pacing beast below.

Meanwhile Joe wanders over to the tape recorder. *"Pillar of Fire* is still on from last night," he remarks, half to himself.

Mrs. Sternberg's beast gives her a nip. "Please! I am almost finished."

Mrs. Sternberg's lips are apt to appear smiling when they are not. When they do smile, there is a dazzling burst—teeth diving through the curtain before their cue like a row of clowns.

Joe's friend Saul reminds Joe from time to time that he is without doubt the only dentist in New York who would hire a nurse with a bad bite. Joe anticipates the remark now, while Mrs. Sternberg reads. He expects to hear it again this evening when Saul comes to the office to pick up his wife, Betty, who has the last appointment of the day. The three of them will then go to dinner, and there will be ample time for Saul to say:

"Shall the skin specialist hire the lady with psoriasis? And shall the surgeon employ the amputee? Ah, my brothers, shall they not!"

146

Levity like this inspires Joe with deep humorlessness. "Her bad bite," he wants to say, "in no way impairs her efficiency." He feels the weight of it, his humorlessness. Humorlessness hangs from one shoulder and sincerity hangs from the other— two straps that support a knapsack of unavoidable traits, visible as a hump. They intrude into his encounters the way Mrs. Sternberg's teeth do in hers.

Instead of staring at Mrs. Sternberg's teeth, Joe looks at his equipment, surrounding him like a Swiss guard. The arm of the drill peaked and angled in a salute, the X-ray machine, the tanks of analgesic gas, the case of bayoneted hypodermics for painless dentistry that enable him to be swift and economical of the patient's time and his. And since his patients are either euphoric from nitric acid or tongue-numbed from novocain he has, also, a hi-fi phonograph and a library of labeled and indexed tapes. Although at the moment he stands stock-still, pretending to listen to Mrs. Sternberg, he is, in action, a busy man. He pictures himself. His foot is on the power pedal, his hand restrains the water-spurting borer, or else he is scraping, probing, modeling. And at the same time aware of the cello part of a string quartet. Every once in a while he says, "Open," or "Wider," but mostly his patients, swimming in sensations inside and out (the shelves, trays, and cupboards are enclosed in a well-grained dark wood that contrasts dramatically with the scrubbed whiteness), respond to a touch. The tape-wheels turn, the drill motor buzzes, and the oxygen and nitric acid pumps (the yes and no twins, clarity and befuddlement) hiss in balanced duet.

Safe and in command. His work. His *living*. He is grateful for dentistry—that limited field of trouble with almost infinite possibilities for care. The microcosm that reverses the ratios of the larger world. Outside this office he hangs by threads.

Mrs. Sternberg is through. She heaves a sigh as if she has, by her efforts, created the day. "There!" she says. "I think you will believe me that you have a busy day." She helps him into his jacket. She picks from their trays the mouth-mirror, pliers, and explorer and lays them in the flutes of the enamel table. She starts the water going in the expectorant bowl, fills the fresh paper cup in the metal holder, and readies a hypodermic needle.

While Joe washes his hands, his assistant leads the first patient to the chair—old Mr. Kidder, who travels in from the country. Mrs. Sternberg drapes him, tilts him, places his head in the headrest like an egg in an eggcup. The last thing she does before leaving the room is to flip on *Pillar of Fire*.

"There!" she says. "I know you are dying for it like for a cigarette." She smiles as wryly as her malocclusion allows.

"If you'll turn that thing down I have a present for you." Mr. Kidder removes from a paper bag he has kept on his lap a bunch of thickly clustered blue grapes. "I grow these myself, you know."

"Wonderful. What a marvelous thing." Joe sees that his thumb has erased the pearly etching from some of the grapes. He sets the bunch down carefully.

"I knew you'd appreciate them," Mr. Kidder says. "You ought to move your family out to the country."

Some of his patients know Mary has died. Most do not. Having revived painful memories, the grower of grapes inhales deeply and goes to sleep. Joe resists the urge to review his life with Mary—erased grape-bloom—and works intently on the demolition of Mr. Kidder's molar, then on Mrs. Dawson's bridge, then on and on, carefully along the road laid down for him early that morning by Mrs. Sternberg.

Betty comes in looking beautiful. She *is* a beautiful girl and knows how to dress, to walk, even to rest her legs in the legrest of his dental chair with grace. She has already recouped, so soon after the birth of her child, a triumphantly slender-waisted body.

She has a broken tooth.

"I must be in ghastly condition," she says dolefully. "I think I was eating Jell-o."

"I suppose there was some calcium deficiency during pregnancy," says Joe.

"I remember my grandmother *saying* it. 'A tooth for every child,' she said. Imagine, Joe. It's actually true!"

"We'll make a nice little cap for it. Nothing to worry about."

She refuses gas because the labor-room experience is too recent. While they wait for the needle to take ("You'll have to be careful about dinner," Joe warns her) she talks to him about her experience of new motherhood.

"Now that I've had the baby I understand something I never did before. How you always want to kneel before a newborn infant. *Any* infant. It's natural and instinctive. That's interesting, isn't it? It helps to understand the myth."

It jars him. Especially the "That's interesting" jars him.

"What the hell, Betty," he says. "You feel you have to think something intelligent to cover up your joy?"

Betty gives him an amused look. He's been humorless again and he can count on his friends to be amused. Betty now pats his arm and smiles at him crookedly but warmly. He actually feels he has endeared himself to her. How devious women are— are they deliberately so or can't they help themselves? First they disarm you. Then they ram you. At the same time he chides himself for his thoughts—that's my whole *trouble.*

He is not sure what he means. Does he mean his whole trouble is that he gives women credit for too much or that he doesn't credit them enough? Or does he mean still a third thing —that his whole trouble is that he attempts to read into the existence of women some meaning for himself, instead of recognizing that they are simply there, like wildlife creatures, some to be approached, some not. Still and all, he reasons, nobody has the final word on who or what is approachable. That is a matter of independent risk. He still feels that way, in spite of the disaster with Mary.

At dinner Saul and Betty graciously divide and realign themselves to counterbalance the lopsidedness of three.

"A tooth for every child," Betty says with mock mournfulness to Joe. "How plain can the meaning get?"

"Oh, Lord, here we go!" Saul pours wine for Joe.

"Deborah is a replacement for me."

"The baby is ten days old, remember." Saul taps Joe on the arm, pretending outrage.

"Yes, she's ten days old. Then she'll be ten years. Then twenty. Then married. I'll be old"—there is no more mockery—"or dead."

"Take this in," Saul says to Joe. "This is *real* maternal feeling."

"It is. I'd die for her right now. If the house were burning I'd jump into the flames for her. But I still know what I know." Betty appeals to Joe. "Philosophers never tell the truth. What they don't say is that more than half of those men in chains they're always talking about are women. While the men sit, the women are busy replacing everybody. Without women there would be no philosophy."

"Without women," Saul says, "who would need it?"

Joe is thinking that Betty and Saul are like each other. They are well matched. He is reminded that in his own marriage he had tried to storm a whole set of qualities in another person— different from his own, fascinating—to take them on and absorb them. A kind of soul-climbing was what he had embarked on and—guess what?—they had not let him in.

Betty's face is very beautiful in the candlelight and Joe accepts with calmness her question, "What was Mary like?"

"A little finesse please, Betty," Saul says.

"Joe knows it's not just curiosity. He knows it's because we love him. You never let us meet Mary, Joe. And you've never talked about her since."

Saul swivels his head around for the waiter. "I think we ought to have another bottle of wine and then—I think—we ought to have another topic."

Joe empties his glass and says matter-of-factly, meaning to be brief. "She was a very pretty girl, like you. A nice, active, happy girl like you, who wasn't happy with me."

Betty takes Joe's hand. "I would have been."

"No, not the way I was then."

"How were you then?"

Joe has been over the matter in his mind a thousand times and can hardly bear to confess again that he doesn't know why anything that happened, happened. It is not possible, on this topic, to be brief.

"I wasn't trying. The whole thing started to slip away down a mountain and neither one of us bothered to catch it before it broke its neck."

Betty and Saul exchange glances and Joe becomes aware of how he has put it.

"You're speaking of—?" Saul says, embarrassed.

"But didn't she die in a fall?" Betty says softly.

"Yes. From a mountain. While climbing."

Hasn't his voice and face been perfectly natural? He is surprised that the candlelight picks out tears in the eyes of his friends.

"Tell us if you want to," Betty pleads. "We don't want to ask any more."

Joe resists the seduction of those tears. He has the feeling Betty would like to see him weep, that she craves magnums of tears. She wants to drink him dry, in order to understand the myth of love. It's very interesting, she can then think. One always desires the qualities that are lacking in one's self. It's perfectly natural and instinctive and there's every chance it will lead to disaster.

But now Joe can't stop remembering Mary all the rest of the evening and it may be that he tells his friends everything. . . .

Joe Bart, city man, first poor and then—through a mixture of industry, love of books, and city-bred one-track-mindedness —thriving in his profession, took for his wife an outdoor girl from the West. "What makes me do this? Do I know who I am? Am I free to choose?" On the brink of marriage, his zeal for self-seeking transformed itself into a seeking out of self. Too late. Blue-eyed and fresh-faced, Mary looked to Joe to be lit up like a moon, whose dark side he felt himself to be. He dreamed that their opposite natures would come together in some grand but not, he hoped, obliterating eclipse.

He loved her optimistic belief (it sprang not from reading— she didn't read—but from her young, fresh-air-filled viscera) that life was lovable. She, in turn, groped among his book and record libraries, glancing from them to him as if the two were synonymous, an error of her innocence that he took advantage of.

With his dental equipment and his hi-fi, his busy, air-conditioned waiting room, he courted Mary, a skier and a hiker, taller than himself by one inch. He had good foreknowledge, in the midst of his love, that they would give each other plenty of hell. But he shook with rage when the warning— "Excuse me, Dr. Bart"—came hissing at him through Mrs. Sternberg's malocclusion—"are you trying to punish yourself for something?"

Punishment wasn't long in coming. And began, as a kind of warm-up exercise, with Mary's ticking off Joe's friends—to whom he introduced her after, not before the wedding. (Some, like Saul and Betty, never got to meet her at all.) There wasn't one friend with whom Mary felt comfortable. Not one whose self-absorption she cared to try to penetrate. For their part, the friends tried at all her windows and doors with their storms of words, rattling the clear glass panes of her being.

"The people you pick!" she cried.

"Be careful." He was astonished at her. "Did you forget I picked you? Let's go easy," he begged. "That's what people live with in marriage. They picked each other."

Still, he couldn't pass up his turn. "Okay! My friends don't barbecue in their back yards. They don't look like and their wives don't look like a bunch of beer ads. They stay indoors and read. Ever hear of it, Miss Rheingold?"

He was astonished, equally, at himself.

They began to glare at each other like two cliffs overhanging a drop. Joe felt the pull of the chasm and longed to fling over some kind of rope ladder. But Mary, younger by ten years, throve on danger. Finally Joe himself lost patience for reconciling. "That's the woman's job, damn it."

Mary began to find things to do that he'd never heard of in the city he'd been born in. First it was nature walks in Central Park at seven-thirty in the morning. Then Sunday excursions ("All meet with lunch and walking shoes in Van Cortlandt Park. Raine or shine"). Then weekends with knapsacks and sleeping bags on the Appalachian Trail in Connecticut. He felt sorry for Mary—sprinting back to dim-witted nature—and for himself—dropping morosely into his books. One night he dreamed an empty landscape, banks and streams and woods, a regular impressionist canvas, which moved him strangely. "If things don't work out on my ground," he said to himself, "why not try them on Mary's?"

The following weekend Joe accompanied Mary to the woods. When they got to the trail they found Mary's new friends waiting, sitting on a rock by a white-blazed tree, eating Gruyère cheese and raisins. The leader of the group was loaded down like a donkey. A bigger knapsack than anybody else's, two blanket rolls under that, canteens knocking on his hip and a guitar slung over all, strumming itself occasionally on a twig.

The next thing Joe saw was that Mary was no general nature lover. She was a specialist, a cultist—exclusively a wild-flower woman. Or at least the guitar player was, and Mary followed. She and the young man, despite his load, went on quests, making sudden scrambles from the paths while the rest leaned their packs against trees. They scraped under dead leaves, squelched around the edges of bogs, tumbled into mosquito-y glens and climbed difficult rocks, blazed with warning blue. They snatched the harmless specimens from the earth—the pale, weak roots spread like fingers—and popped them into the leader's knapsack, later to crush them in some Domesday Book. At night, after Joe made the fire, the guitar player sang, without a care in the world, about his worried mind. When the fire was out and Joe reached a hand to Mary, he found her zipped into her bag. His wildlife creature had safely pouched herself. Joe silently went off a little ways and lay down on a plank shelf in the racoon-gnawed shelter.

He gave up going after that, staying home weekends to study, burying his disappointment in books exactly as he had done before the marriage. The term "nature lovers" took on a cruelly comical meaning. Not that he suspected the guitar player would ever manage to unzip or unload, but that in his marriage he had somehow been cuckolded by flowers, trees, a pair of binoculars.

It was the guitar player who came, one Sunday when it was raining, to tell him of Mary's accident. She had been shrugged off the shoulder of a mountain like an unrequited lover, and had gone down clutching bloodroot.

Mary, plunging, grabbed Joe's hand. Down he went into some terrible descent in which everything seemed to break but

154

his neck. Where gone? Why gone? What and where and why everything in this life?

His friends, whom Mary had used to tick him off, came to comfort him.

"Having made it," said Emanuel, the securities analyst, "now unmake it. Having been with it, now be without it."

"Having misled yourself that you were at home," said Herb the city planner, "now go out and get lost in order to know that you have everywhere and nowhere to go."

"Oh, you scurfy bastards," Joe yelled, "when are you going to cut out the reading and start to feel something?"

"Go forth," they said, leaving him. "Joe, the experiencing one."

"All reincarnation in one short life, don't you feel that? If you slough it off back it comes, Joe, right? Obligation to transcendence."

"What book did you get that from?" he shot after them.

"What's the difference?" his friend Morty called back. "You'll come across it elsewhere."

Joe took, self-consciously, to chewing Sen-Sen in those days for fear his bitterness would repel his patients. . . .

Betty's face, rosy with motherhood and candlelit weeping, moves close to Joe.

"Call Susan," she says softly. "She's a lovely, lovely girl. Anyway you'll put me in an awkward position if you don't. Because I said you would."

She kisses his cheek, squeezes his hand, tells him the novocain has worn off and she is famished for something to eat.

"What do you do weekends, usually?" Joe asks Susan. This follows their second mid-week theater date, once to a satiric revue and once to the ballet and both, what with the smoke and

155

drinks of one place, the blue-lit interior landscape of the other, impeccably shut in.

Betty has not let him down. Susan has an apartment, a studio, an independence. She is a pretty girl. By some oversight, she has never married, and seems only lately to have realized that fact. There is a small, fresh furrow between her attractive brows and she answers him with cool vagueness. "I sometimes go camping. Why don't you come?"

Joe, also cool, mentions patient appointments. But inwardly he stares with recognition at the course of his own life. "Again!" he thinks. "Again!"

He paraphrases Betty (is she deliberately devious or can't she help herself?): without shocks there would be no philosophy. Then he reflects that throughout his life there have been repeats. In one sense, at least, they seem to him welcome. They are like a hint of form in what might otherwise appear to be a floating mass of events. There is, for example, the seemingly random way new patients have walked into his office and turned out to be connected with his life. Husbands of ex-girl friends, sometimes, who revive names, faces, feelings. In one case, an ex-boy friend of his dead wife, making him think of an early, unfinished version of some well-known work, discovered posthumously.

The repeats have entered Joe's life to an extent that some of his friends find comic. He himself gives them serious attention. The eternal return of Joseph Bart's . . . what? Not nemesis. Task. He is not sure of the exact nature of his task, but he feels it has to do with that stumbling-ground in his life where women stand. He is curious to know how the task will be accomplished. Will he be forced (punishment and pain he respects—reconstructors of character without benefit of anesthetic) to evolve?

There remains the question of which challenges to refuse. How does the hero in love behave? He enters the briars, cuts them down, and liberates love. Those who try the same thing and are trapped there can be dismissed as would-be heroes. Too bad. Go further. What about the hero in holy deeds? Also unpredictable and baffling. Percivale got the Grail. Lancelot did not. Moreover, even from the true hero the grace to make right moves can be withdrawn without notice. Theseus fell on evil days over the simplest exploits and Astronaut John Glenn slipped in the bathroom.

Joe mulls it over through a Ravel quartet, superimposed upon a carious bicuspid, and then tells Mrs. Sternberg to reschedule his appointments. What can anyone do except choose from among his choices? He goes home and packs the knapsack he hasn't touched since the hike with Mary.

From the beginning of the trip with Susan, Joe has a good, even a jubilant, feeling. The trail, he knows, is not one that has been walked by Mary and her friends. It is an easy, pleasant path, a beginner's way. Susan is quiet on the hike. She doesn't peer too closely at things. She seems to take everything in at a glance and let it go at that. Joe even feels moved to make a few comments. He knows no names, but he has always appreciated the difference between delicate trees and big heavy crushing ones. The first seem to him feminine (pretty—which would have driven Mary wild) and the other are the kind that travel straight up till you nearly fall on your back looking at them, with branches like commandments.

Joe and Susan stop for lunch under a delicate tree with an arrangement of leaves like fish skeletons. "Well it *is* pretty, damn it, whatever it is," Joe says.

Susan nods agreeably. When lunch is over Joe salutes the tree, says, "Thanks," and pats its bark.

"Don't you want to talk to the tree, too?" he says, putting his body closer to Susan's.

She gets to her feet and walks to another tree, one of those

157

giants with crushing limbs held aloft by the great power of the torso. "As a matter of fact," she says, "I do."

"Go ahead," he encourages her.

Tilting her head back she calls out in a clear voice. "Tree!" She waits a second, then calls out again. "Tree! Sky-flowerer! Old hope of mine, I see you."

He feels the stoppage of his blood. Christ! A loony. He greets the old and familiar suspicion that he has doomed himself to the alien. His heart sinks and his interest quickens. But a moment later Susan walks matter-of-factly back and heaves up her knapsack. She offers him his dessert of half a chocolate bar for the march.

They make early camp, for which he is grateful. His eyes, while there is still light, save up landmarks for his night blindness. Susan gathers them an excellent bed of pine needles. He had packed a shaker of Martinis in dry ice for them and when he zips himself in at last he is feeling pleasantly drowsy. The minute his hooded head touches earth, though, a drama begins. He hears hoofs pounding and awaits trampling, trussed. Then he thinks of the ant holes he is stopping up. He listens to mosquitoes, sweats and freezes in his bag, is furious at himself, miserably lonely under the stars, and, finally, with a last desperate image before his eyes of his expensive dental equipment, gives way to the imminence of his destruction. At the same moment he feels on his face a gentle breeze and with it a melting peace in which he is close to weeping, close to death with his grave under him before it is over him. After that he sleeps miraculously to wake in the morning with dew on his face and a hero's feeling because he has survived the night with nothing between him and emptiness but the vigor and strength of his own sleep.

Lifting a mosquito-bitten eyelid, he sees that Susan's bag is empty. He gets up and walks with the sunlight, following a stream to its dammed pool. Susan is bathing there naked. He decides he will do the same, but before he can advance even a step, Susan is up and striding off to their camp like a vigorous nymph. She dresses, makes breakfast, packs their gear and starts them off on the day's hike. He follows joyfully. "Lead away, my wild one." He would embrace her perhaps in a tree. In the crotch, he sings to himself, of a beautiful something tree, a tree, of a beautiful so-omething tree.

For a short time, where the path bends, she is out of sight. He finds her resting her pack on a rock.

"Where to, my fringed gentian?" Joe asks.

She consults, frowning, a geodetical map with curving lines drawn over the surface, very dense in one part. "Dark Entry Ravine."

"Where?" he asks again, not liking his sudden thought that they might get lost and he be utterly dependent on her. "Is that a real name or did you just make it up?"

"It's real."

"I like those sexy names," he says. But he experiences a warning. Like the signal of a dying nerve, something ticks painfully once, twice in his jaw.

Susan shoves her pack up off the rock and falls against him with a weight that nearly topples him, rear-slung as he is.

"Let's start," she says. "Otherwise we'll have to hike in the dark."

"Listen," he says lightly. "Everything's so pleasant and fine today. Let's not kill ourselves"—he wishes he had chosen other words. "Suppose we just take the easiest path and save the hard work for another time."

"We can't," she says, already moving ahead.

The change is subtle. It is only after they have walked for several minutes that Joe perceives, indignantly, that the innocent beginner's way has turned into a pilgrim's way—stony,

159

with an abyss. On his left the ground is slipping away to form a cliff beneath which runs a torrential, rock-beaten stream. On his right the pleasant meadow has been humping itself into a rocky wall. The path is narrowing, and root sinews fret it, so that it's necessary to walk watching your own footsteps.

Ahead of him Susan, with a cry, loses her footing and slumps awkwardly down onto her right hip. Her right hand has grabbed a root, arched like a handle, that projects through rock.

"Susan." Joe whispers her name, as if he might jar her loose. He has a wild notion that this nightmare now is the price extracted for his witless sleep of last night.

"Not hurt," Susan calls back in a reassuring tone. He watches as she carefully pulls, in and under, the leg that had been sticking out over the cliff. For a minute she squats like a Russian dancer and balances her pack. Then slowly she straightens, shakes one leg at a time and turns carefully on the path, showing him a rueful, unafraid face. "Slippery here."

When she moves forward again he calls, "Wait a minute. Time out."

She waits, keeping her back turned, giving him all the privacy she can on the path. He tries taking a few steps. Forward movement is impossible, the downward pull almost irresistible. He fights an urge to drop onto all fours. To goad himself, he recalls the delicacy of Susan's naked body in the stream, forces himself to recognize the slightness and weakness of her figure —a girl. He, on the other hand, is in good physical shape.

"This is just some damn neurotic thing," he says to himself. The purpose of the neurosis, he has read, is to be a bulwark, a fortress into which the unbearables of life cannot penetrate. Since this information, which he quotes to himself, does not help, he addresses his neurosis directly. "All right you, parasite, function! You damn tick-bird, pecking at my jugular, sing!"

160

But the bird will not sing. The neurosis, that luxury for which he is so heavily taxed, will not defend. All is silent. Over and through the rubble of his collapsed fortress, icy serpents slide. His feet freeze.

All the same, when Susan turns and calls to him lightly, he steps toward her. The leaves and roots on the path move under his feet like the running floor of a funny house and he slips and slides a yard down the trail before he halts, his fingernails scraping rock.

"Why the hell"—he gasps—"did you do this?"

"What are you talking about?" Susan says through her teeth. "Do you think I like it?"

"Didn't our friend Betty tell you—Mary died in a fall, out climbing, something like this?"

After a while Susan says, "Try. Drop off your pack and just leave it. Just come." She holds out a hand. After another little while she says, "Lots of people have this fear."

She even climbs up the few intervening feet to tell him this. He feels close to tears at her sacrifice. Meanwhile the air grows darker and chillier. The sun is leaving this high place. "I think you'd better go on," he says. "No, I'll stay with you," Susan says. His failing spirits lift. But then Susan peers down the path. "No, what I ought to do is go on to the shelter. There are bound to be campers there. We'll come back with some rope."

She seems determined on the course of bravery for herself and he cannot beg her to stay. She puts a bar of chocolate in his hand and without a word begins to slip and slide down the descent. He stays in the spot where his slide landed him, one hand clutching the arched root that saved Susan, the other holding the chocolate bar.

"I'll follow Susan," Joe thinks. "I'll be like her, I'll slip and slide and give myself over to it."

He thinks a while longer about who he can be like. Not as himself will he get out of here. Knapsack or no knapsack, the weight of himself is strapped on. Like a camel he silently sinks down onto the path. From below comes the sound of perpetually falling water and in his nose is the corrupt smell of the leaves. In this fertile, fetid place, breeder of earliest and simplest life forms, he awaits transfiguration.

After a while, there is a commotion behind him on the path. A long string of young hikers, some kind of club, comes jogging, swooping, yodeling down the trail. They salute him, hopping nimbly around him. "Wow!" they call out to each other. "This is a head cracker!"

They make a very long line, well spaced out. As he watches their rhythm, descending, he begins to feel it in his own body. He feels he can do the same. He can follow them to safety, not looking at his feet, just follow their bobbing heads, their rhythm, their singing voices that call back. Dance over the void. I'll be like them. I'll jog right down the mountain. I'll put my mind out of my mind and let my body take over.

He has already pushed to his feet, the strength is already returning to his legs, by the time the second inner voice begins.

I'll twist my ankle. I'll be flipped over the cliff like a cigarette butt. I'll be like Mary.

The argument of his yes and no voices goes on as he takes off. He feels, somehow, balanced in the center of their opposing claims, spinning away like a disk on a string. Pebbles fly from under his sneakers. He feels—it is not unpleasant—the inner shakeup as he jogs, with the joggers, down.

He is the next to last to arrive at the shelter, where all Susan has been able to round up are some of the advance young hikers. She is trying to persuade them to go back up the trail.

Susan throws her arms around his neck. Her voice trembles with feeling. "You did it, Joe! You beat the mountain! You made it!"

At that moment, Joe feels and shares Susan's evaluation of

him: Joe Bart, down from the mountain, is somebody infinitely precious and dear. At the same moment another more professional appraiser registers with a kind of stupefied joy that there has been no trauma. No excision. No extraction of Joe Bart's bloody roots from the universal jawbone. He is still to be a point of contact for his opposite number (he sees the fierce light of interest in Susan's eyes), still to be ground against (he appreciates, at this moment, the sexual suggestion of his own professional imagery) and to grind.

The full surge of exhilaration that comes over him now is delayed reaction to what has just happened and equally appropriate, he senses, to what is to come. That night, in the city, Susan admits him to the bed she has reserved for a hero. Then, in the morning, Joe telephones Susan from his office under the very teeth, so to speak, of Mrs. Sternberg. Susan's voice comes over with delicious warmth and newness. Joe drinks it in like a man who has been thirsty a long while. At the same time, he has the odd feeling of being in the presence of one of those stone goddesses of antiquity (Mrs. Sternberg stands rigid with impatience, waiting for the phone call to be over) whose faces occasionally signaled to men some omen of fate, some leakage of news from higher up. In their struggle against the terrible odds of her unspeakable occlusion, Mrs. Sternberg's lips seem to tremble on the verge of expressing something—possibly pleasure, possibly pain.

Part Three

✣

Green with Child

❖

Sheltering a Life

After Margaret Lowenstein gave birth to her first child she hired a sleep-in baby nurse from a good agency in the usual way. That is, Margaret didn't see the nurse until the day the nurse moved in.

The woman was nothing Margaret had hoped for. Instead of being a retiring person, she was obtrusive. Instead of tactful, outspoken. Instead of a calm, reassuring presence, she was a woman whose life was swamped with troubles. Margaret, recoiling on that first day of the nurse's arrival, telephoned her husband at his office to whisper what they were in for.

The nurse brought it all with her, her whole life, into Margaret's home, where Margaret gave it shelter for five weeks. In return, the nurse gave Margaret's son a virtuoso's care. It was an absorbed and yet, somehow, displaced time. Margaret had the impression that while she was quietly minding her business one day a hand had grasped her shoulder to make her turn and bear witness to the soul of a stranger's life. "Why us?" she asked. "Why here?" "Why now?"

Nurse Hasared was a big, brown-skinned, heavy-breasted woman. But on the first day, Margaret compared her to a bird. She had watched, invited by the nurse's flow of talk, the un-

167

packing of the nurse's case. "I have this," the nurse had said, looking into it tenderly, "so many years." Out had come the candy box that held the hair rollers. Then the shower-curtain box that held underwear and change of drip-dry uniform. There was a gilt-back mirror, its jagged edge pieced with adhesive ("Not broke by me, thank God," the nurse explained. "But I said to my cousin sister-in-law, 'Now you have got to throw that thing away you might as well give it to me . . .' ") and more boxes—candy boxes, stationery boxes, cigar boxes, pressed closed by crossed rubber bands—in which the nurse kept photographs and letters and other mementoes. Without them, the nurse said, she could not sleep in a strange bed.

Look, Margaret told herself. After so many years of roaming she makes her nest with pecked-up bits, like a bird.

But then after thinking of the nurse as a bird Margaret thought of her as a desert wanderer making camp. With the air of an experienced nomad the nurse seemed to sniff her way about the house. She seemed to ask, "Where is water?" "Where is fire?" Then she made her decisions about how she would live. "I will not disturb you to use your bath. I will have my kitchen sink and my lavatory next to that. It is like my private apartment."

But in fact what the nurse really looked like, Margaret decided that first day, was an Indian woman. It was a special, attractive thing about her—that she retained, after years in America, the skipping Jamaican speech, and had also extracted from that polyracial place the look of an Indian woman. She had a big head that swayed laterally as she spoke, in what seemed to Margaret an Indian way. It swayed and then settled and sank—chin into neck and neck into chest—in the centering motion of a dancer. She had the Indian woman's smudged eyes, the flared nostrils, the full, top-pointed lips, the flat swaying walk. Though that walk might have also been her habit from the nights and nights of infant-walking.

The nurse had asked at once for a table to do letters on. Margaret had brought the card table into the nursery and Hassie had spread her fingers over the table as if to prime it for its work.

"I will be honest with you," she said. "You are my last, last job."

While she set out her slippery packs of airmail stationery, her boxes and bundles of photographs, she added, "And my poor relatives, who are crying after me day and night, must be weaned from me like babies." She sighed with distress, then she giggled with pleasure. She rolled smudge eyes to heaven while her head began to center itself. "What will you think of me? I do look forward to a different life!"

After the nurse was with them one week, Margaret took to lying for her. The telephone would ring and there would be a woman's voice. Margaret recognized it as the voice of the nurse's half-sister. Or else there would be a man's voice. That was the nephew. The voices were rich and interesting, but Margaret was brief. If it were daytime and not raining, Margaret would answer, "I'm sorry, the nurse is out with the baby now." Or if at night, "She's taking a few hours off." It was, Margaret thought, like stabbing Polonius. She thrust and then heard, from behind a curtain, the groan of the unseen relative. Meanwhile, Nurse Hasared breathed at her back, just making out, through the receiver, the uninhibited swing and flair of her relatives' Jamaican accents, like an arranged musical background through which their fear could sing.

At the start of the second week, the nurse gave up trying to fish Margaret's name from the pond that teemed with the names of all the other families the nurse had lived with. She called her, simply, Mother.

Margaret then had to resist the thrilling summons of that name—newly christened with it as she was—while the nurse, without mercy, invoked it.

169

"My husband that I lost, Mother, was a good man. Long, lonesome years ago. I was a young girl still, with my three babies. I put those babies into school in Jamaica and I put myself into this night-and-day baby work here. Oh, Mother dear, I have buried my years in these babies. Without them Hassie would have died."

Then, in a different mood—the year before, Hassie had at last returned to Jamaica, had picked a husband and was now waiting for him to come—"Mother, I am a bride!"

When Margaret passed the nursery at night, she saw the nurse rocking the baby from step to step while she walked at her swaying pace. The hem of her nightgown flapped, beneath her robe, against the white stocking-rolls at her ankles. Margaret saw that it was not the nurse's rest the baby had disturbed, but her letter-writing.

Catching sight of Margaret, the nurse wrenched her mind from visas, pounds, and passage. The years she had buried in babies had yielded up a harvest of babycraft (and how beautifully Margaret's son throve with the nurse—the birth weight regained and more, the circumcision wound dry and healed, the blackened umbilical cord fallen cleanly off). Hassie began to instruct.

"When babies cry, Mother, you lay them here." She put the baby on her shoulder. "But if they are still crying, then you put them here." She slipped him down to her breast. "But there will be times when you will just say to him, 'Bundle, come to bundle!' And you will lay him here." Margaret's son and the nurse rocked belly to belly. "They feel that comfort."

But who, Margaret asked herself, was comforting whom?

"She's had to live through every crisis in someone else's house," Margaret said to her husband. "Her whole life has been like that. Unfair."

170

"Well, as to that . . . as to unfair . . ." her husband said. It threw them both into a somberness until her husband reminded her, "It's going to get better."

But Margaret worried that that might not be true.

In the evenings, when her husband worked late knowing that Margaret had Hassie for company, she and the nurse watched television. "Candid Camera," "What's My Line?" "This Is Your Life" did not bare the stranger's bosom half so much as the nurse herself who sat across from Margaret on the sofa. Sometimes Hassie took out the worn boxes, uncrossed the rubber bands and showed Margaret the pictures.

Mostly the pictures were of children. Children Hassie had cared for and lived with, mingled with her own. "This is the first baby I took care of that time I began to bury my life. This is my son, he is quiet and good like his father. This is my first, this is my youngest, this is the people I stayed with a year when their baby was sick. . . ." Her memories trailed along until they confronted her decision. "I am satisfied, Mother, that I have done the best for them that I could do. What is left of me now will take care of myself."

Hassie had also shown the new husband. Margaret took one look and had her doubts. His high white collar was heavily starched, his thick wavy hair carefully side-parted and brushed, his glance braced for the camera. Hassie explained that he was not much younger than she, had never married before, and was the only son of a many-daughtered house. Margaret had an instant picture of slavish sisters polishing, brushing, and flattering at every glance of those uncertain, demanding eyes.

"He will be a spoiled boy." Hassie smoothed the picture, nurselike, with her thumb. Then as if to silence her fear of the future, she pricked herself with the past. Margaret was the last of Hassie's tormentors. It delighted Hassie to remind her of that.

171

"No more nights on my feet! Poor Hassie! For years she has not got her sleep."

As if to prove it, the nurse would slip into a doze in the middle of a sentence. "My man I lost was a good man, Mother. Long, lonesome years." Zzz! She would be snoring, then wake herself with a burst. "This man now that I have married—will he be good to me, Mother? I want some man now who will help me carry the burden." Zzz! Up again, giggling at herself asleep and in her sleep having heard herself snoring. "I do look forward to being a bride."

The next minute she might cover her face with her hands. "But I will miss the darling babies. I will miss my own life, too."

And so it would all go round again and Margaret, half watching, half ignoring "This Is Your Life," "Candid Camera," and "What's My Line?" had a dizzying sense of lives laid upon lives.

"You ought to get out," Margaret's husband said. "If you listen to her stories all day you'll only brood."

Margaret thought, but she kept it to herself, that that was a funny word for him to use—"brood." Because lately she had felt that between them, herself and the nurse, they were hatching an egg. The nurse's new life, still locked in its shell, was waiting to be born.

All the same Margaret went out and Hassie gallantly called in her high, creamy voice, "That's right, burn up your free paper!" But after an hour away Margaret missed home. It was not, she had to admit, because of her son, whom Hassie sheltered like a dove. What called to her was the hatching of the egg. The warm, protective feathering that the two women together made.

The days—close with the closeness of the nest—slipped away. Hassie would bring the baby, asleep in the bassinet, into the living room with them. It was good for babies to hear women's voices, Hassie said. "It is good for him to hear he is safe in the world." Margaret's days seemed lit by twin moons, one dark, one light. The baby moon-face slept smooth-browed. The big moon-face schemed furrow-browed.

Toward the last days, Hassie began to look at things in Margaret's apartment with new interest, as if assessing what made people comfortable and what did not. Their conversation would wander about the rooms and stop at unexpected points.

"That is a very good color you have for a rug," the nurse would say. Or she suddenly pointed. "Do you think that magazine will be a nice one for my husband to start life in this country?"

Dumb cane had been growing in a pot at the foot of the sofa all those weeks, but it was only in the last days that Hassie said, "That is a plant we have also in Jamaica. It is called Mary-Eye-Water."

While Margaret groped at the relationship between Mary's tears and the leaf that numbed the tongue the nurse, pursing her lips, considered. "I may get one to grow in my apartment."

"I wish I could give you a cutting of that plant," Margaret said. "But there's only the single spike. It never shoots." After a moment she added, "I will look for a plant like that to send you."

"Oh, thank you, you are not to trouble." Hassie's tone, with a small nip to it, reminded Margaret of the legion of mothers, close while Hassie lived with them but strangers after all, who must have made such promises.

Margaret's husband had already paid Hassie the full wage of her time and had rounded it out with a sum. But what can *I* give you?—Margaret suddenly asked herself, looking straight across the living room at the nurse, the night before she was to leave—in memory of this time?

They were watching "Stump the Stars." But Hassie was gloomy. She leaned back against the armchair, covering her forehead with her arm. The plump brown elbow peaked itself above her white-uniformed bosom.

"He is writing me now that he would like me to take one more job. Maybe two." Her voice was faint and flat, confiding mostly to the crook of her arm. "Can you tell me, Mother, where I will get the strength to start that all over again?"

"You only have the jitters, Hassie, like any bride." Margaret, stirring nervously, felt the egg beneath them growing cold.

But by morning—the last morning—Hassie had recovered herself. Her head swayed peacefully, centering itself, while she did her last chores. Bathed the baby, then rocked him against her belly for the last time till he sank into a lightly snoring sleep. She did the baby laundry and sterilized the bottles and nipples and filled up a two-day supply of formula. Finally she went to wash and dress herself in the kitchen, clinging till the last to her inconvenient cozinesses. While she was pulling the bamboo drape for privacy she poked out her head and called a last request. "If the phone rings for me, Mother, I will be happy if you will say I have left."

When, a few minutes later, the doorbell rang, Margaret thought what a joke it would be on herself if one of Hassie's relatives—she almost had a foreboding—was standing outside. And that will be my parting gift, Margaret thought grimly. One last, barefaced lie to some desperate relative. But it was only the diaper man.

On her way back through the living room, Margaret involuntarily threw a glance at the bamboo drape—as if to tell Hassie everything was all right—and saw, through a chance combination of angle and light, the naked nurse bathing at the sink. Margaret hurried past to her bedroom, sat on her bed, and looked vaguely around. Finally she got up and looked, without

174

seeing anything, through her glove and scarf box. If she could draw, she thought, she would be able, from that startling glimpse of Hassie, to draw her years from now. She felt she had already done the drawing, or someone had done it for her. Softly etched through the matchsticks of bamboo, lit by yellow kitchen sun, the nurse, big and supple, was a dark-blossomed tree, swaying on the heavy trunk of legs together.

Ribbons? she asked herself. My beaded bag?

Hassie was calling that she was ready, and Margaret, feeling empty-handedness like a weight on her arms, left the bedroom. But when she got to the kitchen, the gift was waiting.

A noble-looking pineapple, its long head jeweled and plumed like a king's, stood on the table. Hassie and Margaret leaned there, hands clasped, their heads a little to one side, and let their glances rest on it.

"You can make a very good drink from the rind," Hassie said. "You would need ginger, too. I will mail you the recipe."

Margaret sensed the nurse had made the promise before. "You mustn't trouble yourself," she said. Then pineapple and promise seemed to leap together. "You make the drink, Hassie!" she said. "You take the pineapple."

"No," said the nurse. "I will not jostle myself with that thing in the subway. But thank you. I will take the rind."

And so, already dressed in her red coat and wool hat, Hassie took Margaret's bread knife and guillotined the plumed head twice more, once at each end. Standing the head on one of its lopped ends and bearing down on the knife, she trimmed the rind. After all the pieces fell Margaret put them in waxed paper and sealed them around with tin foil.

Hassie unsnapped her bulging case. She opened a pocket among her things to slip the package in, then burrowed a little more and took out a man's picture. The face was gentle, bony and—Margaret knew it before she'd been told—dead.

175

GREEN

"That was my good man that I lost, Mother." The nurse stared and smoothed the picture. "Look, Mother, he is young. And Hassie is still going on. Going over all the rough bumps."

"I wish you every happiness, Hassie," Margaret said.

And Hassie answered, "I always pray for all my children."

Margaret turned from her closed door. She wandered from room to room, tasting the nurse's absence, waiting for loneliness to overtake the feeling of relief, behind which it lagged.

In the nursery, her son slept on the good schedule Hassie had established for him. The card table was bare of letters and stationery boxes stuffed with pictures. Margaret snapped the legs under and put the table back in the closet. In the living room she pushed to its place near the window the armchair that Hassie had pushed to the TV. In the dining room, in the kitchen— she touched her things, straightened and restored them and erased from them also.

"Oh, Hassie," Margaret said into the air, "I'm sorry about your buried years." The nurse had lived them—sighing, giggling, weeping, writing her letters home—each time under eyes that saw everything and then blinked everything away.

Just where she stood, Margaret hatched from the egg they had cherished between them a home for Hassie. The taking man turned giving. Hassie laughing and resting.

It was when Margaret began to walk about her house again that she saw the nurse walking about another house as well. The nurse twanged the crossed rubber bands off her picture box. She found a snapshot of herself holding a baby. She smoothed the baby's face and smoothed her own. Little moon, big moon. She said, Margaret heard, to the fascinated mother from whose roof she borrowed shelter, "This is the baby I was caring for at that time. Lonesome nights, Mother. Long, lonesome nights . . ."

The dumb cane, Margaret found, was dry. She filled the kettle and carefully, not floating any sand, let it pour.

176

"Under whose eyes, Mother"—she was speaking to the dumb cane now—"are we?"

The water swelled, rose up full, then withdrew itself into the earth like a receding spirit.

✤

Plantain Shoot, It Want to Die

She is called Sister Gertrude because she is saved. But at first we know her only as Mrs. Burke, recommended by a friend's friend, and we have the idea that she is coming to save us. It is not easy to secure a baby nurse, especially in the seventh month of pregnancy—at the first clue or the final moment, seems to be the unwritten law. Either be a planner or a cheerful potlucker. I am somewhere in between—a planner with slothful tendencies, about which I am not cheerful. Because this is a first child and nothing seems quite real in the early months, I do nothing until an urgent sense of late! late! drives me to the telephone. Mrs. Burke speaks out strongly. "Don't you worry about a thing, girl, you hear? I'll be there!" At the same time she makes it clear that we are not to see her before the baby arrives. She hasn't a minute free.

For the next two months I cherish Mrs. Burke's "Don't you worry about a thing." Her voice holds a hint of Jamaican gallop-and-trot that on the telephone may pass for Irish brogue. In my mind I hear her stranger's voice repeat her words—"You hear? I'll be there!"—until both words and voice are well-known to me. I take this to be a privilege of my condition. The familiar, beginning with my body, has become strange. Then why shouldn't strangeness be allowed its own familiarity?

"We don't know yet how good she'll be," my husband says, sketching in a fence against possible disappointment. I feel I do know, but I don't admit it. I make a face that shows I agree life is full of disillusionment.

Our daughter is born in a white-hot August. One week later Mrs. Burke is to meet us at the hospital for the homegoing. She does not appear. But perhaps when she said, "I'll be there!" she had meant home? The taxi ride to our city apartment is for me almost as full of suspense as the one a week earlier to the hospital. Mrs. Burke is not waiting at our apartment door either. I can still hear the definite way she says, "I'll be there!" and I am convinced she *is* there. But where is "there"? In my fuddled state I have misplaced it.

Late in the day Mrs. Burke telephones. In an accent now trotting, now lazily shuffling, she explains a complication neither my husband nor I understands. It is something to do with her job in New Jersey. She will still, definitely, come. But first there is to be a night and a morning.

"I think it's good to have this experience first on our own," my husband says encouragingly. He has stayed home from his office. In a gesture toward "upness," I wear a light cotton dress rather than a robe. But I am still more down than up. And still fuzzy in the head—in the morning I had used the word "vacation" when I meant to say "valise."

"Don't you worry about a thing, girl!" I can still hear the words, but as there is no Mrs. Burke to be seen . . . "If I weren't so tired . . ." I tell my husband.

To bed at once, then. My husband waits while I creep in, wincing and sighing. My daughter stuns me. This new creature who lies in a room of her own, making sounds—where did she come from? Every part of my body aches, but that's no answer. From what corner out of time and space did this spirit fly to

179

me? I find, despite the first disappointment, that I can look forward again to the arrival of the nurse. I trust that knowledge of the body will cope with mysteries of the soul.

"Mrs. Burke's the kind who will quietly and capably take over," I say to my husband. "I sensed it on the phone the very first time. It's the force of her personality."

I am myself feeling at the lowest point of my own force. The aftermath of childbirth is a surprise to me. For the first time, and possibly too late in life for good acceptance, I feel the oneness of body and soul. Physically I am drained and emptied. But the part that comes as a surprise to my sheltered self is that my spirit feels so thin, so stripped of its layers. In soul as well as body I feel not worth looking into. Only my daughter can lift me from my lethargy, and then to such heights that I am dizzy. From where? My daughter sucks and stares through twelve stories up to heaven.

I rest. An earlier puzzle takes hold. Was it real or hallucination—in the hospital, when the body writhed its agony, and into that agony the mind occasionally woke and stared with piercing clearness—did I dream or live the waking? I grasped the bars of the bed and cried to the sweet-faced young nurse, "What's happening, please!" She looked up once from her book, then down again. She thought my lucid moment not worth acknowledging, since I would soon be submerged in darkness again.

The homecoming, though we try to keep all serene, exhausts our daughter. She gives the impression that she intends to sleep through the night. My husband and I do not. It is as if some unknown yet benign human voice has taken hold of our everyday tied tongues and we talk—of the perfection of the newborn, of our joy. At last my husband fumbles to my head in the dark. He raps my nose and says, "Sleep. Sleep. Do you know what time it is?"

But I, who all day am down, at night am so up I can feel myself, with my new flimsiness of body and soul, flying beyond the self I've known till now. My stripped, layerless spirit billows like a net and captures a vision. Flower-fresh babies, and hags. Circles of the old—newborn once—shuffle round. The room goes round. The earth whirls, too, turning time as a harrow turns earth. *In the springtime, the only pretty ringtime.* And then? *John Barleycorn is dead.* From there I plunge into my own mortality. And from there, impossibly, into a deeper abyss. This new flesh will age, this moist petal will burn and be ashes. In order not to feel despair, I muster anger. Why, why, should a single glimpse of perfection open endless vistas of death?

"What is it?" My husband shudders up from sleep. "What's going through your mind?" He reaches out a hand and strikes my cheek. "Oh, rest," he sighs, and sinks down again.

I whisper into his ear, "We're mortal."

My husband groans for sleep.

"Mortal!" I cry.

Wide-awake, my husband flings out a hand as if to hold me back, while with the other he fumbles for the night light.

"I can't bear it," I say.

My husband now sits quietly, holding both my hands. "Did you think we would live forever?"

I withdraw my hands and lock them beneath the cover. "I know it's late. It's late in life for me to have such revelations," I say falsely. I haven't known it. I don't know it yet. I am astonished to hear myself add, " 'When the bough breaks the cradle will fall.' " I hear, for the first time, the meaning of the nursery words.

"You're tired," my husband says. "Tomorrow Mrs. Burke will be here."

My husband has again taken hold of my hands and I draw

181

them away again to show the rocking song. I whisper the tune, " 'Rock-a-bye-baby on the tree top . . .' "

"I suppose"—he muses over my shoulder—"there is something to what you say. . . ."

"No, it's a nursery thing," I insist. "It goes: 'When the wind blows . . .' "

"It's possible," my husband says, "that your mind stayed sheltered against certain things. . . ."

I lean back on the pillow. I begin to run through the rest of the rhyme, to see what else I will hear. " 'When the bough breaks the cradle will fall, and down will come baby . . .' "

My husband puts his head down too. "This is," he says softly, "a joyful time for us. What could be more? Feel joyful."

In the night light my husband's face, older than his years, is happy.

At midmorning Mrs. Burke arrives. I had pictured her as thin and long-armed and work-handed, to go with the sweetly vibrating Mildred Dunnock voice. Instead she is enormously fat, with a Charles Laughton gravity to her black face that suggests, also, comical deceit.

She gives us handshakes, sets her very small traveling case outside our sleeping daughter's room, which will also be hers, and sits with us in the kitchen over glasses of iced tea, prepared by my husband. It is now near noon, and we suggest lunch before showing her around. She says she has no appetite for food. She wipes perspiration from her rough-skinned face with a crumpled handkerchief that she draws from her belt. Her blue skirt and white, transparent blouse are crushed and sooty. She has traveled, she tells us, straight from her job in New Jersey. Before that she had come straight from Connecticut. Before that she had been on Long Island. And come straight from there.

"In between, I went home this many times." She holds up two heavy, creased fingers and then pulls her nose with the knuckles, laughing in snorts.

"I just put down my suitcase and the phone rings! Off I go. Don't even unpack."

In fact, Mrs. Burke looks as if she has been sleeping in this same skirt and blouse through her last confinements. Also she is plainly exhausted. And suffers lately, she says, from a stomach ailment, so that no food agrees with her. When she has finished her tea, she takes her small bag to the bathroom.

"I like her," I say immediately to my husband, to forestall his objections. "I can tell you exactly why."

"I like her, too," my husband says. "But it's too soon to tell how good she'll be." After that we sit and wait.

When Mrs. Burke returns from the bathroom, I look nervously to see what changes she has made in her appearance. At first I detect nothing. Then I can see only that her crushed blouse and skirt are liberally sprinkled with water. And in her right hand she carries a flyswatter. Not the old-fashioned, wire-mesh kind one still sees in hardware stores, but a new type for sale in the supermarkets—all plastic, with a hard plastic handle and a flexible plastic swatter end that has sharp-edged, open-work designs like a paper doily. The flyswatter is painted gold.

Our daughter snores lightly through a nap and my husband says to the nurse, "I hear they've a fine climate in Jamaica."

"Oh, I left that place years ago." Mrs. Burke reseats herself at the table, and we, who have been standing uncertainly, do also. "My husband died. I married again. Then that husband died. I said to myself, 'Girl, why don't you travel!' And that's what I did. You can go just so far on fine climate."

She smiles pleasantly at my husband and then lets out a sudden big laugh. My husband laughs, too. Mrs. Burke raps the table with the golden flyswatter. I haven't seen a fly, but with all the windows open it's possible we have some. It is a good thing for the baby, I feel, that Mrs. Burke is so fly-conscious.

"And children?"

"Five." The flyswatter, which had been held straight up, wavers. Her manner does not. "I traveled around," she says largely. "Cuba. England. I saw some things."

"American now?" my husband asks.

"Me, no!" Down comes the flyswatter again, this time against the side of her chair, like a riding crop. "I am an independent Jamaican, sir. With a British passport."

The pursed lips and drawn eyebrows in the heavy face make me wonder if she feels offended, except that there is still the hint of comedy in the exaggerated flesh with its exaggerated expressions.

"An English passport is a very good one," I say carefully.

Mrs. Burke sweeps the flyswatter up at me, level with my chin. "I've got better than an English passport. I've got a passport of the British Empire! With lions and a gold crown and my face on it! The sun don't set on my passport!"

While she speaks, Mrs. Burke's arm lifts. Finally, on the last "passport," the flyswatter is again pointing straight up. I am reminded of school engravings of certain British monarchs. The flyswatter descends and suddenly Mrs. Burke begins to shake. Her whole pyramid body, broader at the base than the chair seat, goes up and down while it also rocks forward and back, like a jazz singer's. A shocking, wild laughter breaks out for a few seconds and then is choked off as Mrs. Burke's chin, convulsed into four or five layers, throttles down on her neck. Her mouth is still open; her body still heaves up laughter; but it makes no sound. The audible laughter now comes from my husband. And then there is a duet. Mrs. Burke laughs *ironic triomphado;* my husband, in some shrouded key. I remember then his account of how he traveled to this country, passportless, through half a world.

I sit tight in my chair, crouched over my thin spirit and my aching body. Mrs. Burke and my husband laugh so hard that I am the first to hear the baby's cry. "Passports!" Mrs. Burke gives a final drill of laughter and then she goes to work. She walks with a quick waddle, scoops the baby from the bassinet and seats her atop her mountainous breast. She gives commands: "Up, now!" and "There, see?" and "Hush up, darling" and "Let's go, lazy!" The baby seems to absorb them all. Mrs. Burke carries her swiftly through the rooms. I totter after, calling, "Is there anything—"

From the bathroom, where water is running, I hear an encouraging shout. "Come on, Mommy!"

My husband has his notecase. "I see everything's under control," he says, "so I'm going." He waits. "Are you pleased?"

"Oh, yes."

"Then rest now."

"I don't know whether I should rest or whether I should watch first, to learn, and then rest."

"I think rest first," my husband says. "You can learn next week."

"That's right," I say. And with that reassurance my body surrenders its last watchfulness. "Please tell her," I mumble. I creep toward bed and am asleep by the time I am down.

I awake into silence, feeling bereft. "Where's the baby?" I call out. I attempt to jump from bed, am stabbed and fall back.

Mrs. Burke has changed into a uniform, less crumpled than her traveling outfit, and has rolled up her hair. She seats herself at the foot of my bed. The golden flyswatter is cradled in the crook of her arm. She watches me.

"Where's the baby?" I ask again, in a humbler tone.

"She is sleeping sound."

"I—wasn't I supposed to nurse her?"

"I gave her the bottle. I wouldn't wake you, looking so weak."

"Won't my milk dry up, then?"

Mrs. Burke hits her leg with the flyswatter and examines the rug for a corpse. "Milk don't dry up so fast. Your milk going to come back and make you feel sore after you want to give it up. That's nature." She surveys me dispassionately again. "You do look weak."

I take a chance with this five-times life-worn mother and admit, "It's my stitches."

Mrs. Burke raises her golden flyswatter. For a moment I imagine she will bring it down on my bed with a flap. Instead she holds it aloft, so that her answer seems to hang suspended, too. Her words, when they finally come, descend like a dread but just decree, a meting out of equal sorrow: "Everybody get the same cut."

I fall back on my pillow. "Tell me about your life in Jamaica. Tell me about your children. Are they still there?"

"No." She shakes her head and fans herself with the flyswatter.

"Some here? Some in England?"

"Not one child."

"Where are they, then?"

"They dissolve on me." Mrs. Burke hunches over and moves the flyswatter in a flat, slow sweep before her. "All dissolve a-way." A small echo of that Gargantuan laugh I had witnessed earlier shakes silently through her body and she rolls once over my toes. Involuntarily I jump, and then tears burn my eyes. Mrs. Burke turns to me with a pursed mouth. "You too soft, girl," she says.

I am given early supper on a tray and then my daughter is brought to my bed. Gracious words spring to my mind. "Laying the babe to breast" and "giving the child suck." But what I say to the nurse is—reproachfully—"It's painful. Because of the skipped feeding."

"It better be," she answers. "That shows that baby needs you."

As my daughter drinks the pain dissolves. I discover that my body needs hers as much as she needs mine. I feel both less and more than I was. I am one half a being, one end of some timeless, two-ended creature, with itself in its mouth, and consider saying so to Mrs. Burke. But she follows her own thought and is there before me. "Anything don't need its mama," she says, "going to push it off the vine."

Without knowing when it was I dozed, I find myself waking again in the yellowish summer twilight—later than it looks—that fills the room. I hear a pleasant murmur of voices. I wash my face and put on lipstick, comb my hair, and tie a ribbon in it. My husband's voice now and then breaks into a held-down laugh. I put on a new robe and go into the dining room, where the yellowish glow takes on an amber light. My husband and Mrs. Burke are sitting over coffee. A sharp laughter dies when I come in.

"I'm so glad you feel better," my husband says, drawing up a chair for me. His face has gone shades whiter than its normal tone, but he seems unaware of his fatigue. "I looked at her," he says. "She is so sweet!" He has brought fresh mimosa, and their powdery brightness stands on the table between two brown bottles of beer.

"What were you laughing about?" I nibble at the remains of his bread.

My question reminds Mrs. Burke to laugh again, a short drum roll. From the look of the table she has prepared a good dinner for my husband and has not stinted on covered serving dishes, which she later will wash. All the same, I've begun to

187

dislike her. I wait for my answer. "What was the joke as I came in?"

"A saying of the island," my husband says. "Plantain shoot, it want to die."

"Oh," I say.

"It's funnier the way Mrs. Burke tells it." My husband tries again. "It comes from the way plantain farming is done. Applied to people."

"How does it apply to people?"

"Oh, if they strut or brag, they need to be cut down."

"Or if they send up a shoot, I suppose." I look toward Mrs. Burke. She is beginning to clear the table and is absorbed in that.

In the privacy of our room my husband tells me, "She's done just about everything. And what she hasn't done herself, she's seen. And she is saved, she says—although the way she says it . . ." Appreciating ambiguity, my husband smiles at one corner of his mouth. "But what do you think?" he asks. "You're the one who has to spend all day with her."

"Fine," I say. "She's very good with the baby."

On this second night of my daughter's homecoming, I go to bed in the grip of the most futile feeling there is—I am miserable over the way the world is made. Misery provides the sleep that the first night's joy withheld. But in the morning I wait for my chance with the nurse.

Heat has accumulated in the closets and corners of the rooms, and Mrs. Burke comes in wiping her face and fanning herself with the flyswatter. She sits at the foot of my bed and appraises me.

"You don't look strong," she says. "But you don't look so weak."

"Mrs. Burke, what does it mean, 'Plantain shoot, it want to die'?"

Mrs. Burke nods her head at me, as if I have caught on to some essence she would like to impart. "That's right," she says. "You were talking about that last night."

"That's right," she says again. The little golden shovel warps over her knee.

"Why do they say that about a poor plantain?"

"The men come with big knives," Mrs. Burke says. "Sharp. When they see the new shoots rise they walk up to that old plantain and—" She levels off the flyswatter and gives a mighty cut. Then she lays it down again. "I've seen it done a thousand times." She bounces my bed with laughter. "All those big men with knives . . ."

"But why? Must they?" I want to argue with her as I could not argue with my own vision. "Must they?" I insist. But Mrs. Burke does not argue. She gives an impatient cluck as if I weren't learning well after all, and mops her face with her handkerchief. "I do prefer to be in the cool in the summertime," she says. "But a promise is a promise. I promised to be here these few days and here I am."

"What do you mean, few days?"

"Girl, I'm not finished with that job in New Jersey."

"But you promised you'd stay here!"

"No, not stay. Come. And I did."

I begin to cry.

Mrs. Burke raises her golden stick. "Girl, that girl in New Jersey is sick. Feel pity for that girl in New Jersey," she commands me. Then she glares and whispers, "She might die!"

I feel myself go cold and then hot. "Are you sure it's that?" I say at last. "Or is it just cooler in New Jersey?"

Mrs. Burke shakes my bed again with her laugh. "You health improving!"

With Mrs. Burke watching, I telephone a nurses' agency and extract a promise of someone for the next day.

Mrs. Burke then says reflectively, "I am wondering if my daughter-in-law could come to you."

"I thought you had no children."

"My stepson," Mrs. Burke says. "As dear to me as any of my own."

A silent cheer for Mrs. Burke rises above my rage. *A stepson. As dear as any of her own.* She has struck water from rock, joy from misery. "But no," she adds, calmly examining the flyswatter, "I believe she is too busy."

Next day there comes to us from the agency a Mrs. Johnson. Although she is also from Jamaica, it is another Jamaica. She is neat, bustling, with a high, quick voice and a collection of stiff uniforms. She and Mrs. Burke (who astonishes me with her formality and her uniform at nine in the morning) meet and exchange glacial smiles. Then Mrs. Burke changes to her blue skirt and transparent blouse, ready to travel. She gives my husband a royal handclasp and me a motherly hug. My husband carries her case to the door, where I hear them laughing one last time.

I follow Mrs. Johnson to the baby's room. She begins carefully to sponge my daughter in the bathinette.

"Oh, I see," I say. "Mrs. Burke just bathed her in the bathroom sink."

Mrs. Johnson makes a disparaging sound. Then she deftly wraps the baby in a towel. Everything else, for the rest of Mrs. Johnson's stay, is managed in the same regular way.

One day I ask her, "Do you know the saying 'Plantain shoot, it want to die'?"

"Oh, the country people might say that. I'm from Kingston, dear."

"Mrs. Burke said—" I begin.

Mrs. Johnson laughs, a high-pitched sound with which she is

190

as nimbly and quickly done as with any of her duties. "Her! You're lucky she left." Then she gives me a shrewd look. "Every woman feels a little down after she has her baby, you know, dear. Best to smile and shake it off. Just smile and shake it off."

And that is what I do. My body revives. My spirit's paraphernalia is reassembled. The narrow, lucid moment with its wracked questions is over. I catch no more visions. I am busy. I make plans. The future is not just a dark corridor leading to another dark corridor. For a while, as if to make up, it is as though the future can seem nothing but a bright blur, a colorful voyage whose end I cannot foresee. It is hard, even for self-protection, to brush in a few shadows.

Months later, as it turns out, Mrs. Burke's daughter-in-law, Mrs. Cooper, does come to us to help with the baby. Her coming stirs a vivid ghost of Mrs. Burke and unveils an imagined portrait of the man who is dear to both women—the husband and stepson. A man of scope is how he appears, and on good, full terms with life. For they are opposite as night and day— the slow, shy, backward-glancing wife and the dauntless traveler, Mrs. Burke, the one who has lost everything, and is saved.

✛

What Must I Say to You?

When I open the door for Mrs. Cooper at two in the afternoon, three days a week, that is the one time her voice fails us both. She smiles over my left shoulder and hurries out the words "Just fine," to get past me. She is looking for the baby, either in the bassinet in the living room or in the crib in the baby's room. When she finds her, she can talk more easily to me— through the baby. But at the doorway again, in the early evening, taking leave, Mrs. Cooper speaks up in her rightful voice, strong and slow: "I am saying good night." It seems to me that the "I am saying" form, once removed from herself, frees her of her shyness. As if she had already left and were standing in the hall, away from strangers, and were sending back the message "I am saying good night."

Maybe. I know little about Mrs. Cooper, and so read much into her ways. Despite the differences between us, each of us seems to read the other the same—tender creature, prone to suffer. Mrs. Cooper says to me, many times a day, "That is all right, that is all right," in a soothing tone. I say to her, "That's such a help, thank you, such a help." What can I guess, except what reflects myself, about someone so different from me?

Mrs. Cooper is from Jamaica. She is round-faced and round-

192

figured. She is my age, thirty, and about my height, five-five. But because she is twice my girth (not fat; if there is any unfavorable comparison to be drawn, it may as well be that I am, by her standard, meager) and because she has four children to my one, she seems older. She is very black; I am—as I remember the campus doctor at the women's college I attended saying— "surprisingly fair." Though, of course, not Anglo-Saxon. If you are not Anglo-Saxon, being fair counts only up to a point. I learned that at the women's college. I remember a conversation with a girl at college who had an ambiguous name—Green or Black or Brown. She said in the long run life was simpler if your name was Finkelstein. And I said it was better to be dark and done with it.

Mrs. Cooper has been coming to us, with her serious black bulk and her beautiful voice, for some months now, so that I can get on with my work, which is free-lance editorial. The name is lighthearted enough, but the lance is heavy and keeps me pinned to my desk. Mrs. Cooper's work, in her hands, seems delightful. Though she comes to relieve me of that same work, it is a little like watching Tom Sawyer paint a fence—so attractive one would gladly pay an apple to be allowed to lend a hand. Even the slippery bath, the howls as my daughter's sparse hairs are shampooed, become amusing mites on the giant surface of Mrs. Cooper's calm. They raise Mrs. Cooper's laugh. "Ooh, my! You can certainly sing!"

I sneak from my desk several times an afternoon to watch the work and to hear Mrs. Cooper speak. Her speech, with its trotty Jamaican rhythm, brings every syllable to life and pays exquisite attention to the final sounds of words. When she telephones home to instruct the oldest of her children in the care of the youngest, it is true that her syntax relaxes. I hear "Give she supper and put she to bed." Or "When I'm coming home I am going to wash the children them hair." But the tone of her voice is the same as when she speaks to me. It is warm, melodious. Always the diction is glorious—ready, with only a bit of memorizing, for Shakespeare. Or, if one could connect a woman's voice with the Old Testament, for that.

"God is not a God of confusion." Mrs. Cooper says that to me one day while the baby naps and she washes baby clothes in the double tub in the kitchen. I have come in to get an apple from the refrigerator. She refuses any fruit, and I stand and eat and watch the best work in the world: rhythmic rubbing-a-dubbing in a sudsy tub. With sturdy arms.

She says it again. "God is not a God of confusion, that is what my husband cousin say." A pause. "And that is what I see."

She washes; I suspend my apple.

"It is very noisy in these churches you have here." She has been in this country for three years—her husband came before, and later sent for her and the children, mildly surprising her mother, who had other daughters and daughters' kids similarly left but not reclaimed—and still she is bothered by noisy churches. Her family in Jamaica is Baptist. But when she goes to the Baptist church in Harlem, she is offended by the stamping and handclapping, by the shouted confessions and the tearful salvations. "They say wherever you go you are at home in your church. But we would never do that way at home."

She lifts her arms from the tub and pushes the suds down over her wrists and hands. "But I will find a church." The purity of her diction gives the words great strength. The tone and timbre would be fitting if she had said, "I will build a church."

Again she plunges her arms in suds. "Do you ever go," she asks me, "to that church? To that Baptist church?"

Now is the time for me to tell her that my husband and I are Jewish—and so, it occurs to me suddenly and absurdly, is our three-month-old daughter, Susan.

194

It is coming to Christmas. I have already mentioned to my husband that Mrs. Cooper, who has said how her children look forward to the tree, will wonder at our not having one for our child. "I don't feel like making any announcements," I tell my husband, "but I suppose I should. She'll wonder."

"You don't owe her an explanation." My husband doesn't know how close, on winter afternoons, a woman is drawn to another woman who works in her house. It would surprise him to hear that I have already mentioned to Mrs. Cooper certain intimate details of my life, and that she has revealed to me a heartache about her husband.

"But I think I'll tell her," I say. "Not even a spray of balsam. I'd rather have her think us Godless than heartless."

My husband suggests, "Tell her about Chanukah"—which with us is humor, because he knows I wouldn't know what to tell.

Mrs. Cooper stands before my tub in the lighted kitchen. I lean in the doorway, watching her. The kitchen window is black. Outside, it is a freezing four o'clock. Inside, time is suspended, as always when the baby sleeps. I smell the hot, soaped flannel, wrung out and heaped on the drainboard, waiting to be rinsed in three pure waters. "We don't attend church," I say. "We go—at least, my husband goes—to a synagogue. My husband and I are Jewish, Mrs. Cooper."

Mrs. Cooper looks into the tub. After a moment, she says, "That is all right." She fishes below a cream of suds, pulls up a garment, and unrolls a mitten sleeve. She wrings it and rubs it and plunges it down to soak. Loving work, as she performs it—mother's work. As I watch, my body seems to pass into her body.

I am glad that my reluctance to speak of synagogues at all has led me to speak while Mrs. Cooper is working. That is the right way. We never, I realize while she scrubs, still seeming to be listening, talk face to face. She is always looking somewhere

195

else—at the washing or the baby's toy she is going to pick up. Being a shy person, I have drilled myself to stare people in the eyes when I speak. But Mrs. Cooper convinces me this is wrong. The face-to-face stare is for selling something, or for saying, "Look here, I don't like you and I never have liked you," or for answering, "Oh, no, Madam, we never accept for refund after eight days."

The time Mrs. Cooper told me her husband had stopped going to church altogether, she was holding Susan, and she uttered those exquisite and grieved tones—"He will not go with me, or alone, or at all any more"—straight into the baby's face, not mine.

Mrs. Cooper now pulls the stopper from the tub and the suds choke down. While she is waiting, she casts a sidelong look at me, which I sense rather than see, as I am examining my apple core. She likes to see the expression on my face after I have spoken, though not while I speak. She looks back at the sucking tub.

When Mrs. Cooper comes again on Friday, she tells me, as she measures formula into bottles, "My husband says we do not believe Christmas is Christ's birthday."

I, of course, do not look at her, except to snatch a glance out of the corner of my eye, while I fold diapers unnecessarily. Her expression is calm and bland, high round cheekbones shining, slightly slanted eyes narrowed to the measuring. "He was born, we believe, sometime in April." After a bit, she adds, "We believe there is one God for everyone."

Though my husband has told me over and over again that this is what Jews say, Mrs. Cooper's words move me as though I have never heard them before. I murmur something about my work, and escape to my desk and my lance again.

Mrs. Cooper has quoted her husband to me several times. I am curious about him, as I am sure she is about my husband.

She and my husband have at least met once or twice in the doorway, but I have only seen a snapshot of her husband: a stocky man with a mustache, who is as black as she, with no smiles for photographers. Mrs. Cooper has added, in the winter afternoons, certain details important to my picture.

Her husband plays cricket on Staten Island on Sundays and goes on vacations in the summer without her or the children, sometimes with the cricketers. But to balance that, he brings her shrimps and rice when he returns at 1:00 A.M. from cricket-club meetings on Friday nights. His opinion of the bus strike in the city was that wages should go up but it was unfair to make bus riders suffer. About Elizabeth Taylor he thought it was all just nonsense; she was not even what he called pretty—more like skinny and ugly.

In most other respects, it seems to me, he is taking on the coloration of a zestful America-adopter. There are two kinds of immigrants, I observe. One kind loves everything about America, is happy to throw off the ways of the old country, and thereafter looks back largely with contempt. The other kind dislikes, compares, regrets, awakens to *Welt-* and *Ichschmerz* and feels the new life mainly as a loss of the old. Often, the two marry each other.

Mr. Cooper, though he still plays cricket, now enjoys baseball, the fights on television, his factory job and union card, and the bustle and opportunity of New York. I mention this last with no irony. Mr. Cooper's job opportunities here are infinitely better than in Jamaica, where there aren't employers even to turn him down. He goes to school two nights a week for technical training. He became a citizen three years ago, destroying his wife's hopes of returning to Jamaica in their young years. But she dreams of going back when they are old. She would have servants there, she told me. "Because there aren't enough jobs, servants are cheap." Her husband, in her dream, would have a job, and so they would also have a car. And a quiet, gossipy life. She likes to move slowly, and this, as she herself points out, is very nice for my baby.

Christmas Week comes, and we give Mrs. Cooper presents for her children. And since Christmas Day falls on the last of her regular three days a week, we pay her for her holiday at the end of the second day. "Merry Christmas, Mrs. Cooper," I say. "Have a happy holiday."

Mrs. Cooper looks with interest at the baby in my arms, whom she had a moment before handed over to me. Suddenly she laughs and ducks her knees. Her fingers fly with unaccustomed haste to her cheek and she asks, "What must I say to you?"

"You can wish me the same," I say. "We have a holiday. My husband gets the day off, too."

I am glad that Mrs. Cooper has not grown reticent, since her embarrassment at Christmas, in speaking to me of holidays. Soon she is telling me how her children are looking forward to Easter. The oldest girl is preparing already for her part in a church play.

I fuss with the can of Enfamil, helping Mrs. Cooper this way when what I want is to help her another way. "Will your husband come to the play?" I ask casually.

"I am not sure," she says. After a while, "We haven't told him yet." Another little while. "Because it seems also he is against these plays." Then, with just enough of a pause to send those tones to my heart, she says, "I think he will not come."

Because the Judaeo-Christian tradition will have its little joke, Passover Week sometimes coincides with Easter Week, overlaying it like a reproach. It does the year Mrs. Cooper is with us. First, Good Friday, then in a few days is the first day of Passover.

198

"This year," my husband says, "because of Susie, to celebrate her first year with us, I want us to put a mezuzah outside our door before Passover."

"I'm not in favor." I manage to say it quietly.

"You don't understand enough about it," my husband says.

"I understand that much."

"Do you know what a mezuzah is? Do you know what's in it?" Taking my silence as an admission of ignorance, my husband produces a Bible. "Deuteronomy," he says. He reads:

"Hear, O Israel: The Lord our God, the Lord is one Lord:
And thou shalt love the Lord thy God with all thine heart,
 and with all thy soul, and with all thy might.
And these words, which I command thee this day, shall be
 in thine heart:
And thou shalt teach them diligently unto thy children,
 and shalt talk of them when thou sittest in thine house,
 and when thou walkest by the way, and when thou liest
 down, and when thou risest up. . . ."

All this and more is written on a parchment that is rolled up tight and fitted into the metal or wooden mezuzah, which is no more than two inches high and less than half an inch across and is mounted on a base for fastening to the doorframe. My husband finishes his reading.

"And thou shalt write them upon the door-posts of thine
 house, and upon thy gates:
That your days may be multiplied, and the days of your
 children, in the land which the Lord sware unto your fa-
 thers to give them, as the days of heaven upon the
 earth."

The words might move me if I allowed them to, but I will not allow them to.

My husband closes the Bible and asks, "What did your family observe? What was Passover like?"

"My grandfather sat on a pillow, and I was the youngest, so I found the matzos and he gave me money."

"No questions? No answers?"

"Just one. I would ask my grandfather, 'Where is my prize?' And he would laugh and give me money."

"Is that all?" my husband asks.

"That was a very nice ceremony in itself," I say. "And I remember it with pleasure, and my grandfather with love!"

"But besides the food, besides the children's game. Didn't your grandparents observe anything?"

"I don't remember."

"You sat at their table for eighteen years!"

"Well, my grandmother lit Friday-night candles, and that was something I think she did all her life. But she did it by herself, in the breakfast room."

"Didn't they go to a synagogue?"

"My grandmother did. My grandfather did, too, but then I remember he stopped. He'd be home on holidays, not at the services."

"Your parents didn't tell you anything?"

"My parents were the next generation," I say. "And I'm the generation after that. We evolved," I say—and luckily that is also humor between my husband and me.

But my husband rubs his head. It's different now, and not so funny, because this year we have Susan.

My husband was born in Europe, of an Orthodox family. He is neither Orthodox nor Reform. He is his own council of rabbis, selecting as he goes. He has plenty to say about the influence of America on Jewishness, Orthodox or not. "The European Jew," my husband says, "didn't necessarily feel that if he rose in the social or economic scale he had to stop observing his

Jewishness. There were even a number of wealthy and prominent German Jews who were strictly observant."

"I'm sure that helped them a lot!" This is as close as I come to speaking of the unspeakable. Somewhere in the monstrous testimony I have read about concentration camps and killings are buried the small, intense lives of my husband's family. But why is it I am more bitter than my husband about his own experiences? And why should my bitterness cut the wrong way? It is the word "German" that does it to me. My soul knots in hate. "German!" Even the softening, pathetic sound of "Jew" that follows it now doesn't help. All words fail. If I could grasp words, I would come on words that would jump so to life they would jump into my heart and kill me. All I can do is make a fantasy. Somewhere in New York I will meet a smiling German. In his pocket smile the best export accounts in the city—he is from the land of scissors and knives and ground glass. Because I am surprisingly fair, he will be oh, so surprised when I strike at him with all my might. "For the children! For the children!" My words come out shrieks. He protests it was his duty and, besides, he didn't know. I am all leaking, dissolving. How can a mist break stone? Once we exchange words it is hopeless; the words of the eyewitness consume everything, as in a fire:

> "The children were covered with sores. . . . They screamed and wept all night in the empty rooms where they had been put. . . . Then the police would go up and the children, screaming with terror, would be carried kicking and struggling to the courtyard."

How is it my husband doesn't know that after this there can be no mezuzahs?

"It's too painful to quarrel," my husband says. He puts his

hands on my shoulders, his forehead against mine. "This is something I want very much. And you feel for me. I know you feel for me in this."

"Yes, I do, of course I do." I use Mrs. Cooper's trick, and even at that close range twist my head elsewhere. "Only that particular symbol—"

"No, with you it's all the symbols." My husband drops his hands from my shoulders. "You don't know enough about them to discard them."

I don't have the right to judge them—that is what I feel he means. Since I was not even scorched by the flames of their futility. As he was, and came out cursing less than I.

"But besides everything else"—I take hasty shelter in practicalness—"a mezuzah is ugly. I remember that ugly tin thing nailed to the door of my grandmother's room. If I spend three weeks picking out a light fixture for my foyer, why should I have something so ugly on my door?"

Then, as my husband answers, I see that this shabby attack has fixed my defeat, because he is immediately reasonable. "Now, that's something else. I won't argue aesthetics with you. The outer covering is of no importance. I'll find something attractive."

The next night my husband brings home a mezuzah made in the East. It is a narrow green rectangle, twice the normal size, inlaid with mosaic and outlined in brass. It does not look Jewish to me at all. It looks foreign—a strange bit of green enamel and brass.

"I don't like it," I say. "I'm sorry."

"But it's only the idea you don't like?" My husband smiles teasingly. "In looks, you at least relent?"

"It doesn't look bad," I admit.

"Well, that is the first step." I am happy to see the mezuzah disappear in his dresser drawer before we go in to our dinner.

When Mrs. Cooper comes next day, she asks, "What have you on your door?"

I step out to look, and at first have the impression that a praying mantis has somehow hatched out of season high on our doorway. Then I recognize it. "Oh, that's . . ." I say. "That's . . ." I find I cannot explain a mezuzah to someone who has never heard of one.

While Mrs. Cooper changes her clothes, I touch the mezuzah to see if it will fall off. But my husband has glued it firmly to the metal doorframe.

My husband's office works a three-quarter day on Good Friday. I ask Mrs. Cooper if she would like time off, but she says no, her husband will be home ahead of her to look after things. I have the impression she would rather be here.

My husband comes home early, bestowing strangeness on the rhythm of the house in lieu of celebration. I kiss him and put away his hat. "Well, that was a nasty thing to do." I say it lazily and with a smirk. The lazy tone is to show that I am not really involved, and the smirk that I intend to swallow it down like bad medicine. He will have his way, but I will have my say—that's all I mean. My say will be humorous, with just a little cut to it, as is proper between husband and wife. He will cut back a little, with a grin, and after Mrs. Cooper goes we will have our peaceful dinner. The conversation will meander, never actually pricking sore points, but winding words about them, making pads and cushions, so that should they ever bleed, there, already softly wrapped around them, will be the bandages our words wove. Weave enough of these bandages and nothing will ever smash, I say. I always prepare in advance a last line, too, so that I will know where to stop. "When mezuzahs last in the doorway bloomed," I will say tonight. And then I expect us both to laugh.

But where has he been all day? The same office, the same

203

thirty-minute subway ride to and from each way, the same lunch with the same cronies. . . . But he has traveled somewhere else in his head. "Doesn't anything mean anything to you?" he says, and walks by me to the bedroom.

I follow with a bandage, but it slips from my hand. "I know a lot of women who would have taken that right down!" It is something of a shout, to my surprise.

He says nothing.

"I left it up. All I wanted was my say."

He says nothing.

"I live here, too. That's my door also."

He says nothing.

"And I don't like it!"

I hear a loud smashing of glass. It brings both our heads up. My husband is the first to understand. "Mrs. Cooper broke a bottle." He puts his arms around me and says, "Let's not quarrel about a doorway. Let's not quarrel at all, but especially not about the entrance to our home."

I lower my face into his tie. What's a mezuzah? Let's have ten, I think, so long as nothing will smash.

Later, I reproach myself. I am in the living room, straightening piles of magazines, avoiding both kitchen and bedroom. A woman, I think, is the one creature who builds satisfaction of the pleasure she gets from giving in. What might the world be if women would continue the dialogue? But no, they must give in and be satisfied. Nevertheless, I don't intend to take back what I've given in on and thereby give up what I've gained.

I am aware of Mrs. Cooper, boiling formula in the kitchen, and of my baby, registering in sleep her parents' first quarrel since her birth. "What must I say to you?" I think of saying to my daughter—Mrs. Cooper's words come naturally to my mind.

I go to the kitchen doorway and look at Mrs. Cooper. Her face indicates deaf and dumb. She is finishing the bottles.

When Mrs. Cooper is dressed and ready to leave, she looks into the living room. "I am saying good night."

"I hope you and your family will have a happy Easter," I say, smiling for her.

I know in advance that Mrs. Cooper will ask, "What must I say to you?"

This time she asks it soberly, and this time my husband, who has heard, comes in to tell Mrs. Cooper the story of Passover. As always in the traditional version, there is little mention of Moses, the Jews having set down from the beginning not the tragedy of one but their intuition for the tragedy of many.

When my husband leaves us, Mrs. Cooper takes four wrapped candies from the candy bowl on the desk, holds them up to be sure I see her taking them, and puts them in her purse. "I do hope everything will be all right," she says.

"Oh, yes," I say, looking at the magazines. "It was such a help today. I got so much work done. Thank you."

I hear that she is motionless.

"I will not be like this all the days of my life." It is a cry from the heart, stunningly articulated. I lift my head from the magazines, and this time I do stare. Not be like what? A Jamaican without a servant? A wife who never vacations? An exile? A baby nurse? A woman who gives in? What Mrs. Cooper might not want to be flashes up in a lightning jumble. "I am going to find a church," she says, and strains her face away from mine.

I think of all the descriptions of God I have ever heard— that He is jealous, loving, vengeful, waiting, teaching, forgetful, permissive, broken-hearted, dead, asleep.

Mrs. Cooper and I wish each other a pleasant weekend.

Part Four

✣

Green in New York

❖

George Wag in New York

George Wag was fond of his parents, fond of his sisters. But his nature was different from theirs. The life his family now led suited them wonderfully. But such a life didn't attract him. They had originally lived in Kansas and had moved, when he was a boy, to Iowa and from there to Illinois and, finally, to the outskirts of Terre Haute, Indiana, where they had relatives and began to do better. But wherever they lived, they led what George Wag thought of as Kansas lives. And George Wag's nature, he felt, was different. His father joined the Rotary. Though formerly a reticent man, he now said, "Swell to see you!" at the drop of a hat. His mother was a Rotary Ann and his married sisters either were already, or meant to become, the same. The nature of George Wag's wife, whoever she might be, would also be different from all that.

George Wag had gone to the state university. His build and height were good, and he played some football. He even won a certain stardom on campus. But then he thought, Where is this taking me in relation to my goals? And so dropped out. He often did things like that. Cutting in on the enjoyment of something with a question. But then losing track of the question when something else, a girl or a great movie, overtook him

209

again. He was serious in his studies, majoring first in English, then History, with some Economics and Art crammed in. He was aware that he had no talent for anything special. It was painful knowledge; he would have liked to shine.

He had nothing namable to set against his uncle's insurance business. It wasn't that he foresaw anything brilliant for himself. But he had had, for years, a desire to continue his family's early wandering and to finish it, for himself, in New York. In that free city, he felt, he would have the chance to develop in some unforeseen way. Not until it happened to him would he know what he was meant for.

Though he was an only son, his mother let him go at twenty-three. His older sisters cried and hugged, adventurous boy, and kissed him one by one, standing on the round braid rug in the living room, with young leaves waving in the windows. And he escaped from his childhood sweetheart, who had counted on marriage, with a short, though painful scene.

He packed a pair of golden leather suitcases with brass snaps, an extravagant, chip-in gift from his family. Then he flew, bird-free, to New York. Except for his nature, of course. But he hoped that would loosen up and fly free also, once he got there.

With no trouble at all, since he was an intelligent, courteous, and well-appearing young man, he landed a trainee's job. It was in the underwriting department of a large insurance company, whose employee benefits were written up in a thick booklet he read from time to time in the evenings. He found himself a furnished apartment in a transition area of Third Avenue, neither too rich nor too poor, but on the way up, with skinny plane trees new-planted in the sidewalks. The tiny apartment was comfortable and clean, equipped with newly sprayed metal furniture, a gray rug, and a red armchair. His only complaint was that he had noticed, through open doorways, that all the other rooms in this four-story remodeled house were furnished in exactly the same way. He would have thought that the owner, who ran a children's toy and bicycle shop on the street floor, might have more feeling for variety.

There was absolutely no difficulty meeting girls. He picked them up—perfectly decent, clean, college-caliber girls—looking at outdoor art shows in Greenwich Village. Or at paid parties, thinly disguised as protest rallies, or in reforming political clubs that drew volunteer envelope-stuffers. The abundance and variety of all that helped to take away much of the bad feeling of the final scene with his sweetheart. See! he told himself. What if I had married Jeannie? The limited man picking from the limited field. Only from variety can a person make free choice. My tastes are changing already.

Whenever he had a little spare money, he replaced a suit or pair of shoes from home with a new one, simpler and more stylish. He went about things quietly and with a certain stubbornness. His nature included that, too. For example, he studied his way through the subway with maps and guidebooks, rather than ask questions. He would become a New Yorker in his own way.

He was doing so well at it that he was taken by surprise when, one day during his second month on the job, he suddenly threw down his pencil and said to the trainee who sat at his right, "These desks make me sick!"

He was talking about the metal, formica-topped desks, of which his was one, in the block of sixteen identical desks.

"These desks look like something the farmers back home feed the pigs from," George Wag said heatedly. "Not something for a man to sit at every day of his life. I like wood," George Wag went on. "Wood's all right. I could take a wood desk."

Then he stopped, astonished with himself. Because it was not

211

his way to blurt things out to strangers, Middle-West background or no Middle-West background.

"Oh, listen," said the trainee on his right, whose name was Sanford, "that's going to change! It's only here, with us slow beginners, that everything's so speeded up. So plastic and modern."

George Wag, who was working to eliminate his Midwestern twang, listened to this Southerner's pleased-with-himself drawl.

Sanford kept his light eyes fixed on George Wag, and his face began to twitch here and there with laughter at the elaborate thing he was passing off, straight-faced, except for the twitches.

"When you get to be an executive," Sanford went on, "everything around you slows down."

"Is that so?" George Wag said it stiffly, to make up for the outburst.

"Listen," Sanford said, still enthusiastic. "I went up to fourteen once, just to look around? They have rosewood, oiled rosewood paneling in the offices. Teak desks that you can't just run a rag over with polish on it; they have to be rubbed down with oil, like a horse. And handwoven Turkish rugs, this thick. Everything's real there, believe me."

Sanford lifted an index finger to show he had come to the important part. "After you wear out your soul to get ahead, everything around you slows down so much it gets old-fashioned. Upstairs, it's all old-fashioned and real."

Sanford's grin zipped out, boyish and handsome and don't-give-a-damn. "That's my fake-furniture paradox." The way he said the word, it came out "paddocks."

George Wag, who had been feeling lousy about feeling lousy in New York, now found himself laughing.

"Thanks for the paradox," George Wag said.

"Here's another. If you're very New York, it's perfectly all right to be not New York."

George Wag wondered if his nature, which puzzled him, might be quite clear to others.

"I've got lots more paddockses," Sanford said. "I survive on them."

They took to talking at coffee breaks and at an occasional lunch. Sanford was often engaged for lunch, George Wag much less so. He had to learn his own nature and get the hang of New York at the same time. Sometimes the combination got him down, and then he was not much good as company. But Sanford, to a newcomer, was excellent company, because almost everything struck his funny bone.

In the next few weeks, there were times when George Wag felt he also survived in New York on Sanford's paradoxes. A strange thing was happening to him. It seemed to him that his fervor toward New York had inverted itself, so that he now felt a passionate anger toward the city. At home he had countered all argument by saying, "I know, I know." He had forgiven New York all its faults in advance. But now that he was here alone and with no one to contradict him, the New York faults—coldness, greediness, filth, all that triteness; he groaned to be wasting his time minding them—struck him squarely in the eyes.

George Wag told Sanford how he felt about New York girls. They were very alive. Their eyes reflected some glow as if New York itself were burning. But their eyes never glowed so brightly, it seemed to him, as when the girls mentioned expensive restaurants, or co-operative apartment houses on the river, or cream-colored Jaguars that somebody they knew had. At least the girls he met. If there were others, he said to Sanford, he hadn't met them yet.

"Oh, listen!" Sanford said, his face twitching against the grin that wanted out. "Listen! Those aren't the New York girls. Scratch the surface and they're from Omaha. They'll all go home after two years. I save myself a lot of trouble by sticking

213

to older women. Thirty-seven? They're all weeded out by then."

George Wag laughed and again felt relief. After that, if a girl made him uncomfortable on a date, he was able to smile in one corner of his mouth and think of Sanford: "In a couple of years she'll be weeded out."

Sanford was a stylish dresser. In the matter of button-down shirts and trouser-leg widths and red madder ties, Sanford knew what was what. And clothes, it so happened, was one of the things on George Wag's mind. Clothes in New York. At home, where the loosened tie, the trouser cuffs pleating over shoe tops were the mark of the man, he had been an anxiously natty dresser. But here in New York, which was the very eagle's nest of natty dressers, he found in himself an unfamiliar urge to be, not seedy or unpressed ever, but oblivious to the turn of fashion's screw: pants, ties, jackets, hat brims, squeezing narrower all the time. He didn't want to look into the mirror and not know himself.

Sanford, at lunch, disclosed the snob paradox. You had to be a snob, but be so much and so conscious a snob that you detested "straight" or "unconscious" snobs. This was similar to the high-style paradox. You had to care deeply about dressing well, but be conscious every minute that it was stupid to care. If you knew that what you cared about was absurd, it saved you from being absurd yourself. The same thing applied to "unconscious" good dressers as to "unconscious" snobs. If they had no more notion than a certain Duke of what asses they made of themselves, then they might as well wear smallpox.

"Ivy League is the greatest armor," Sanford said to George Wag. He pointed to his jacket, lightly herringboned. "My shield." He cupped his hand around his tie below the knot and pulled his fist quickly down, letting the narrow silk run through: "My sword." He pointed under the table to the big oxblood shoes: "My buckler." He reached to the seat beside him for his little curly-brimmed green hat and slapped it over his neat brown hair and exploded, "My cocked—my cocked—" He sputtered and choked while his wide grinning mouth grabbed the straight-faced joke away from him, ". . . hat!"

Sanford's hands were always moving about his clothing, straightening his tie, settling his collar, brushing the cuffs of his trousers, feeling behind, whenever he stood up, to the vent in his jacket to make sure the flaps were down, adjusting the Madras plaid watch band on his plumpish wrist.

"I'm a clothes horse!" he said to George Wag. "Isn't that crazy? Is that a thing for a man to be?" His slightly bulging blue eyes watered a bit from suppressed laughter. "But I know it. I know it!" He raised his index finger. "That's the difference, son!"

Sometimes Sanford's humor caught George Wag up short in an uncomfortable way. What's so funny about that? George Wag would ask himself while Sanford laughed hard. It might be an anecdote about Sanford's own family, on the sad side, George Wag might think.

One day a new trainee said to George Wag in the men's room, "Do you think this guy Sanford is a fruit?"

George Wag shrugged his thickly muscled shoulders. But to himself he supposed that it was likely. That was likely the off-kilter thing that could make Sanford not give a damn about the things other people gave a damn about. At the same time, he cautioned himself. Because a guy was off-beat and dressed in a stylish way was no reason to jump to that conclusion. That was the sort of conclusion people at home jumped to all the time.

In any case, George Wag was now having fewer lunches with Sanford. The girls he had been dating had rented summer places and he was invited for weekends. Fire Island, the Hamptons. The girls lived well, summer and winter. His weekend chores had to be done during the week, and he brought laundry and shoes for repair to the office in his attaché case, to take care of on lunch hour. Weekends, he made good use of his new luggage. He packed his smaller case on Friday morning, brought it to the office, and took off after work.

"Very handsome," Sanford said, looking at his new suitcase.

"Oh, thanks," George Wag said. "It was a gift."

"Um, very nice."

The weekends kept him busy if not yet happy. He had to admit he still missed Jeannie, and he wondered how long before he would feel at home.

One day, Sanford, whom he hadn't talked to much lately, except during coffee breaks, said, "George, may I ask a favor?" Then without waiting, he went right on, "If you're not using it this weekend, would you lend me your handsome suitcase?"

No spoke itself at once. Clear and direct from George Wag's nature, displeasing him. I am too tight about things, he said to himself. I need to loosen up. Lend and give more.

"I'll be glad to," he said to Sanford. "I'll bring it in tomorrow."

On Friday, Sanford brought the suitcase back to the office with him, packed for his weekend. And that was the last the office saw of Sanford.

On Monday, it wasn't yet a confirmed disappearance. Sanford simply didn't appear at his desk and didn't phone in an excuse. George Wag felt at an outsider's disadvantage. He didn't know whether people in New York disappeared from their jobs as a regular thing or not. His co-workers, the other underwriters, all assumed a disappearance on the first day. But that was mainly so they could express their wish to disappear also.

Bert Pratt, who was the father of two small children and hard-pressed for cash, said, "No more underwriting for him, lucky stiff. Boy! He escaped, lucky stiff."

216

And Bert's side-kick, Lucas Bloocher, also a father of small children and a sandwich-bringer, said, "That's the way to do it."

Martin Phelps agreed. "Walk out on Friday and never come back."

And that was all the opinion George Wag, who preferred not to ask questions, could gather on Monday.

On Tuesday, George Wag's co-workers turned their Monday statements into questions. "Do you think he quit? Do you think that's what he did?" Bert Pratt asked.

And Martin Phelps said, "Just walked out on Friday and decided to never come back?"

"Just decided," Lucas Bloocher said, "no more underwriting?"

The following day, someone suggested that Sanford had behaved irresponsibly, but that was talked down. The underwriters all agreed that the company wouldn't think twice about tossing someone out if they didn't need him.

Finally, someone said, "I wonder if anything happened to him? An accident, or something?"

George Wag, who was growing so weary of wondering if New Yorkers were normal, wondered it again. He himself was counting on some catastrophe (which he hoped, nevertheless, Sanford would survive) whose enormity would take away his grief at the loss of his suitcase. Since Monday, when his suitcase disappeared along with Sanford, he had been hit with a wretched homesickness. Mama, he'd thought, like any kid. The names of his sisters—Hattie, Dotty, Lily—could bring tears to his eyes. The thought of Jeannie, who had become a golden girl of the West, never to be found again, was almost unbearable.

"Nah, accidents don't happen to types like Sanford," someone said.

The underwriters reviewed their case.

217

"Where does a guy, twenty-five and foot-loose, as good-looking as that, disappear to?"

"Some millionaire's widow found him and took him on a cruise to Greece."

"Are you kidding?" A meaningful glance, which most of the underwriters seemed to understand.

"Ah, come on," said an underwriter who was tired of the meaning of that meaningful glance. "Come on, he's not."

"I don't think so, either," said several underwriters.

"What are you talking about?" said others. "He is!"

"Look at how he dresses. Those fairy watch bands. Those plaid cotton ones."

"I beg your pardon." Lucas Bloocher shot out his wrist and pointed to his watch band.

"Well, you know what I mean. It's everything together. The waistcoat. The tight pants."

"That's style. You can't hang him for style."

There was a pause, while several underwriters weighed it.

"His speech was kind of effeminate," someone began.

"That's just Southern."

"He talked a lot about girls. He had a lot of dates."

"That could be a cover-up."

"Look. The guy's not here to defend himself." That was Bert Pratt. "Not only that, but he could really have had an accident."

Lucas Bloocher said, "His private life is his private life. He was a good-natured kid. Cheerful. Nice to have around."

I'll never see my suitcase again, George Wag thought. Mom. Hattie, Dotty, Lily. He could not even bring himself to say that other name.

"I didn't say he wasn't a good-natured kid. But I also say," someone else insisted, "that there's a fine line between dressing well and dressing like a fag. Even if it's not the swish kind of fag."

"What's the difference?" a couple of underwriters wanted to know.

"The fag always wears the latest. And the good dresser always waits about a year."

"I don't know about that," said Lucas Bloocher.

"Look. Nobody but a fruit would have been caught dead in a cummerbund when they first came out. Now you can't get away in a tuxedo without one. But there's always that lapse of time."

"I wouldn't be caught dead in a tuxedo."

"And I still wouldn't be caught dead in a cummerbund."

"Well, the President of the United States wears one. Okay?"

"And a ruffled shirt?"

"Lots of diplomats do."

"Don't get me started on diplomats."

The following evening George Wag found a letter from his mother telling him that Jeannie was engaged to be married. "So it seems she had another fellow up her sleeve all the while, George dear. I hope you won't be hurt, but will learn from this. There is something a little deceitful about all women, and the sooner you learn it, the better off you'll be, though I am a woman myself. . . ."

There's no going back, George Wag said to himself. That's what losing the suitcase means, too.

The next day, Friday, George Wag worked hard all morning. When he looked up for a breather, it was suddenly past twelve and the underwriters had cleared out for lunch. George Wag was without a date or an errand, having been invited nowhere that weekend. No suitcase, no trip, he thought, feeling, for the first time in his life, hard-luck prone. The only thing that was traveling was bad news.

He decided he would get a quick sandwich and take a walk, and had already left his desk, when Bert Pratt's phone rang.

The heck with it, he thought. I'm out to lunch. Then he turned back. I can take a message for Bert. But when he was

219

halfway there, the ringing stopped. After a short pause, it started again in the far corner of the block of desks. "I've already left," he said to the phone. He headed out for the second time, walking down an aisle between the desks toward the door. The ringing stopped and then resumed at a desk near the end of the aisle. George Wag put his hand on the phone at the second ring.

"Underwriting," he said. "George Wag speaking."

"George? George! I'm delighted! I was going to call you next." The familiar drawl was pitched slightly upward by telephone.

"Hello, Sanford." George Wag saw his suitcase in his mind's eye like a beloved face. "Are you okay?"

"Dandy, thanks. George? Would you mind taking all my silly stuff out of my desk for me? Put everything in a big envelope and bring it over. To where I am now. I'll give you my new address."

"I didn't know your old one," George Wag couldn't resist saying. At the same time he remembered that Sanford knew his.

"Well, I've moved and that's not why I quit the job but I got real involved in the moving and had to miss a few days and I just thought, who cares? Those old trainee jobs are a dime a dozen."

George Wag was angry again. Oh, the weight of always being a stranger and always angry. It was not only that Sanford had abruptly changed his tune about how good this particular job was, and many a time had persuaded him to stay when he had been all for leaving, but it was also because, George Wag felt, Sanford had no intention of giving him any explanation about the suitcase.

"I'll be happy to bring your stuff, Sanford," George Wag said. He copied down Sanford's new address with a certain bitterness, thinking: This is how things in New York are.

"Can you make it this evening?" Sanford asked. "Otherwise, the rest of the weekend, I won't really have a minute."

George Wag decided to clean out the desk first, before he got his sandwich. He went to the big metal supply locker at the side of the room and took two of the largest Manila envelopes. Then he opened all the drawers of Sanford's desk, step-fashion, so he could have an idea what was in them. Scattered through the drawers was a disorder of leavings: numerous letters, folded back into their slit envelopes; an electric razor; a squeeze bottle of deodorant, labeled "He-Man"; two nickel packs of tissues; a stick of lip pomade; a clotted linen handkerchief, stained by nosebleed; a silver-mesh-case fountain pen; a wrapped cake of soap labeled "Savon for Sirs"; and a small square of mirror. He didn't know why the mirror should shock him so much, but it did. There were also packs of sweet biscuits, a few opened, one of the biscuits bitten into, leaving a crescent shape, a smiling cracker. George Wag nibbled one, chucked the rest into the wastebasket, and began to fit things into an envelope. He had almost filled the first envelope when Martin Phelps came back from lunch and moseyed over.

"Sanford call?" he asked.

George Wag nodded.

"I thought he'd call somebody. I saw his desk was full of stuff. And he knows how fast Personnel starts interviewing."

He watched George Wag pushing objects into the second envelope—the first was by now misshapen with things—and then he said, "Well, you'll be in a position to clear up the mystery after you deliver the stuff. What the place is like, who he lives with, all that."

George Wag was embarrassed. "He borrowed my suitcase. I'd like to get it back."

"I wish you luck," Martin Phelps said.

When George Wag left with his two envelopes at five, everybody in underwriting seemed to know where he was going.

"Take a good look around," one of the underwriters said. "We'll want a full report." His laugh turned self-conscious at the end, almost a giggle.

Bert Pratt said severely, "Give Sanford my best. Tell him I wish him good luck."

Twenty minutes later, George Wag walked with his bundles up a quiet, tree-lined, expensive street he hadn't seen before. The houses were small and fancifully decorated. A wrought-iron arbor of grapes and grape leaves before an entryway, a fanlight of stained glass over a bright red door with a polished brass dolphin door knocker, stone balconies with wisteria vines twisted over, casement windows with sparkling diamond-shaped panes, coach lanterns, pots of geranium and fuchsia fastened to the grillworks of façades. The façades themselves painted pink, lavender, yellow ocher, olive green, charcoal.

Near the end of the street, he found Sanford's new address. He pushed open the outer door—black, with panels, and a huge engraved brass knob set as high as his shoulder—and rang the inner door buzzer below the name he had been told. Henry Durwood, an engraved calling card in a row of bright-polished name plates on a wall of blue and tan shepherds in the papered hall.

There were two buzzes back. Uneasy as he was about his reception—Sanford had never mentioned a word about the suitcase—he overinterpreted. Not long, gracious buzzes to say: "I'm making sure you get in," but short, hurried ones that said: "Grab it, or you lose."

He caught the doorknob just in time. He climbed a red-carpeted stairway that rose from a darkly wood-paneled hall with stone statues in niches and rang another buzzer, outside a red door.

"How is New York treating you, George?" Sanford's face, poked in the open doorway, was mischievously grinning. As if he knew that without him, George Wag could only be baffled by New York, gnawed at and jostled.

"Just fine," George Wag said. He stepped inside and then he saw what Sanford was wearing. Sanford was wrapped in a long garment of brown-and-white print material that hung from his waist to the floor. His chest, plump and pale-skinned, with reddish hairs, was bare.

"Do you like it?" Sanford said. "It's from a dear friend in Hawaii and it's worn by Hawaiian men."

"Ah," said George Wag.

Sanford then took the two bundles and, raising his index finger, moved it like a metronome. "George—Henry." Then he reversed the metronome. "Henry—George."

A pale young man sat on the sofa, gazing into his drink. George Wag gave him a stiff bow and then left it at that. The young man did not look up.

Sanford handed George Wag a chunky glass filled with gin and ice cubes and pointed, there was no mistaking the indication, to a large, flat, orange cushion on the floor. Sanford then disappeared to rummage behind white draperies at the right.

George Wag lowered himself to the cushion on the floor, leaned his back against the wall and, while the cushion slid slowly under him, looked around the room.

Not only were the draperies white, everything else in the room was immaculate white also. The walls were white. The louvered shutters, like old-fashioned hinged gates, fencing the long windows of the high-ceilinged room, were white. A low chest of drawers, that had Oriental-looking medallions for pulls, stood against a wall, painted white. On the chest was a milk-glass bowl holding large white tulips that looked both real and fake, in the way of tulips. Against another wall stood a black bench with white cushions. Before it was a small, round, deep-piled white rug. The rest of the floor was polished and bare. In the center of the room hung a huge-bellied white lantern that, lit, shone out like the ectoplasmic spirit of the air-conditioned, white room.

White, that's no color, George Wag thought. He liked a nice blue, or a nice green. White, that's for whitewash, or a prime coat, before the real paint goes on.

George Wag looked cautiously over his shoulder. He saw no door other than the one through which he had just entered. This was it, he supposed, one large room, with an entryway and a kitchenette concealed behind those white drapes and beyond that a bathroom. There wasn't any bedroom.

The one real piece of furniture in the room was a large black sofa with red and black velvet pillows. That must be the bed, he thought. It must open up to a double bed.

It was on this sofa that the silent young man sat. George Wag had looked at everything else in the room, and now he looked at the young man on the sofa.

Henry Durwood sat with legs crossed, still gazing down. He was, to George Wag's great relief, not wearing anything Hawaiian, but just plain slacks, light green, and a sweater.

A lock of black, wavy hair had slipped down over the pale forehead. The face was still except for the nostrils. First they flared into peaks, and then they pressed themselves flat. Then they repeated what they had just done. It unnerved George Wag to think what strong speech was going on behind that still mask.

George Wag saw no sign of his suitcase.

Sanford came out from behind the white draperies, carrying a plate with a wedge of cheese on it and some strange, shreddy crackers. He set the plate on a wicker stool which he placed halfway between George Wag on his cushion and the young man on the sofa. Then Sanford placed himself a fair distance away from both on a flat black cushion on the floor. He sat cross-legged, arranged his Hawaiian whatever-it-was, and looked at George Wag.

"And how are things at Durable Life?"

Sanford had barely finished his question before his glance slid off to the young man on the sofa. The young man's lips seemed to flicker for a moment. George Wag couldn't be sure. At any rate, the young man's nostrils had flared. Then they pressed flat.

"Why, things are going along, Sanford," George Wag said.

"Have I been replaced yet?" Again Sanford began with a look at George Wag and ended with a look at the young man.

George Wag shook his head. "Ernest Toufer's getting married."

"I told you about him," Sanford said to Henry Durwood.

The young man on the sofa glanced up for a moment, his eyes wide and gleaming. He looked toward the tulips. He said, "The good-looking one," articulating slowly and carefully. Then he looked into his glass again.

Sanford seemed worried. He continued to look at Henry Durwood, but Henry would not look at him. Sanford's wit and cheer seemed gone. There was heavy tension in the room and it finally came through to George Wag as something that existed apart from how he felt about his suitcase.

Suddenly, Sanford said, "Ooh!"

He jumped up and rushed, in his brown-and-white Hawaiian business, to rummage behind some more white curtains which must have concealed a closet, because he came out with George Wag's suitcase.

"There!" he said, and settled himself on the rug once more, George Wag's suitcase beside him. It lay on its side on the rug. With its good golden-brown color and its gleaming snaps, it seemed to George Wag the most welcome sight he had ever seen. Not only that, but the realest, most substantial thing in the room.

225

"Oh, listen!" Sanford said. "I had more compliments on this case. . . ."

And suddenly George Wag imagined that Sanford was beginning a paradox. "Oh, listen!" he imagined he heard Sanford saying. "This is the way it is only at the beginning. Only the beginners have to accept substitutes. Afterward, the fake flowers bloom. One of the guys turns into a woman. A real, *real* woman. Realer than a woman who's a woman from the start. They really get married. They can have real children. They are really happy."

At once George Wag's spirits lifted. Hope for everybody, he thought. Then he almost laughed out loud. Paradox for all.

Henry Durwood cleared his throat. When Sanford and George Wag had both turned to him, he rotated his delicate wrist and looked at his small round watch on its black suède band.

"Our dinner appointment is for seven-fifteen. We'll have to dress," he said to his watch, in his carefully articulating voice.

"Have dinner with us, George," Sanford said. He leaned back and rested his elbow on the side of George Wag's suitcase.

But Henry Durwood nagged. "The reservation is for four, with Peter and Jack. Chico's place is just tiny."

George Wag thought he heard the fibers of his suitcase crack.

In his mind, George Wag was long since up and out the door, with a formal nod for all. But to do it was another matter, down on the floor on his cushion.

He set his drink down carefully on the floor beside him and pulled his back away from the wall. "Very pretty place you've got here," he said politely. He continued to roll his weight forward and brought one palm down behind him on the cushion. "Those are pretty tulips there." He pulled his right foot toward him and was getting his leg weight onto the shoe when, to his surprise, Henry Durwood said something to him.

"We're fabulous fakes," Henry Durwood said in his slow, clearly enunciating voice, giving a long sound to the "u" of fabulous.

At least that was what, at the moment, George Wag could have sworn Henry Durwood said. Later, he realized it must have been, *"They're* fabulous fakes." Meaning the tulips.

But at the moment, George Wag, with one knee half off the floor, politely agreed, "Yes, you are."

Then there was a screech and a rush and the spilled dregs of gin with ice cubes skittering, and a stinging smack to his left cheek. George Wag was knocked off the orange cushion onto his back.

One minute he was in a rage, ready to kill with his fist. The next, he was appalled to dream of hitting a weeping woman. He struggled off his back and considered. He could not say he'd been knocked down. He'd been down to begin with. The difference between cushion and floor was an inch, so an inch was what he'd been knocked down.

Sanford was standing up and twisting the hem of his brown-and-white Hawaiian thing in his hands. The pale young man went and stamped his feet in a corner.

George Wag crawled away on his hands and knees in the wet. Where have I wandered to? he asked himself. When he got near the door he stood up, walked out, and went meditatively down the stairs.

What if, he asked himself in the street, the ugly episodes in his life were not the accidents he took them to be, but the central reality? The shouting near fist-fight with his father, the shouting near-hysterical breakoff with his sweetheart, the contemptuous leave-taking of his job in his uncle's office with the shouted recriminations there, and this farcical slap from a nerve-shattered fairy who found his presence on the orange cushion intolerable. What if all this was not, as he had thought, the accidental dust his foot raised as it carried him forward, but the real stuff of his life? Not until he was home did he realize he had left the suitcase at Sanford's.

He went to a double feature on Saturday and another double feature on Sunday, sitting right through, even when the air conditioning broke down. He couldn't think of an answer, neither could he get the questions out of his head.

On Monday, there were more questions.

"Does he live alone, or does he share?"

"He shares."

"Girl or guy?"

"A guy."

"See?"

"See what, for God's sake?" Lucas Bloocher said. "Didn't you ever share an apartment before you got married? I did."

"All right, ask George then. What was this guy like?"

George Wag shrugged. "On the nervous side."

"Who's not nervous? Everybody here is nervous."

"Nice place?" somebody asked.

"Yes."

"Naturally."

"What was he wearing, the latest?"

George Wag hesitated. "Yes, I suppose it was."

But it was all inconclusive, and the underwriters drifted back to their desks.

Martin Phelps stayed to ask, "Did you get your suitcase back?"

George Wag told him, "Yes."

As if in reward for his honorable reticence, that evening George Wag found his suitcase standing before his door. Stuck in the catch was a one-word note written in green ink in Sanford's big, loopy writing: "Sorry!" The note, as he expected it would be the minute he saw it, was written on finest paper—

deckle edge, handlaid, impeccably white. In contrast, his suit-case—now that he saw it up close—was streaked and discol-ored and the edges looked chewed. The suitcase looked as if it had been pulled through openings that were too small for it. Narrow, George Wag thought. He felt it was a bitter thing to travel around in a country that was wide but where, for a paradox, the doors all squeezed so narrow.

✤

A Thousand Tears

Twice in one day Sandra Loeb, who lives a careful life in New York City, hears a tale of murder close by. The day, as it happens, is one during a newspaper strike. People feel a need to tell what they hear, some revived obligation to pass on news of the world's woe. That, at least, is Sandra's explanation to herself, and afterward to her husband Ben when they get a chance to talk. On top of everything else, this day is Sandra and Ben's tenth wedding anniversary—a time of welled-up feelings that, in the rush of things, must be swallowed again, making a hot friction around the heart. One tale in the morning, one in the evening, form brackets around Sandra's well-ordered hours and squeeze from them drops of blood.

Ben never brings flowers. They are in the same category as tears, and to be avoided. Sandra understands this. All the same, to be sure there will be no gap into which hurt feelings might stumble, on her way home from work the evening before the anniversary she buys armfuls of fresh greens—rhododendron and magnolia leaves—and fills all the vases in the house. Then late at night she remembers that Lily, their day maid, has asked for extra cream to make the cake. So early in the morning, while Ben can still be home with their two preschool children and before Sandra herself must leave for work, she hurries out to buy some.

Now! How stupid! The moment Sandra is in the street she sees what she has done—quite automatically put on the new fur coat that she means to wear to work today. For a moment she hesitates, then decides, "No, I won't go in."

Sandra has lived all her life in or close to this part of New York's West Side, where great blocks of buildings line the avenues from park to park. "Democratic people" were her mother's words for those who preferred the West Side's rich population mix to the distilled elements of the East Side. The description holds good, Sandra feels, although she has added to it her own: "Hopeful people." Hopeful of education. Renewal. Good will. Above all, good will. "We're all idealists. . . ." Sandra frowns. Who was it who said that to her quite recently?

The store she does not enter is a small *bodega* where she often goes for dairy items and bananas. The Puerto Rican woman who keeps the store has pictures of her grandchildren taped to the counter. The woman is unquestionably better off, in money as well as English, than most of the Puerto Ricans Sandra sees on the streets. No doubt the friendliness between them would survive the interpolation of a fur coat. But it might not, Sandra thinks, survive the effort they would have to make to convince each other that the fur coat did not matter. She hurries on, annoyed with herself, to the specialty grocer's, half a block farther on.

The store is cold. Along with the new coat, Sandra has hastily pulled a scarf from the closet and tied it around her head. A black alligator shoulder bag, which Ben calls "the survivor" because it is as old as their marriage, hangs at her side like animal armor. All the same, an iciness creeps in at her shoulder blades and travels down her back. A policeman—in

231

Sandra's youth a symbol of order as substantial as the West Side itself—is speaking.

"So the Puerto Ricans got up a little excitement around here last night." He takes a quick check of the faces in the store. Then he goes on, telling the grocer, "Some guy runs with a gun to an apartment on Eighty-first Street and he shoots two bullets into a guy, and then he finds out he shot the wrong guy so then he runs to an apartment on Eighty-fourth Street and shoots the guy he thinks he wants. Meantime the first, *wrong* guy runs down into the street and then runs up Amsterdam Avenue but in the middle of running he drops dead."

The policeman stops for another quick look around. He then says his last word: "Well, at least as long as they only kill each other . . ."

The grocer, whom Sandra knows for a simple man, looks bewildered. "Why'd he do it? For what reason?"

Sandra by now has placed the policeman—a traffic cop from a Broadway corner in the Seventies. He is a serious-faced young man. His open-air life has not yet given him the invulnerable look of ruddy-faced policemen. He shakes his head in a quick movement that is almost a shudder. "How much does it take in this town to send somebody nuts?" His words seem to hold an angry sympathy that softens his earlier, callous remark.

Is the remark callous? Sandra hears it again and again: "As long as they only kill each other . . ." It is the West Side's policy of containment. In this the West Side is like the world, holding its skirts lest they brush against intolerable dangers: the small war ("As long as it doesn't get big"), the cold war ("As long as it doesn't get hot"), atomic stockpiles ("As long as some maniac doesn't set one off"). But even "as long as they only kill each other," there is always the chance of the stray bullet, the miscalculated knife throw, the splashing drop of acid, the warring gangs made up of "each other" who may fall on a boy of no gang at all. It is infuriating to live, in the world, with the fear of the bomb that some maniac may set off. And along with one's hope one lives, on the West Side, in a state of anger as well, because of this overflow of danger that cannot be contained.

Sandra's hope now, at this early hour, is to be spared any encounters as she strides quickly home. But at the corner of Seventy-fifth Street she crosses paths with a Puerto Rican boy of four or five. One hand holds his wedge of breakfast pizza; the other is fisted against his chest as if to beat out the cold there. He gives her a brief, brown stare as he passes and she, before she knows what she is up to, turns her head after him to check. She learns nothing she didn't already know. There are no socks in his shoes, no jacket over his shirt, and from the flapping around his skinny thighs, no underwear under his dirty white shorts with a green stripe down the outer seam—a discard from the camp outfit of some boy who lives in another world.

What will become of him? Sandra finds herself paying out the question like a toll before she can pass along. *Mira! Mira!* What will become . . . Then her first thoughts repossess her and she hurries. Shooting in the street not ten blocks from us! That is what, if there is time, she must tell Ben.

But as usual, there is no time. Lily arrives, Ben goes, and soon Sandra is hurrying after, swinging her gloved hand in the street for a cab. She has a picture of herself standing in this spot morning after morning, waving the same hand, differently gloved with the seasons. Then she takes the short ride, made dear by the waits at intersections, to her desk.

At lunchtime Sandra is again in a cab. This time she is going farther downtown to meet a friend who particularly wants Sandra's advice because the friend is about to vacation in Puerto Rico.

"I know you went there on your honeymoon," Elizabeth had said on the phone the previous week when they made the date.

"Do you know what that Tuesday we're meeting will be? My tenth anniversary," Sandra said.

"Congratulations. You must remember something about the place."

"As a matter of fact, I remember quite a bit. I've even got some folders somewhere, and a journal—I kept a journal in those days."

"Oh, bring it! That's my idea of *lunch*." Then Elizabeth asked, "Was it a good honeymoon?" and when Sandra stopped for a thoughtful moment, added: "Aren't they all sort of sad?" Elizabeth is divorced, so there was nothing to say but yes.

At lunch Sandra warns Elizabeth, who lives singly and elegantly East, "You're in for some heartbreaking sights. We see them every day in our neighborhood, so things can't have changed that much in ten years."

Elizabeth raises mildly reproachful eyes. "I no longer travel as the shocked American. Haven't for some time."

"Worst of all is when you *don't* see them. Sometimes they walk right by and you don't see them."

Elizabeth nods and sips her drink.

"I'm talking about my *own* neighborhood." Sandra gropes and shrugs helplessly. "It's like—"

"Blindness," Elizabeth supplies. "I loathe that in me too. But it's indispensable. I know it is."

Sandra then tells Elizabeth about the shooting.

"How horrible for you," Elizabeth says. "I *loathe* their being here."

Sandra wonders if it is possible to hate the sympathy of women—that good trait with its own reverse image stamped to its back.

"Although I would hate to see you move . . ." Elizabeth says.

"No. No suburbs, thank you."

Because Sandra is engaged in the working woman's race to stand for Home and Mother in the nick of time, she suggests to her last cab driver of the day that he try the route through Central Park. Soon they are rounding the curves of the road at a good speed. Sandra, watching the movement of the snowy landscape, is suddenly aware that this evening looks more like dusk than the pitch-black it was a few weeks before, around Christmas. A thin purple lifts the sky above the filamented trees.

When the driver stops for the light near the Seventy-second Street exit she sees a small parade of mounted police coming along the bridle path in twos. They do not, as she expects they will, turn off at the cross-park highway. Instead they allow their horses to trot across the highway and take the bridle path on the other side. The policemen chatter and gesture within their pairs like pilgrims to Canterbury and their horses converse in steam.

"I didn't know," Sandra says to the back of her cab driver's head, "that there were all these mounted police in the park at night. I'm so glad." She feels a rising hope—because the evening sky is lifting—that this lovely, lost park is to be reclaimed.

"Sure," says the driver. "Since what happened."

Sandra notices that the ear pieces of his glasses are taped with adhesive, one white, one black.

"I guess you don't get the chance to know these things during the strike," says the cabbie. Stimulated by her silence, he half turns toward her while his hands and feet, at the light change, work out the rhythm of shifting into first. "They found some guy in pieces. Some Puerto Rican." He gestures at a snowy hill. "Right around here someplace."

While she is still blocks from home Sandra estimates the fare, adds the tip, readies her money and finds when they get to

235

her door that she has guessed close enough so that she needn't open her purse again, and she is already swinging one leg to the curb when the driver's words catch her—one foot in, one foot out and back absurdly bent. "At least," he says, "as long as they only kill each other."

What in the world makes her wonder at this moment if they have candles? Surely they have some left over from a birthday. But if they haven't? Sandra is scrupulous about these ceremonies. She can't, as a mother who gives her day to her children might do, fob them off with some story—"Anniversary cakes don't *need* candles." They must have candles, and it's simpler to get them now than go upstairs first and check. She heads again—it's a day of repetitions—for the little grocery store.

Near the corner, in front of the doughnut shop, the nightly group is forming. Henna-haired boys, with hips fined down to a sole suggestion, converse in clattering Spanish. Sandra gives them the barest side glance as she passes. They are what they are—the oldest no more than seventeen, perhaps—as stoical and tough as a band of Elizabethan mummers. But on the walk back, having bought her candles, she sees a new boy has been added, with the face of a dark angel—beauty with no place to go but down. He stands with his hands in his pockets, watching the charade to be learned.

What will become of him—the voice inside Sandra's head begins its chant—when he's twenty? Then she stops in the street for a moment because the obscene parody jumps with such force into her head: "At least as long as they only seduce each other."

Sandra's clean, beautiful children, whom Lily has dressed in brother and sister outfits of red velvet, race each other to her arms. Almost as soon as Sandra is in, Lily is out—she has her own dinner to fix at home. But first, quickly, information passes from Lily to Sandra: The children ate good lunches,

236

they were good about their rest times, and Lily kept them in the sunny part of the playground where it wasn't so cold.

Sandra steps into the hall for a minute with Lily. "I heard about—an accident in the park today," she says.

"Oh, my," Lily says. "Was it a car?"

"No." Sandra is whispering now. "Someone was murdered."

Lily's eyebrows lift at the inner edges, making downcurves of pity. "It's hard to raise children in the city," she says. A ring of grayish-white rims the iris of each eye. How old is Lily? Her black face seems ageless, no gray in her neatly bunned hair. Good Lily, lend us your protection for a few more years. Why should you? But do it.

"I was thinking, Lily, perhaps you could keep the children out of the park for a while. It must be awfully cold there, anyway. Just—go window-shopping with them?"

"Yes, I'll do that, Mrs. Loeb."

Moments after Lily goes, Ben is home.

"Oh-oh!" Ben says when he sees the faces of the children, pale with excitement above the red velvet.

They hang their arms around his neck and bow his head with their weight. Content for now to let the children's greeting stand for their own, Sandra and Ben exchange a look above the shouts and then Sandra slips back to the kitchen to keep her eye on Lily's roast. Unexpectedly—the children are busy in the hall dividing Ben's spoils of rubbers, muffler, and gloves—Ben appears. Sandra intercepts the myriad possibilities of his greeting with a thick whisper: "Two people were shot right around here last night. And somebody else was chopped up in the park. Near where the children play!"

"All right," Ben says quietly. He takes a quick turn around the kitchen and his loose arms bang against the dishwasher. Sandra wishes she had spoken differently. She had forgotten (how could she?) that Ben longs to protect them—against bullets, maniacs, bombs. But he can't, so his voice gets quiet and thin and his arms throw themselves uselessly about. "We'll leave. Let's go. Move."

"Well, we can't say it happens often." Sandra pays double dues now to the tact she forgot. "There are *hundreds* of police out now." After a short wait she asks, "Do you ever think about Puerto Rico?" It sounds so coy, though she hadn't meant the honeymoon part, that she doesn't blame Ben for looking as if she'd rolled marbles under his feet.

"No," he says. "I've forgotten. Is that where we went?"

This is silly, Sandra says to herself. She supposes hurt feelings show in her face. Now it is Ben's turn to weave and spin. To show how much he remembers—every moment, in fact—he begins to hum, in an appropriately dying voice. After a quick glance at her, he goes to change. The children follow him, asking in loud whispers to see the box with the present. Sandra takes up Ben's tune while she looks after Lily's dinner: *"Mil lágrimas, mil lágrimas de amor."* She fishes in her apron pocket for a tissue. It is something, after all, to be able to blow your nose unobserved.

She knows what the trouble is. It's the research she did for Elizabeth. Her memories of ten years ago have been freshened. Unless you were Proust there was little point in having memories come back so fresh. The blessing of passing time—that it could carry off foreground and dwindle it into background—was lost. If everything came back stark, staring and foregrounded again, like a primitive painting—well, there was little point to that either. All it led to was a lot of secret nose-blowing in the kitchen. Idiotic. She and Ben and everybody else live, as any moron could point out, in difficult times. It's time to get used to the times. But her memories have been freshened. . . .

Their room in the hotel had a balcony that overlooked the sea and the mountains beyond the distant town. There was one wall of glass through which they could, while lying in bed, look out at the large, unbroken clouds. Below were the coconut palms and the pool. Next to that was the dining plaza, mosaic-floored, open on three sides to the trade winds and the view. At lunch the tables and the waiters wore white starched cloth, but the guests could sit like pampered children with dripping suits and bare feet. Next to this alfresco delight was the evening dining room—as enclosed, carpeted, and muffled as this one was open and fresh. The three guitarists and the girl who wore purple lipstick came to the dining room twice nightly to shed their thousand tears—"*Mil Lágrimas*," the song with which they opened and closed their program. So twice each evening (their contempt made them tireless) Ben and Sandra clutched each other's hands and monkeyed up anguish into their faces. They did so well that one night the group came and sang at their table. Afterward Sandra was ashamed. But Ben said they deserved to be fooled.

"*Mil lágrimas*, for God's sake!" Ben said. "That's no way to talk about sorrow."

"What is, then?" Sandra had asked. She thought that Ben, who knew a great deal, would also know that.

But Ben only scowled and rummaged in his crew cut. "It's just no way!"

After that, *mil lágrimas* was shown its place. When the unfamiliar rum drinks went to Ben's head in a night club and they had to leave before the dancers came on, Ben told her with mock gravity that he was suffering from *mil lágrimas*. And when Sandra got sick on the twisty ride up the mountain to El Yunque, the rain forest, it was the same thing.

The Sandra who stands in the kitchen over Lily's dinner now sees, with idiotically pricking eyelids, the other Sandra and Ben. She no longer sees them tiny, through ten years' distance. But still they stumble and suffer like children. She sees the

other Sandra and Ben signing up for the trip to the rain forest
—their one and only venture into organized sight-seeing—with
disdain, naturally. Then, half hoping they will miss it, they are
late, the last ones to enter the shiny black limousine parked at
the entrance to their hotel.

Their driver and guide is a tan-skinned man of athletic
though portly build. His hair is well brushed; he wears a natty
sports shirt and slacks. Down here, until he speaks, he might be
mistaken for an American businessman with a really good tan.
But of course he is not. He is only the driver and guide, with
much good will toward the United States.

In the back of the car are two young men close in age, possibly brothers, the older no more than twenty. They sit tall and
look clean, with long, clean fingers wearing gold college rings.
Sandra sits beside the younger brother and Ben takes the well-
padded jump seat ahead, turning halfway round to her. A
plump, dark-haired woman, perhaps in her middle forties, sits
up front and is quickly classified, by signs and looks, as one of
the dreadful drawbacks of sight-seeing trips. She wears more
jewelry than she ought with a cotton dress, and she rivals the
guide for cheery chattiness in a situation that obviously, unless
you are a guide, calls for aloof silence. Other than that it is not
clear why Ben and Sandra make their uncompromising judg-
ment of her, though they seem in perfect agreement on it.

Aproned Sandra now gives her nose another blow. Poor,
talkative woman, worried all during the trip about their being
so young and possibly coldhearted, and trying to rouse
them. . . .

They drive through the open country that connects the
towns. Words flow from the driver as easily as miles from the
wheels.

". . . Here was once coconut plantations. Now no more.
Why? Pay very little. Coconuts not so much any more in de-

mand. What they get? A man who pick a thousand coconuts . . ."

Sandra and Ben crane necks upward, following the curving
trunks, to the fruit high above. Then how many trees would he
have to climb to pick . . . They calculate, are shocked by
their own arithmetic. He must climb all day, monkey-fashion,
with only the aid of a band of cloth tied ankle to ankle.

". . . An' how much you think the man who chop the coconut get?" the guide goes on. "Chop off the husk with the ma-
chete?"

Ben and Sandra listen, stricken again. He must chop all day,
all day, never straightening his back.

The woman in front gives her bracelets a jangle. "And let's
hope," she says, "he doesn't lose a hand in the process."

More flatness. They begin to see at intervals some cement-
block buildings. Stuck in the earth before each is a sign with a
picture of a spoked wheel, like a party symbol. One of the
brothers wants to know what that is. The plump woman in
the front looks knowingly around to the back and then up at
the guide.

"That is *Fomento*," the guide says. "That is our government's effort to establish our own industry on the island. With
the help, of course, of the United States. But is a wonderful
effort to help the people by giving them industry here."

The older brother wants to know if it is working out. He
doesn't see much going on.

"Is going on," the guide says. "Sometimes wait for machines
from the United States, sometimes wait for people to show how
to use machines, sometimes wait for material, but is going on.
Fomento is the same in English—to rouse the people?"

The woman up front moves restlessly and then twists to the
back. It is going on, you can take it from me," she says.

The two brothers continue to gaze out their near window as

241

if to show that no matter how baffled they may be, *her* reassurance is not wanted.

Soon the car begins the slow climb up the mountain that leads to the rain forest. They see clumps of bamboo and ferns grown into trees—long, slender trunks leaping up, absurd as giraffe necks. Now and then they see wet in the road. Spatters of rain fall all the time, but never for very long, the guide tells them, as if he has arranged everything for their comfort. Suddenly, at a bend, there is a lovely waterfall, a flat cutout for cars, with a few people standing around and several little boys with wooden crates that serve as tables for bananas and flowers. The driver pulls over to the cutout and parks.

"Only a few minutes . . ." The driver is already out the door, pursing his lips in a very Latin, very deprecating manner. "To stretch, to look at the water, eat a banana, smell a flower . . ."

The little boys chatter at the tourists. They lift up their wares —brown-skinned bananas, some so ripe their seams have burst, and the heavy-scented, white ginger flowers.

Nearby, a couple from the States are arguing. The man has heard the fruit is not safe to eat. He stands balky as a child while his wife stares at him with fury. Ben draws Sandra away. They are so newly married they feel that any quarrel between husband and wife diminishes their honor. *"Mil lágrimas,"* he whispers to her, his voice doleful with irony. *"Ay-ay-ay,"* Sandra whispers back.

The car resumes its twisting climb. The flower stalk Ben tosses onto Sandra's lap ("I just boomed the economy," he says, frowning) begins to ooze. Scent hangs in the humid air, bringing on a memory of the near-nauseating excitement of their wedding and translating itself into *mil lágrimas* in Sandra's stomach. Ben sees, then rolls down his window and leans forward so she can get the air.

At last they are at the top of the road. Of course it is disappointing. Of course there is nothing to be seen there that they have not already seen on the way up. The sole point of this forest on the mountain seems to be to draw more height from its plant stalks. Everything Sandra has seen at home, growing nicely as a plant in a pot, is here a tree.

In the silence of the descent the woman in the front seat grows restless again. She alters her position, gazes more than once at the guide, jangles her bracelets above her head and consults her watch. At last the guide clears his throat. "We are going to make an extra little sight-seeing today. At no extra cost. Something very interesting for you."

Ben, Sandra's protector against *mil lágrimas*, strengthens his shy voice to give it authority: "It's out if it means additional riding."

"No additional riding," the guide says, holding up his brown hand. "We go back to the hotel another way, that is all. Through some villages in the mountains. There we make one little stop. You will see our sad poor people and also what we do for them. Very interesting for you."

After the car twists down some more of the mountain, he parks at the side of a narrow road. They all sit in the car and stare. Sandra is not well traveled, but she is willing to accept as truth the guide's sad boast that "nobody has less than they do." The stilt village of crazily sloping walls and roofs (made of what—paper? tin cans?) is dark with the darkness of a forest and of the faces that seem to sleep with open eyes. The bodies to which the faces belong sit in the dirt, leaning against a tree trunk or, like last straws, against a hut whose side already leans halfway to the ground. Children peep from every corner, some wearing little filthy shirts, some naked. They are testimony to the fact that there is one activity that still goes on in the motionless village. The children, though they do not know it yet, are its thousand tears.

The plump woman in the front seat begins to instruct them,

243

her voice breaking in like the voice in a documentary. "This is how they live. This is the meaning of *Fomento*. From this village and from others like it the workers will come."

They all look at her. She flushes, shakes her bracelets, rocks her head a little in nervousness and pride.

"My husband has a factory," she says. "He gave up a thriving business in New York to start again here. It isn't easy. He has to teach everything. Machines are broken, cloth is ruined."

She puts her hands to her cheeks, mottled with excitement. "Americans should see this. To know what's being done. . . ."

Sandra feels the young man next to her take a deep breath. "I suppose," he says coldly, "it has nothing to do with the fact that it's tax-free. Nothing to do with cheap labor."

The woman looks stunned. Her eyes shine with tears of disappointment. "I resent that," she manages to say. "I resent that very much." Her voice trembles under its weight of feeling. "These people will have an industry, these children will have a future. . . ." She twists to the back, reaches out a bangle-jangling arm to the brothers. "I understand your feelings. You're afraid a few will do something to disappoint you." The brothers' faces redden. No one looks at the plump woman and no one answers her. "We're all of us idealistic. All Americans . . ."

To the guide's credit it must be said that he gets them home as fast as he can—without chatter, without slowdowns and with nothing but a no-no wave to a little brown boy who calls frantically to him from behind a pile of ripe bananas. But it is hardly fast enough for Sandra. As soon as they are back she flings herself on the bed.

"I think I'll sleep," she mutters to Ben. "Why don't you go down and swim?"

"Good idea." He watches from a chair, his hands wrung together. "Maybe I'll stay and just be quiet."

"No—go down, go down!"

Ben gets up slowly. It is as if she had depressed one side of a scale and he were rising with the other side, to be weighted. Just before he leaves, Sandra pats her belly and whispers, *"Mil lágrimas."* In a way it is true. The dinners *en brochette,* the icy rum drinks, the dessert-heavy luncheons by the pool, all curdle in her stomach. Beyond their honeymoon, surrounding it like plague outside the walls, has been all the while, running like fire, this terrible cycle of the people who have no luck.

She has already heard, in New York, stories about Puerto Ricans. But now—what if some of these forgotten ones she has just seen are to become the unknown ones about whom the tales in New York are told? What if, when *Fomento* rolls on, some of these people, roused from their lethargy, go north with their new trade? Or with no trade? Killed in brawls; killed when the gas heaters fail or fire breaks out, overwhelming ten children at once; killed with bullets or clubs. It is like terror in childhood. A giant hand covers the universe. "I'll get you in your bed or I'll get you on the ship or I'll get you . . ."

Next morning they take the plane home, where Sandra promptly develops flu. Watched by her mother, who had hoped to see her fatted and calmed by the mystery of consummation, Sandra hacks and sneezes and loses her tan. It is all very satisfying. When she recovers, everything is normal again. Ben is Ben and Puerto Rico is far away. The bits of it that have come to New York sink easily from her sight. . . .

The children shout, "Happy anniversary!" at her again. Her son stops to joggle on one foot as he follows his father into the kitchen.

"Why," Ben asks without warning, "were you thinking of Puerto Rico?" He pretends to grumble. "It wasn't that long ago."

245

Sandra isn't looking at Ben. She is peering into the oven at Lily's roast. But she is sure that Ben is smiling at the children to show them: "This is nothing serious. Your mother and I have this joke."

In the same way Sandra turns to smile at them when she answers, "I was thinking of the people we saw in the villages there. Remember how they looked?" And in the same way again she smiles at the children after the gifts are opened, because a queer feeling has taken hold of her. It seems to Sandra that as the children's eyes shift from one face to the other, doting on their parents' pleasure (Sandra's bangle, Ben's cuff links), they are foreshadowing their own far-off time as parents. Sandra's heart thuds once, as if it had run ahead of itself and collided with something. *Mira! Mira!* What will become . . .

When the children are in bed Ben pours brandy. He fits the glass into Sandra's lifted hand and kisses her. "Anyway, darling, happy anniversary. . . ."

"Happy anniversary anyway, darling," Sandra says.

Ben sits beside her on the sofa and stretches his legs. "Do you remember . . ." he begins. At the same time a hoarse wail pierces the room. It is the siren of a police van or an ambulance, racing along the freezing streets. "Do you remember . . ." Ben begins again. "We took a tour. And there was this woman . . ." The siren reaches full cry, as if at their door. Elsewhere at that moment—Sandra feels it with a resonant certainty—klaxons scream; bombers roar aloft. From the city and from the world, the clamor that goes up fills the house. Ben and Sandra sit in silence, waiting for it to recede.